HOTSHOT HERO ON THE EDGE

Lisa Childs

HARLEQUIN
ROMANTIC
SUSPENSE

HARLEQUIN®
ROMANTIC
SUSPENSE™

Recycling programs
for this product may
not exist in your area.

ISBN-13: 978-1-335-73804-2

Hotshot Hero on the Edge

Copyright © 2022 by Lisa Childs

For questions and comments about the quality of this book,
please contact us at CustomerService@Harlequin.com.

Harlequin Enterprises ULC
22 Adelaide St. West, 41st Floor
Toronto, Ontario M5H 4E3, Canada
www.Harlequin.com

Printed in U.S.A.

Ever since **Lisa Childs** read her first romance novel (a Harlequin story, of course) at age eleven, all she wanted was to be a romance writer. With over seventy novels published with Harlequin, Lisa is living her dream. She is an award-winning, bestselling romance author. She loves to hear from readers, who can contact her on Facebook or through her website, lisachilds.com.

Books by Lisa Childs

Harlequin Romantic Suspense

Hotshot Heroes

Hotshot Hero Under Fire

Bachelor Bodyguards

His Christmas Assignment
Bodyguard Daddy
Bodyguard's Baby Surprise
Beauty and the Bodyguard
Nanny Bodyguard
Single Mom's Bodyguard
In the Bodyguard's Arms
Close Quarters with the Bodyguard
Bodyguard Under Siege

Visit the Author Profile page at Harlequin.com for more titles.

For my husband, Andrew Ahearne, who always offers unwavering love and support, but who especially helped out with the Hotshot Heroes series. Love you, my hotshot hero!

Chapter 1

Everybody looked at him like he was a killer. Like they had already tried and convicted him.

Coming to the Filling Station, the bar around the corner from the firehouse, had been a mistake. Luke Garrison knew that, but he'd felt so damn alone back in the bunkroom. Since Willow had thrown him out, he'd been staying with fellow Hotshots, but once his best friend, Dirk Brown, had died, he'd no longer been welcome anywhere. So he'd been bunking at the firehouse.

Stanley, the kid who cleaned up around the place and serviced the engines, had been staying there, too. But now he had his bedroom back at their friend Cody Mallehan's house since Cody's soon to be sister-in-law no longer needed it. The fire damage to Courtney's apartment, and the store beneath it, had been repaired.

Everybody probably thought Luke was responsible for that fire, too. But the only fires Luke had ever set had been controlled burns—and only on the orders of his superintendent, Braden Zimmer.

There was nothing controlled about the firestorm of gossip raging through the town of Northern Lakes, Michigan, right now. But Luke was the only one getting burned—by every scorching look directed at him. Coming to the Filling Station had definitely been a mistake.

Hell, coming to the bar too often after Willow had tossed him out was probably what had caused his current issues. If he hadn't been drinking too much, he might have realized what the hell was going on, that he was being set up…to look like a dead woman's accomplice to murder and attempted murder.

How could these people—team members he'd thought were his friends—believe that he was capable of such atrocities? That he would have in any way betrayed Dirk?

As always, Luke's mind went to his wife. Had Willow heard the gossip? Did she believe it, too?

His stomach lurched at the thought, and he pushed away the plate with his barely touched burger. He hadn't come to the bar to drink. He'd stopped drinking the night his car had been used to run down his friend and team member, Owen James, and Owen's girlfriend, Courtney Beaumont. But Luke wasn't sure if he couldn't remember much from that night, a few weeks ago, because of the alcohol, or because someone had slipped something in his drink.

He knew he hadn't driven his car, though. He'd left it in the lot and staggered back to the firehouse to sleep off whatever the hell had hit him so hard. And alcohol never hit him very hard. Despite his best efforts, he had never been able to drink enough to numb the pain of losing their babies before they were even born and then losing Willow when she threw him out.

Nor had he ever been able to forget all that he'd lost even before them. And now it wasn't just Willow and the babies, but every last one of his friends in the world as well…

Because nobody that could suspect him of betraying Dirk was actually a friend. A true friend would know that he was too loyal to betray his best friend, let alone the woman he loved more than life itself, his wife.

He pulled some money from the pocket of his jeans and tossed it onto the bar next to his plate. Then he slid off the stool and headed toward the door, crushing peanut shells beneath the soles of his boots. He felt everyone's gazes following him, boring into his back.

The skin between his shoulder blades tingled and ached. He felt like a knife had been buried in his back, hilt-deep. Somebody had set him up to look complicit in Dirk's murder.

But who?

Could it be someone in this bar? He glanced over his shoulder, but as soon as he did that, people looked away from him instead of at him, as if they didn't want to meet his gaze. Some of them were the local shop owners and service workers. Some were members of his Hotshot team. Even though the wildfire season hadn't started yet, many of them were in town to help with the fire breaks the local Hotshots had been working on when Dirk had died.

Ethan Sommerly was here from his ranger post in the upper peninsula of Michigan. He sat in the corner booth the Hotshots always used along with Rory VanDam, who'd come over from the island in Lake Michigan where he worked as a ranger, and Trent Miles, who'd come up from Detroit, where he worked as a firefighter.

The new guy, the one who'd taken Dirk's spot on the team, didn't sit with the others. But since everybody figured nepotism was the reason Braden had hired his wife's brother, Patrick "Trick" McRooney hadn't been accepted yet.

Luke didn't care about Trick. The guy hadn't been around long enough to form an opinion about Luke and vice versa. Luke was more concerned about a member of the team being the one behind the attempts to frame him. Why would any of them hate him enough to try to destroy him? Hadn't that person realized he'd already been hurting enough? That he'd already lost more than he'd thought he could survive losing…?

Willow…

His chest ached with missing her. But he wasn't what she wanted. She wanted the babies they'd lost—the babies she'd blamed him for losing. She had blamed the stress of being married to a Hotshot for the miscarriages.

And she was probably right. They'd lost their first baby a couple of years ago, when he'd been off in California battling a wildfire, and they'd lost the second during that terrible time when an arsonist had been in the middle of a reign of terror in Northern Lakes, over six months ago. So many of his friends had become targets of that arsonist.

Willow had feared that he would be next. That either the arsonist would come for him, or that Luke would leave to fight another wildfire and never return.

Guilt gripped him along with the pain. She was probably right that she never should have married him. And every day he waited for the divorce papers to arrive; he waited for her to file and officially end their marriage.

He couldn't give her the peace and security that she wanted. And even if he left his job for her, like he'd offered that horrible morning she'd raged at him four months ago, she'd said that it was too late, that she would never forgive him for what he'd already cost her.

The knife in his back from whomever had framed him was nothing compared to the pain of the sharp blade he'd felt her bury in his heart that morning. Maybe that was why he'd been framed—because he'd been an easy target. He'd been too distracted to even notice.

And his friend had died because of it. If Luke had been more aware of what was going on with everyone else in his life, instead of drowning in his own despair, he might have been able to warn Dirk—to save him.

But Dirk had died.

The burden of that hung heavy on Luke's shoulders. He stepped out of the bar without looking back again. He didn't need to see the looks following him—the ones of suspicion or, from those already convinced of his guilt, disgust.

He could have walked back to the firehouse. But he headed to the vehicle he'd parked down the street. This wasn't the same one that had run down Owen and Courtney. That car was still in the state-police impound lot.

This was an old truck that, ironically, he'd inherited from Dirk. His friend had decreed in his will that Luke should get it—since they'd spent so much time working on it together. Driving it was probably a mistake, was probably just making everyone more suspicious of him, as if Luke had helped kill Dirk to get a truck.

But he'd loved his friend. And he missed him nearly

as much as he missed his wife. Driving the truck made him feel closer to Dirk, reminded him that at least one person had truly been his friend.

So instead of heading to the firehouse, Luke drove the old pickup outside of town—past the hospital where Willow would probably be starting her shift soon. That was where they'd met, three years ago in the ER, when he'd come in with a cut from a chain saw that had malfunctioned on him. She'd numbed him, so that the doctor could stitch him up.

But with her touching him, he hadn't been able to feel anything but attraction and awareness. She'd looked so damn beautiful with her blond hair bound up in a sloppy bun, and her green eyes tender with concern.

As he neared the hospital, he slowed down so much that the vehicle behind him gunned its engine and passed in a blur. Luke barely noticed it, since his attention was focused on the hospital lot, where he tried to catch a glimpse of Willow's distinct SUV. She usually parked in the very back row, but there was no sight of the bright teal paint gleaming under the security lights. She usually came in early, but maybe she was running a little late.

Or maybe her shift had changed.

He hadn't talked to her in so long that he knew nothing of her life anymore. Had she heard all the rumors about him?

Northern Lakes was so small that she must have.

And he wondered again, like he had at the bar, if she believed what everyone else did about him.

That he was a cheater and a killer.

He hoped not.

But he'd come to accept that his hopes were never realized. He'd been hoping for months that she would call him, that she would ask him to come home. But his cell never rang.

It vibrated now and, his heart racing, he pulled it from his pocket. But she wasn't calling him. His boss's name was the one lighting up the screen of his cell. Braden was probably calling to fire him—because nobody else wanted to work with him.

He should ignore it.

But what if there was a fire and Braden was just calling him to the house to suit up for it?

He couldn't ignore it, so he accepted the call. But he didn't know how to greet his boss, so he said nothing.

"Luke?" Braden asked, concern rumbling in his deep voice. "Are you there?"

"Yeah, sorry," Luke said. "I'm here. Why are you calling?" Because nobody else was. Not Willow. Not anyone else that Luke had ever considered a friend.

"You're not here at the firehouse," Braden said.

Was his boss keeping that close of tabs on him?

"No, I'm not," Luke confirmed.

"I need you to come back here," Braden said.

"Do I have a curfew?" Luke asked. Or maybe Braden, like the state trooper, Marty Gingrich, wanted to put a GPS ankle bracelet on him, so he would always be aware of where Luke was.

Fortunately a judge hadn't signed off on Marty's request to monitor him, since no charges had actually been brought against Luke. Yet.

He suspected it was only a matter of time before Gingrich convinced the prosecutor to file charges. If not as an accomplice to murder, then at least to the hit-and-run that had injured Owen and Courtney since Luke's car had been used in that attack.

"I'm not your father," Braden said. The superintendent was younger than some of the team members and only a few years older than others. But there was something very paternal about him. "I'm your boss. And I need you to come to my office."

Dread gripped Luke. He was going to get fired. "Now? Isn't it kind of late?"

If he was Braden, he would have been home with his wife. Sam McRooney loved her husband.

Willow hated Luke. That was the last thing she'd said to him, the thing that had convinced him to walk away. That their marriage was really over; the love was gone. On her side at least...

"Yeah, it is late," Braden agreed. "So get here fast."

Luke swallowed a sigh. "Okay..." He clicked off his cell with a finger that shook slightly. Then he dropped the phone. It slid off the seat onto the floorboards. He glanced down at it for just a second. When he glanced up, lights blinded him. Something was heading straight toward him.

He squinted and confirmed that his truck was between the yellow line and the ditch. He hadn't veered out of his lane. But the vehicle, meeting him around the curve in the country road, had. He didn't have time to tap his horn.

Didn't have time for anything but the instinctive reaction of jerking the wheel and heading straight for the steep ditch and trees on the right side of the road, and oblivion, as his head struck something hard.

He was innocent. Or she...

Willow Garrison's palm pressed against her swollen belly. The baby was too small to kick very hard yet, but she felt a flutter. More like wings than feet...

Like an angel...

Willow already had angels: two babies she hadn't been able to carry to term. Would this baby join his or her siblings?

Tears stung her eyes and pain gripped her heart. She hadn't lost just those babies. She'd lost her husband, too. But had she ever really had him?

Had she ever really known who Luke was?

She moved her hand from her belly to curl her fingers around the pewter frame of the picture on the mantel—their wedding portrait. Luke looked so handsome with his dark hair cut short, and his blue eyes gleaming with love as he stared down at her.

But was it really love in his gaze? He hadn't fought to stay when she'd asked him to leave. He hadn't fought for them. Was that because he'd already had someone else?

Louanne Brown?

She shuddered as she thought of what the woman had done to her own husband. An ER nurse, Willow had been working the day that paramedics had rushed Dirk Brown to the hospital. He'd already been dead on arrival. He had probably been dead shortly after the cable had snapped on the logging truck and cut him...

She shuddered again, and nausea rushed over her. It was the first time she'd felt it with this pregnancy. With the others she'd been so sick. But not this time...

Was that a good sign or a bad one?

She should know, but she didn't specialize in obstetrics even though she had helped deliver a few babies in the ER. Babies that hadn't been able to wait for their mothers to be moved to the maternity floor.

Her babies hadn't been able to wait to be born either. They'd come too soon to survive. Because of the stress...

She'd been five months along with their first child

when Luke had been called out to that wildfire in California and he and his team had lost contact for so many long hours…

During that time she'd gone into labor, and their baby girl had been too small to survive. Then nearly a year ago when that arsonist had first started his six-month reign of terror in Northern Lakes, she'd gone into labor at twenty weeks again with their son. That had to have been over the stress as well, over her fear of losing her husband, of her baby losing his father to the arsonist who'd clearly been targeting firefighters.

She wasn't sure how far along she was now. Because she hadn't had any morning sickness, she hadn't even realized she was pregnant until recently, and she had yet to schedule an ultrasound.

She wasn't sure that she wanted one…that she wanted to connect to that little image on the screen only to lose him or her again.

"You have to wait," she murmured to this one. "You have to wait…"

Just like she'd been waiting for Luke to come back, to beg her to give him—to give them—another chance. But he hadn't. That was for the best, though. She didn't want to give him another chance. She didn't want to open herself up to that kind of stress and pain again.

But even though he was gone, she couldn't help but worry about him. And wonder…why hadn't he reached out to her?

Because he didn't love her?

Had he loved Louanne Brown? Had he helped her kill her husband?

She'd thought that Luke had loved Dirk like a brother. He cared about every member of his Hotshot team, but he'd been especially close to Dirk—playing cards at his house and working on vehicles in his garage.

How could he have betrayed his friend?

How could he have betrayed her?

Her hand shaking, she put the picture back on the mantel. Maybe she should put it away—smash it, even— but she couldn't quite believe that the man she'd always thought so sweet and kind could be a vicious killer.

For the last four months, she'd been thinking that she'd made a terrible mistake making him move out. She'd been so depressed over the miscarriages that she'd just wanted some time alone.

She hadn't wanted Luke around—hadn't wanted his love or support. She'd rejected so many of his attempts to comfort her, until that last night…

She touched her belly again. The night they must have made their baby. She hadn't told Luke. Hadn't talked to him since she'd tossed him out the morning after that night.

That magical night…

She'd felt guilty for feeling so happy, so much pleasure—she'd felt like she'd betrayed her angels. And she'd turned that guilt into anger…against Luke. She couldn't even remember everything she'd said to him that morning.

But she could remember how he'd looked—crushed and devastated.

And that love she thought she'd seen in their wedding portrait hadn't been in his eyes any longer. But maybe it had been gone long before that morning.

Maybe they'd been over long before then.

Or maybe what they'd had had never been real. Maybe she'd never even known who her husband was.

Could he be a killer?

* * *

"He's not coming back," Patrick "Trick" McRooney said. "He's running. And only guilty men run."

Braden Zimmer ignored the sick feeling in the pit of his stomach, the dread that his brother-in-law might be right. He leaned back in the chair behind his desk, in the small windowless office in the firehouse, and he focused on Trick, who was pacing in front of him. "Give him time. I just called him a few minutes ago, and I don't know where he was. And neither of us know if he's guilty of anything."

"You know, you just don't want to admit that it really is a member of your team," Trick persisted.

Braden led a twenty-member crew of Hotshot fire-fighters—firefighters that battled wildfires on the front lines. His team came together, from the surrounding area, when they were called out to a fire. In addition to being superintendent of the Huron Hotshots, Braden, with a few of his closer team members, manned the firehouse in the northern Michigan town of Northern Lakes.

Braden uttered a ragged sigh. He didn't like it, but he had no problem admitting it. "I *know* it's a member of my team."

He knew because of the damn note—the one he'd received months ago that had warned that someone on his team wasn't who he thought they were.

What the hell did that really mean, though?

It hadn't said that person was responsible for all the *accidents* that had been happening on the job lately, to equipment and to team members. Of course, the arson-ist, whom they'd caught over six months ago, had been responsible for some of those things; and more recently, the wife of a team member had been responsible for that team member's death.

But other things kept happening...

And eventually somebody else was going to get badly hurt or worse.

"Yeah, it's Luke Garrison," Trick said. "He was having an affair with the dead Hotshot's wife."

"That's just gossip," Braden reminded him. "Not fact."

"Fact enough for Luke's wife to throw him out months ago," Trick said.

Braden shrugged. "We don't know that's why..." From experience he knew that nobody outside a marriage really understood what went on inside one. Hell, he'd been inside his first marriage and still hadn't known what was going on, that his wife was cheating on him, or why. Now he knew she'd done him a favor because with Trick's sister, Sam, Braden was happier than he'd ever been.

Luke Garrison was not. He had been miserable since the day his wife had tossed him out. Maybe part of that could have been guilt that he'd caused the breakup, but...

He didn't look like a guilty man to Braden. He looked like a broken man, who had only gotten more broken after the death of his best friend and the obvious suspicion of his team members.

Trick shook his head, and a lock of thick auburn hair tumbled over his brow. He pushed it back with one of his beefy hands. The guy was big, but Braden hadn't brought him into his team because of his size. He'd brought him on to help him investigate—because Trick offered an outside perspective. Unfortunately a spot had recently opened up due to Dirk Brown's murder. His wife had been responsible for that, but some believed she hadn't acted alone.

Trick was one of them. "There's more than gossip implicating Luke Garrison," he said. "There's his car and his gun…"

Braden groaned. Both were hard to explain. And Luke hadn't made much of an effort, just murmuring that he didn't know…

And now neither did Braden.

Had Luke Garrison helped Louanne Brown kill her husband? Had he helped her try to kill the man who'd nearly been killed along with her husband? Had Luke provided the gun with which Louanne had inadvertently killed herself?

She was gone now, so she couldn't explain how she'd gotten the gun and access to Luke's car. Luke had to— he had to prove his innocence.

If he was innocent. And if he *was*, why wasn't he coming back to the firehouse as Braden had asked? Had he gone on the run, like Trick thought?

Chapter 2

Willow had been late to work, but when she'd rushed in moments ago the charge nurse had assured her it was fine. The night had been quiet, but weeknights usually were until summer, when tourists flooded Northern Lakes. Spring in northern Michigan was too cool for water sports. Ice clung still to the surface of some of the inland lakes with temperatures at night often dropping below freezing. It hadn't been that cold when Willow had run across the parking lot a short time ago. But her blood chilled when she exited the locker room to find the head nurse, who was also her friend, waiting for her, with an anxious expression on her face.

"Paramedics are bringing in a Hotshot," Cheryl said, sympathy in her voice and in her warm brown eyes.

"What—what happened?" Willow asked. She hadn't heard about a fire, hadn't smelled any smoke. And it was too late for them to have been working on cutting fire breaks, like they'd been the day Dirk had died.

That wave of nausea crashed over her again as she remembered what had happened to Dirk. All the Hotshots were close, but Dirk and Luke had been especially close, with Dirk visiting their house often, until the miscarriages—then she'd refused to have any company. And after months of awkward silence between her and Luke, filled with all her resentment of him, she hadn't been able to bear his either.

Cheryl shrugged, her shoulders straining against the green material of her scrub top. "I don't know. He's unconscious—possible concussion, maybe internal injuries. He'll need a CT and MRI when he arrives."

He. There were only two female Huron Hotshots, so that left eighteen possible firefighters who could have been injured. But Willow knew who it was. She knew because of the panic that had her heart frantically pounding and her stomach churning with nausea.

It was Luke.

Her friend's look of concern confirmed her fear. "Maybe you should sit this one out," Cheryl advised.

Willow would have refused, if not for the baby. Her head was already swimming, black spots dancing before her eyes. She had to be careful, for the baby's sake. She couldn't lose this child like she had the others.

While a part of her would probably always love him—no matter what he'd done—she had already lost Luke, months ago, when her resentment of him had destroyed any chance of their relationship surviving. But because she still loved him, she didn't want him hurt, or worse.

She didn't want him to wind up like his friend: dead.

Was he dead?

The last thing Luke remembered was the bright light

but it hadn't been leading him to the afterlife. It had sent him careening into the ditch.

The light returned, shining into one of his eyeballs. He fought against the grip on his lid, struggling to close his eyes again as he groaned in protest.

"Pupils are reactive," a deep voice murmured. "He's coming around."

"What the hell...?" Luke murmured, as he tried to move. Pain radiated throughout his chest, though. The old truck didn't have airbags, so he must have struck the steering wheel. The truck...

How was the truck?

More importantly, what happened to the other car?

"Are they okay?" he asked, his voice gruff. His mouth felt like it was full of cotton balls, dry and muffled.

"They?" the man asked. He leaned back, and Luke recognized him.

Owen James. When he wasn't battling wildfires, the former Marine medic worked as a paramedic for the town of Northern Lakes.

"Were there other people in the truck with you?" Owen asked, and he looked away from Luke, probably toward the ditch where Luke had driven the pickup. "Gingrich," he called out, "did you screw up and move somebody else, too?"

"There was nobody else in the truck," the state police trooper replied, his voice coming from close by and not the ditch. The lawman stepped closer to Luke, leaning over the stretcher to peer down in his face. His brown eyes, small and beady, stared at Luke.

Luke tried to sit up, but he'd been strapped to the stretcher. It wasn't just the straps holding him down, though. Something cold and hard encircled one of his wrists. He'd been handcuffed. He struggled against that. "What the hell…?" he murmured again. But he would deal with the handcuffs later. "The other…"

He wasn't sure what the vehicle had been. He'd only been able to see the blinding lights of it. "The driver…" Maybe he'd had passengers, too. "Is he okay?"

Gingrich snorted. "Are you going to try claiming you weren't driving now? I pulled you out from behind the steering wheel myself."

Owen cursed. "And you damn well know not to move an accident victim," he admonished the trooper. "You could have paralyzed him."

Luke wasn't able to move, but that was because of the straps and the handcuffs and the agonizing pain inside his skull. He must have hit his head on the steering wheel or the dash, or maybe the roof of the pickup.

"He's too damn drunk to be seriously hurt," Gingrich said. "I need to take him to jail."

"Not drunk…" Luke murmured in protest. "I haven't been drinking…"

Gingrich snorted. "You smell like a brewery and I found a broken liquor bottle in the cab of the truck."

Luke shook his head, which sent pain reverberating through his skull. He flinched and grunted. "I haven't had a drink since that night…"

"What night?" Gingrich asked. "The night you tried running down your *friend* here and his girlfriend? Are you finally going to confess to being behind the wheel then, Garrison?"

Risking the pain, Luke shook his head again, and his vision went black, as consciousness began to slip away from him. He must have been out for a long time as it was since he'd had no idea Gingrich had showed up and pulled him from the truck. Luke fought his way out of the darkness and pried open his eyes again.

"Draw some of my blood for me," he murmured to Owen.

"What?" Owen asked.

"Yeah, yeah," Gingrich said. "Do that. Test his blood alcohol immediately—before he has time to sober up."

"I'm not drunk," Luke insisted, but even he could smell it now, the overpowering stench of whiskey. His clothes were damp with it. What the hell had happened? How would a liquor bottle have even been in his truck? He never drank the hard stuff—just beer—and never enough of that that he actually lost control.

He hadn't lost control of the truck, or he would have hit that vehicle head-on. Instead he'd veered out of its path to prevent an accident.

But had it been an accident?

Or had the driver of that vehicle been purposely aiming for him? And when Luke had gone off the road, had someone poured that whiskey over him? He sure as hell hadn't.

"I don't think he's drunk," Owen said.

"Your nose broken, James?" Gingrich asked, disparaging the paramedic. "He reeks."

"Is yours broken?" Owen asked. "The smell's coming from his clothes, not his breath. And his eyes are clear, despite probably having a concussion. And because of that concussion, I need to get him to hospital for a CT."

The stretcher moved then, but just a short distance before it jerked to a stop. Luke rallied enough to raise his head and see Gingrich standing between him and the open doors to the back of the paramedic rig.

"Get the hell out of my way!" Owen yelled at the trooper.

"He tried to kill you and Courtney Beaumont," Gingrich insisted. "Why do you want to help him?"

"Because it's my job," Owen said. "And it was Louanne Brown who tried to kill me."

Gingrich snorted. "In his car? Yeah, right…"

"Get out of my way," Owen said again. "And if you want the results of his blood-alcohol test, you better get a warrant."

Finally Gingrich stepped aside, and Owen pushed the stretcher into the back of the van. Someone else must have been driving the rig because Owen climbed in beside Luke.

"Thank you," Luke murmured.

Owen shook his head. "Just doing my job…"

Maybe that was all he was doing. But Luke had hoped it was more—that Owen still considered him a friend. "It wasn't me," he said. "I wasn't driving…"

"Tonight?" Owen asked.

"No…" Luke shook his head, and his vision went black for a moment.

A hand squeezed his shoulder. "Take it easy," Owen cautioned. "You could have pressure building up…"

He did, but that pressure was in his chest, not his brain. He probably had bruises from the steering wheel, maybe even a broken rib. But the pain was more emotional than physical. More panic probably even than pain.

He didn't want anyone to believe that he would betray not just one friend but two. And his wife…

He especially didn't want Willow to think that he'd cheated on her. He tried to reach out for Owen, but the straps around the gurney, and the handcuffs, held him to the stretcher. "Don't bring me to the ER," he implored his team member.

Owen's brow furrowed. "Why not? Have you changed your mind about that blood-alcohol test?"

"No," he said. He was afraid of seeing his wife. He hadn't come to the hospital that day—the day Dirk had died—because of that. And because he'd been out at the accident site. He'd seen how badly wounded Dirk had been, and he'd known there was no way any doctor or surgeon could resuscitate his already dead friend.

Owen skeptically arched a dark blond eyebrow. "Really?"

"I don't want to see Willow," he admitted. And more importantly, he didn't want her to see him like this— battered and reeking of booze.

She would think what everyone else apparently thought about him: the worst.

"I have to bring you in," Owen said. "You could have a bleed…"

In his brain? His head hurt, but it was nothing compared to his heart. That felt like it was bleeding out.

"I'm fine," he lied.

And Owen snorted now, like Gingrich had. Did Owen think he was lying about more than his physical condition, though? Did he think he'd tried to kill him and Courtney? Did he think that he could have betrayed Dirk?

He stared up at his friend, and the suspicion on Owen's scarred face confirmed Luke's fears. The former Marine had been wounded during his last deployment. He was a good man. A hero. Maybe that was why he looked at Luke with suspicion instead of the judgment others did. Owen hadn't already tried and convicted him like Gingrich and some of the others. But he clearly had his doubts about Luke's innocence.

Luke shook his head, trying to protest his guilt. The

pain intensified, threatening to shatter his skull again. And he slipped back into oblivion.

Owen checked for a pulse. It was there, but it wasn't particularly strong. And neither was the sound of breath coming through Luke's parted lips.

"Hurry up," he told the driver.

Owen used to work mostly with another Hotshot who was also a paramedic. But Dawson Hess now spent all his time, not at wildfires, with his wife in New York. If Courtney ever returned to the city where she'd launched her career as a fashion designer, Owen would go with her, too.

He loved her so much. He shuddered as he remembered how close he'd come to nearly losing her. Had it really been Louanne behind the wheel of that car?

Or had it been Luke?

The blood—Owen's blood—found on the cracked front bumper and broken headlight proved that Luke Garrison's car had been used in the hit-and-run. But Luke claimed he hadn't been behind the wheel. Owen wanted to believe him. He'd always considered Luke a friend—a good friend and a good man.

But what if he was wrong?

What if Luke still posed a threat to him and Courtney?

Or, worse yet, to his wife and the baby she was carrying?

When the driver backed the rig into the ER bay and opened the back doors, Willow was the first person Owen saw. Her pretty face was pale with fear. She looked at him, and he saw the question in her wide green eyes.

Is it Luke?

He nodded.

But instead of rushing forward, she stepped back and let another nurse and a young medical resident help him get the stretcher, with Luke's body strapped and handcuffed to it, down from the rig. Of course, hospital rules decreed that she could not work on a family member, but that was a hard rule to follow when so much of the town was related either by blood or marriage, or had friendships that felt like family.

Luke had once felt like family to Owen. But now he couldn't be certain what he was. Owen had been with Louanne in those last moments of her life, when her attempt to take his had ended her own instead. The gun she'd tried shooting Owen with—and inadvertently ended up harming herself—was Luke's. The car that had run down Owen and Courtney before that had been Luke's as well.

If he hadn't been her accomplice, how had she gotten access to his things? From when he'd been staying with the Browns after Willow had tossed him out? And why had Willow tossed him out? Because he'd been having an affair? Louanne had admitted to having one, but she hadn't named Luke as her lover. She hadn't named him or anyone else as her accomplice, but she must have had one.

Luke?

Was he a killer?

Or another victim?

Despite his clothes smelling like alcohol, Luke really hadn't seemed drunk…when he'd regained consciousness. Had someone run him off the road and poured alcohol over him to make it appear like he'd driven himself off the road?

Most of those recent attempts on Owen's life had

been staged to appear like accidents—just like Dirk's death had been staged. When Louanne had died, those attempts had stopped, so Owen had thought he was safe.

That Courtney was safe. But if there was an accomplice that was still alive, would he resume the attempts on their lives? Or had that accomplice found a new target in Luke? While other people, because of the gun and vehicle being his, were convinced that Luke was guilty, Owen wasn't so sure. Maybe he was, or maybe Louanne's real accomplice had framed Luke and was trying to take him out now before he could prove his innocence, which could launch a more thorough investigation.

Either way, Louanne had definitely had help. That meant a killer was still on the loose in Northern Lakes.

Chapter 3

For the first time in this pregnancy, Willow got physically sick. That was one of the reasons why she had rushed off before the stretcher had even been lifted down from the paramedic rig. She'd had to run to the restroom. And even after washing her face and pressing cool, damp towels against her neck, her skin was still flushed and her stomach still nauseous. Another reason she'd run off was because she couldn't give in to the stress; she couldn't let it steal another baby from her. That was why a relationship with Luke was never going to be possible; it was inevitably going to cost her more than she could survive losing. Another baby…

She held on to the sink as she drew in several deep, calming breaths. But it was as if the smell emanating from Luke had followed her into the restroom. The scent of liquor hung in the air, like the cloud of it that had hovered around Luke.

He must have gotten drunk and crashed his vehicle. But in the three years she'd known him, she couldn't remember him ever losing control like that. She couldn't even remember him ever drinking more than a few beers. But if all the rumors she'd heard about him were true, she hadn't known him at all.

Had he been listening to rumors, too? Did he know about…?

She ran her palm over her belly. Even though she wore a big scrub top, she was showing now. If he hadn't heard about the baby, he would see that she was pregnant.

She couldn't go back out there, but she had a job to do. And because of that job, she couldn't be involved in his care. She didn't have to go anywhere near him.

Drawing another deep breath to brace herself, she pulled open the door to the restroom. Her colleagues hovered nearby in the hallway, as if they were waiting for her.

Some looked concerned. A few just looked away, embarrassed for her, but not enough to reserve their judgment. Of Luke.

Everybody in town was gossiping about him. Judging him.

She'd hoped they were wrong about him and that she hadn't been…

But she'd smelled what they had.

One of her true friends stepped up to her. "They've taken him to CT," Cheryl told her. "He's gone in and out of consciousness since the crash."

Her pulse pounded. How badly was he hurt?

"What happened?" she asked.

"He got drunk and drove off the road," a male voice answered her.

She glanced up to see Trooper Gingrich stomping down the corridor toward them. He was short and pudgy, the buttons of his tan uniform straining across his belly and the vest he wore beneath it. His stomping, or maybe his bald head, had his brown trooper hat sliding down his ruddy face until the rim nearly touched his nose. He pushed it up before holding out his cell phone. "I have a judge on the phone authorizing a blood draw to test Garrison's alcohol level."

He thrust the phone toward her, but Willow stepped back. "I—I can't..."

"He's in Radiology right now," her friend informed the trooper. "We'll draw blood as soon as he's back in the ER."

"That could be too late," he protested. "I need that blood now!"

"We're not busy," the nurse pointed out. "So he will be back soon."

Gingrich shook his head. "If he gets out of this, it's on you," he told Cheryl. But he was looking at Willow, like this was somehow her fault.

Was it?

Had Luke started drinking like this because she'd thrown him out?

But was drinking all Luke had started doing? People had been speculating for months why they'd separated, but Willow hadn't wanted to let anyone else into their pain, into their private lives, so she hadn't told anyone about the miscarriages. The gossips had come up with other reasons. Abuse, either alcohol, drug or physical, and then infidelity...

There had been none of that during their marriage. But Willow had no idea what Luke had done after she'd thrown him out.

Her head pounded, like his probably was. Did he have a concussion? How severe were his injuries? No matter how he'd gotten hurt, she was worried about him—worried about both his physical and mental health.

He was still her husband. And he would always be the father of their child…if this child survived…

Luke awoke with a jerk. But when he sat up, pain crashed through his skull, and he flinched. He also couldn't move one arm. He pulled on it and found it was still shackled, or maybe had been again. Was this the stretcher from the ambulance? Or one in the ER?

Fluorescent lights buzzed over his head, the glare blinding him. He flinched again and closed his eyes, trying to shut out the light and the pain.

"Are you okay?" a deep voice asked. "Are you about to pass out again?"

He forced his eyes open, squinting against the light and met his boss's concerned gaze. Concerned? Or judgmental?

Clearing his voice so he could speak succinctly, he said, "I am not drunk."

And, fortunately, he didn't smell like it anymore now. Somebody had changed him out of his clothes into hospital scrubs—ones like Willow wore to work. He glanced around, trying to find her. But the curtains were closed around the gurney—only he and Braden were inside the enclosure.

"You've been going in and out of consciousness," Braden told him.

Luke rattled the handcuff around his wrist against the metal support of the side of the gurney. "Why the hell is this still on me?"

"Gingrich insisted," Braden said with a sigh. "He's hounding the lab right now for the results of your blood-alcohol test."

Luke glanced down at his arm, where someone had taped a cotton ball to his skin. Had Willow drawn his blood?

No. She probably wouldn't have been allowed since they were married. For now...

How soon before she filed for divorce? He suspected that it wouldn't be long now. Even when she learned the results of the test...

"I wasn't drinking," Luke insisted.

Braden narrowed his dark eyes and studied his face. "Some of the team said they saw you at the Filling Station earlier tonight."

He'd suspected they'd all been watching him.

"Eating," Luke said, although he hadn't done much of that either. "I wasn't drinking."

"You still trying to sell that bullshit?" Gingrich asked as he jerked aside the privacy curtain. "I took your clothes for evidence. And I'm impounding the truck, too. Can't believe you'd crash the vehicle your friend left you. But then I guess he wasn't really your friend, anyway, or you wouldn't have been sleeping with his wife."

It was clear that Gingrich had already tried and convicted him.

"I wasn't sleeping with Louanne," he insisted. He couldn't believe that anyone would think that he had, that he would have betrayed his own wife and his best friend for a woman he hadn't even liked that much.

Gingrich snorted his doubt.

"What happened tonight?" Braden asked.

"Somebody ran me off the road," Luke said. "If I hadn't swerved, they would have hit me head-on."

Gingrich snorted again. "There were no tire tracks on either side. You drove right in the ditch—probably after you passed out behind the wheel."

Luke shook his head then gasped at the jolt of pain. What the hell had he hit his head against in the truck? The roof? The side door? He couldn't remember anything but jerking the wheel, then waking up strapped down to that stretcher with Owen and Gingrich standing over him.

"There was another vehicle," he persisted.

"And it just drove off?" Braden asked the question now.

Luke flinched at the skepticism in his boss's voice. He hated that everyone doubted him, but he should have been used to it. His own mother had doubted him when he'd decided to be a firefighter. And then, when she hadn't been able to convince him to change his mind, she'd done what everyone else had recently done to Luke—turned her back on him. Tossed him out just like Willow had...

"No," Luke said. "I don't think the car left. I think whoever drove me off the road also put that bottle of liquor in the truck—because I did not have one with me."

Gingrich shook his head now, and his hat slid down over his bald head, shading his face. He was the same age as Braden—they'd gone to school together—but he looked much older. Like he'd lived harder.

"You're getting a ticket for an open receptacle," Gingrich said. "And for driving under the influence..."

"No, he's not," another voice chimed in as Owen joined them. "The results are back. There is no percentage at all of alcohol in his blood."

"Why the hell would *you* cover for him?" Gingrich asked as he pushed his hat back up.

"I'm not covering," Owen said, and he handed a slip of paper to the trooper. "Here are the results of your warrant. You have no cause to arrest him."

"I told you I wasn't drinking," Luke said, then he tugged at the handcuff on his wrist. "Now you can take this damn thing off…"

"You still had an open receptacle in your vehicle," Gingrich reminded him.

"My fingerprints won't be on it," Luke insisted. "It wasn't mine."

Gingrich snorted. "I *will* check it for fingerprints. In the meantime, you are getting a ticket for careless driving."

Anger boiled up inside Luke. "I don't deserve that damn ticket." He didn't deserve anything that had happened lately—any of the doubts and suspicions his friends and the townspeople had about him—and he was getting damn sick of it. "Find the person who drove me off the road and give the ticket to them!"

"You can protest it if you want," Gingrich said as he ripped a citation from his pad. "But you're going to lose."

Losing was nothing new to Luke. He'd already lost so much—those babies, his wife, his best friend…

And now so many other friends.

But he wasn't going to keep wallowing in his misery like he'd been doing since Willow had kicked him out. He was going to fight back now. He was going to prove his innocence. "Take this handcuff off me now!" he yelled at the trooper.

Gingrich produced a key and unshackled Luke. A red mark and deep indentation encircled his wrist where the cuff had chafed it.

"You had it on him too damn tight," Braden said.

"He was fighting it," Gingrich said.

"No, he wasn't," Owen said. "He was unconscious most of the time."

That was how Luke felt—like he hadn't been fully awake since that morning Willow had tossed him out of their bed and their home. He'd been in a daze, barely going through the motions of living.

No wonder somebody had picked him to frame. He'd made himself a damn easy target. But that was over.

Gingrich stared down at Luke. "You need to get used to that feeling. You're going to be wearing cuffs on both your wrists very soon."

"So much for innocent until proven guilty," Braden murmured as his old rival walked away.

"He's not the only one who's already tried and convicted me," Luke reminded his boss.

Braden turned back to him, but he didn't meet his gaze, staring at the same point over his shoulder that had suddenly drawn Owen's interest. They couldn't look him in the eye.

But he'd already seen their doubts. He sighed. "Sorry I missed our meeting tonight," he told Braden. "But I have a feeling I know what it was about…"

His termination.

"Don't worry about that now," Braden told him. "Just focus on getting better."

"I'm fine," Luke said.

"You have a concussion and some bruised ribs," Owen informed him.

He'd figured as much, so he just shrugged. "I'm fine. I don't have to spend the night here. I want to go back to the firehouse."

Braden and Owen both shook their heads. "You need

to stay overnight for observation," Owen said. "The concussion is serious."

The concussion had probably done him a favor. Instead of addling his brain, it had cleared it up for him. It had brought Luke out of his funk and back into fighting mode. Whoever the hell was trying to frame him wasn't going to find it so damn easy anymore.

Although the indent on his wrist made it feel like the handcuff was still there, Luke remembered he was no longer shackled to the stretcher, so he swung his legs over the side and stood. A wave of dizziness crashed over him, and his knees shook, threatening to give. But he locked his legs and willed himself to stay upright and alert. He couldn't lose consciousness again.

"You can't check yourself out," Owen protested. "You could still develop a bleed or swelling on the brain."

"I'm not staying here," Luke insisted. He had too much to do. He had to prove his innocence, and the only way he could do that was to find out who had really been Louanne Brown's accomplice.

"Gingrich impounded your vehicle," Braden reminded him.

And Luke felt a pang that his boss wasn't going to help him. But it was obvious that Braden had as many suspicions as Owen and everybody else had about him.

"I'll call a cab," Luke said. Of course, he would have to find his wallet to see if he had any cash or cards on him. What the hell had happened to him after he'd swerved to avoid the oncoming vehicle?

Somebody had put that bottle of liquor in the cab with him, but had they taken anything off him? Louanne must have copied his keys at some point while he'd been crashing at her and Dirk's home; that was the only way she could have gotten access to his car and his gun. He certainly hadn't given either to her.

"Why are you being so damn pigheaded?" Owen asked him. "You're putting yourself in danger."

Whoever the hell had been driving that vehicle was the one who'd put him in danger. But why?

He might have believed it had been an accident, that the other driver might have been looking at his phone, or drinking...

But for that liquor poured over his clothes with the open bottle left in the truck. He was being framed all over again. But what the person framing him hadn't realized was that he'd quit drinking.

Luke had wanted the blood-alcohol test to prove it, and Gingrich's insistence on getting a copy of it had helped Luke prove it. At least legally...

He wasn't sure if it had made any difference to Owen and Braden. His fellow Hotshots didn't seem ready to trust him yet.

"I'm putting myself in more danger if I lay around doing nothing," Luke said. "I need to find out who's messing with me."

He saw his wallet sitting on the wheeled cart next to the gurney and grabbed it in one hand. Then he stepped around the partially open curtain, and as he did, he saw her.

She was just slipping behind the nurses' station, but he caught a glimpse of her body—of her belly swelling against the top of her scrubs.

He felt a pang in his chest, like one of those bruised ribs had snapped and poked a hole into his heart. And his knees began to shake.

She was pregnant. Willow was pregnant.

And she hadn't told him.

But then she hadn't spoken to him at all in months—not since that morning she'd told him to leave and never come back.

Maybe the baby wasn't his. Maybe that was why she hadn't told him.

That possibility struck him harder than the truck had hit the ditch. He wasn't sure what would hurt more, though. That she was pregnant with another man's child or that she was pregnant with his and hadn't told him.

Did she hate him that much? Or had she heard all those rumors and believed them?

Did the woman he had thought was his soul mate, his best friend, not know him at all?

Damn it!

Luke Garrison wasn't proving to be such an easy scapegoat anymore. He should have been sitting in the back seat of the state police cruiser, being carted off to jail right now, not hopping into the passenger side of his boss's pickup. Hell, Braden Zimmer should have fired him already; instead he was helping him out.

Letting him stay at the firehouse…

Not that he had anywhere else to go now. Everybody hated him. Everybody suspected him of colluding with Louanne Brown to kill her husband and trying to kill Owen James and Courtney Beaumont. Louanne had been setting up Garrison to take the fall in case anyone figured out that Dirk's death hadn't really been an accident. But when she'd been caught, she'd let it slip about the damn affair. Fortunately everyone had figured it must have been with Luke since she'd used his car and gun.

But it wasn't enough that they suspected Luke. They had to really believe it. Or they might start looking for Louanne's actual accomplice; they might dig even deeper into Dirk's death and figure out who was also responsible. That could not happen. This case had to be closed before the investigation went any deeper and uncovered the truth.

But if Garrison hadn't realized it before, he had to know now that he was being framed after having that liquor doused all over him. When the hell had he stopped drinking? Or had he never really been drinking as much as it had seemed?

Sure, he'd spent a lot of time at the Filling Station, but he could have been nursing the same damn beer the whole night. And with no one drugging it this time, there was no way Garrison would appear as drunk as he had that night his vehicle had nearly taken out Owen and Courtney.

Sure, all that could have been blamed on Louanne... if she hadn't confessed to having a damn affair. Why hadn't the bitch kept her big mouth shut?

Now the mess she'd left had to be cleaned up. And the only way for that to happen was for Luke Garrison to take the fall. But maybe he didn't need to be convicted of a crime. Maybe he just needed to pay for it...

With his life. Once he was dead, the investigation would certainly be closed. Especially if a little suicide note confessing his involvement in Dirk's death also turned up on his computer or his phone or somewhere...

There was no getting to him now, though. Not with Owen hopping into the pickup with them. Garrison had too much protection with the other two Hotshots.

But that left somebody else Luke cared about totally unprotected...

Garrison needed to be distracted again. If he hadn't been, he probably wouldn't have been so damn easy to frame. But to kill him…

He would have to be even more distracted so that he would never see it coming.

Chapter 4

The darkness unnerved Willow. Usually she came home after the sun had already risen. But Cheryl, who was also the head nurse, had insisted Willow leave work early. Maybe she'd thought Luke was going to stay for observation like the doctor had ordered. But he'd walked out of the ER, anyway—without another glance in her direction.

Had he seen her belly?

But if he had, wouldn't he have said something—wouldn't he have tried to talk to her?

Usually she left a light on in the house when she headed out for the night shift. But she must have been so preoccupied with thoughts of Luke that she'd forgotten. The darkness was so encompassing that instead of pulling into the detached garage, she parked near the front door, and used the headlamps to illuminate her way up the brick sidewalk. She'd shut off the SUV, so the lights would only stay on for a minute. She needed to find the lock and slide the key into it quickly. But her hand trembled so much that she had to make several attempts before she managed to get the key in the right way. She'd just turned the knob and pushed open the door when the SUV lights were extinguished. She was afraid. Not of coming home alone to an empty house, but of Luke learning the truth and hating her for keeping it from him.

She should have told him about the pregnancy, but she'd been so angry with him—angry for making her feel pleasure again that night they'd made love, and angry that he'd left even though she'd told him to...

But that was for the best, that they'd separated, especially now. She couldn't handle the stress of being married to a Hotshot. Dirk's death had reinforced how dangerous that job was. But then it wasn't the job that had killed Dirk. It was his wife.

Because all of the Hotshots associated outside of work, Willow had met Louanne Brown. She hadn't particularly liked her. There had been something cold and calculating about her, an insincerity that had kept her from ever getting close to any of the other wives or the female Hotshots. Louanne had seemed much more comfortable in the company of men, working in her husband's garage and playing cards with the guys, than getting to know any of the other wives.

But maybe Willow hadn't been as close to the other women as she'd thought, because none of them had warned her about those rumors, had told her that Luke might have been cheating on her. She'd inadvertently started those rumors when she'd thrown Luke out and not told anyone why. Then after Dirk had died, the gossips had started speculating about a possible involvement between Dirk's widow and Luke. Tammy Ingles, who owned the local salon, had been the one who'd warned Willow about that rumor going around town.

The thought of Luke being with Louanne, being with anyone but Willow, had that nausea churning in her stomach again. She felt so damn sick. But it wasn't because of the pregnancy this time. It was because of the man who'd made her pregnant.

She could remember clearly the day he'd carried her over the threshold of this house, the feeling of security and love she'd felt with his strong arms holding her tightly, as if he would never let her go.

But he had.

And she needed to let go, too. It was for the best, for her and especially for this baby to survive...

Shivering at a sudden gust of wind, Willow knew she should walk over that threshold on her own and get out of the cold. But the chill penetrated too deeply inside her to be just a result of how low the temperature had dropped. A strange feeling crept over her, like she wasn't alone.

But that was crazy. The house was dark. Nobody was inside. But still she hesitated. Instead of walking in, she reached her hand across the doorway and fumbled for the light switch on the wall.

A lamp on the table beside the couch flickered on and cast a glow over the living room. With its brightly patterned rug in the middle of the dark hardwood floor and its big stone fireplace and hearth, the room looked warm and inviting. But when Willow stepped inside and closed the door behind her, it didn't feel any warmer than outside.

Then she noticed the curtains fluttering at one of the windows. She wouldn't have left a window open; it hadn't even been warm enough to open a window yet. Although she had been feeling a bit flushed earlier...

When she'd been thinking about that last night she'd spent with Luke, about how much pleasure he'd given her...

So maybe she had opened it. She had been forgetful lately. During her previous pregnancies, she'd blamed the lapses in memory on pregnancy brain. She had even more reason to be forgetful now—because she had so much on her mind all the time.

The baby...

Luke...

All now those horrible rumors about him.

What if they were true? She couldn't believe that, couldn't believe the man she'd loved so much was capable of betraying her, let alone his best friend.

She shivered again and hurried over to the open window. After pulling down the pane, she locked it. Then as she settled the curtains back into place against the wall, she noticed the wedding portrait on the table in front of the window. At least it looked like the heavy pewter frame the wedding portrait was in, but the picture was turned upside down.

Or maybe the wind had just knocked it over...

But hadn't she left it on the mantel, earlier, where it always was?

Hands trembling, she reached out and picked up the heavy frame. The photo hit her as it always did—right in the heart. How could Luke look at her like that—the loving way he had in that picture—and then just walk away?

Sure, she'd told him to, but he hadn't fought her over leaving. And he had never tried to come back home.

Couldn't he have at least offered to leave his job, to make her and their future family his priority?

Tonight he had done the same thing. She'd noticed that he'd glanced at her, but then he'd looked away and had never looked back again.

So maybe he hadn't noticed that she was pregnant. She had intended to tell him, but she hadn't told anyone yet. Just in case.

If she lost this baby, like she'd lost the others, she didn't want to have to deal with other people's reactions to her loss—with their well-meaning but difficult-to-accept sympathy. Even with only the coworkers who'd treated her knowing about the second miscarriage, she'd gotten too much attention, had had to talk about her loss too much when she'd just wanted to be able to pretend that it had never happened. But she hadn't been able to pretend. She hadn't been able to get over her loss.

And because of that, she'd lost more.

She'd lost her nerve. She'd sworn she wouldn't be like her mother, that she would be stronger, that she would be able to handle being the wife of a man with a dangerous career. But then she'd lost those two babies, after feeling them moving around inside her, connecting with them, nurturing them, and all because of the stress. The fear of losing her husband had made her lose those babies instead. It had been her job to protect them, to carry them to term. But she'd failed them. And the guilt had become unbearable.

And she'd lost Luke, anyway. She stared at the man gazing at her in that photo and she wondered how...

That love looked so real—had felt so real—how could he have just stopped loving her? She hadn't stopped loving him. Not yet...

If he really had done the things everyone suspected he'd done...

Then he wasn't the man she loved. Maybe he had never really been that man.

A loud thud startled her, so much so that the pewter frame nearly slipped from her grasp. She set it on the table and slipped one hand over her mouth, holding back a scream.

What had fallen?

Was it inside the house?

Was someone inside the house?

She reached into the purse slung over her shoulder. Her fingers brushed across her cell phone. But if she called 911, it would take a while for the state police post to send out a trooper. So she skipped the phone and reached for her gun.

She was the daughter of a Detroit police officer, and her father had taught her how to shoot before she'd hit her teens. And when she'd begun her nursing career at hospitals in Detroit, he'd insisted she get a permit to carry a concealed weapon because of the late nights she worked.

When he'd retired up north and she'd moved up to be near him, carrying the gun had become such a habit that she would have felt naked without it. But in Northern Lakes, she'd never had to draw it out.

Until now.

"What do you think?" Braden asked as he closed his office door, shutting Owen inside the small space with him.

"I think Luke should have stayed in the hospital," Owen replied. "He needs to be under medical observation for that concussion."

"He wasn't going to stay," Braden pointed out. "So it's better that he came back here rather than going off on his own."

Owen sighed. "Yeah, we can watch him here." But a muscle twitched along Owen's tightly clenched jaw. He was clearly filled with tension.

"You don't have to do that," Braden said. "I can keep an eye on him."

Owen snorted. "You have that sixth sense about fires, boss."

Braden wasn't sure it was actually a sixth sense, or just years of experience as a firefighter telling him when conditions were right. Of course, there were times when he'd predicted fires set by arsonists, and those had nothing to do with weather conditions.

Owen continued, "But I don't think you could detect a brain bleed or swelling the same way."

"I can figure out something's wrong if I can't wake him up," Braden said. That had been the doctor's orders—to wake him up every hour.

"I've got this," Owen said. "I'll watch over Luke. You can go home and be with your wife."

"I wish I could," Braden said with a heavy sigh. "But Sam's working an arson investigation out west. She's not home. Courtney is. Go—be with her."

Owen edged toward the door as if eager to leave. And Braden realized the paramedic was worried about his girlfriend. But Luke was here.

So Braden reiterated his first question. "What do you think about what Luke said? Do you believe he's being framed?"

Owen ran one of his hands through his dark blond hair. "I hope he's telling the truth," he said. "I'd hate to think a man I considered a friend could have colluded to kill another friend and…"

"You."

"And Courtney," Owen added.

Braden was right. After what had happened with Luke tonight, Owen was concerned about Courtney's safety. If someone else had gone after Luke, he or she could go after Courtney again.

"Go," he told the paramedic again. "I can see you're worried." He opened the door and held it open for Owen to exit.

But his friend hesitated before walking out. "If he's telling the truth, and I'm beginning to believe he might be," Owen said, "then someone tried to kill him tonight."

A shiver chased down Braden's spine; Owen was right. If everything had happened like Luke claimed, then someone had run him off the road and doused him in liquor to try to make it look like the crash was his fault.

Braden had almost lost another team member tonight, and one was one too many. He couldn't lose Luke like he had Dirk Brown.

But when Braden walked into the bunkroom after locking up behind Owen, he found it empty. He hadn't had to worry about not being able to wake up Luke. He should have worried about Luke waking up and taking off.

But had Luke really left of his own will? Or had someone gotten to him, just like they'd tried to get to him earlier?

Guilt hung heavy on Luke's shoulders. But he shrugged it off. That was the problem, the reason he'd been so damn distracted. He'd been wallowing in the guilt Willow had put on him that last morning. He'd accepted the blame for those miscarriages—for the stress his job had put on her and their marriage.

And he'd been hating himself so much that he'd let his life get to the point where everybody else seemed to hate him now, too. But he hadn't done anything wrong—to Dirk Brown, or to anyone else on his team.

He wasn't sure about Willow. He hadn't intentionally caused those miscarriages. He'd wanted those babies so very much that when he'd learned she'd lost them, and he hadn't been at her side, it felt like his heart had been ripped out, leaving a hollow ache in his chest. He had wanted to start a family with the woman he loved.

And he would always love her no matter what.

Even though she wanted nothing to do with him anymore. Even if she hated him so much that she hadn't told him she was pregnant, and she had certainly looked to be pregnant.

No matter how she felt about him, he deserved to know if he was going to be a dad.

That was why Luke had snuck out of the firehouse. He needed to talk to his wife. So he'd borrowed a US Forest Service truck from the lot behind the firehouse, and he'd driven out past the hospital, past the site where he'd been run off the road, to the sprawling ranch house they'd made into a home on the outskirts of Northern Lakes.

Driving past that site, to where his tire tracks had gone off the road into the steep ditch, sent a chill down his spine over how close he had come to being even more seriously injured. Or worse.

How the hell had it happened? Someone must have been following him when he'd left the Filling Station earlier. But the car had come at him from the other direction…

Could it have been an accident after all?

But he hadn't had a bottle of liquor in the truck. He hadn't poured that over himself.

And he thought back to that drive from the bar. There had been a vehicle behind him, one that had passed when he'd slowed down to gaze into the hospital parking lot, to look for Willow's SUV. Because he'd been looking for her, he hadn't paid the vehicle any attention.

He didn't remember what it was or what it had looked like. He'd been too distracted with thoughts of Willow, as he always was. But now he wished he'd paid more attention. He'd been more careful this time. During the drive, he'd kept glancing into the rearview mirror. But he hadn't noticed any lights behind him.

It was so late now that it was actually early, with dawn just a couple of hours away. Usually Willow's shift wouldn't have ended yet, but her SUV hadn't been parked in the lot when he'd passed this time. That was why he'd kept driving, past the crash site, to their house. Like she must have driven earlier, right past where he'd gone off the road, when she'd headed into work. Had she seen his truck? Had she seen the vehicle that had driven him off? Or had it been hers?

The driveway was long, with the cedar-sided ranch house sitting a good distance off the road, behind a thick stand of pine trees, so he couldn't see if any lights burned inside the house. If she'd come home, she could have gone right to bed. She'd been so tired during her previous pregnancies.

Maybe if he'd been around more, and not off fighting wildfires, he would have been able to help her so she wouldn't have been so exhausted, so that she wouldn't have miscarried like she had. Alone.

He was exhausted now. Maybe he should have stayed back at the firehouse. But he hadn't expected to be able to sleep—not when he had so much work to do to prove his innocence. But even more importantly than that, he knew he wasn't going to be able to sleep until he talked to Willow—until he got the truth out of her.

But he didn't want to wake her up if she was sleeping. So he turned off the lights as he turned the truck into the driveway and he nearly struck her SUV. She'd left it parked near the front door instead of in the garage.

Fortunately it was the only car in the drive. Unless someone else had parked in the garage…

Maybe Louanne Brown wasn't the only Hotshot spouse who'd been having an affair. Maybe that was why Willow had tossed him out without a second thought. She'd already had someone else.

Pain gripped him, but it wasn't in his head. It was his heart that ached with the thought of Willow being with anyone else but him.

But she wasn't with him anymore.

She hadn't been with him for months.

Had she been with someone else?

He had a right to know. He was still her husband—at least until she had him served with divorce papers. So he shut off the truck and pushed open the driver's door. The wind caught it and him, the cold slapping him in the face. He pulled up the hood of the oversize sweatshirt he wore, but it wasn't thick enough to keep him warm. He headed toward the dark house.

He didn't have his keys. Gingrich probably had them, along with the truck he'd impounded. Luke suspected there was another set out there, though. That Louanne must have copied them at some time to gain access to his car and his house, to get a hold of his gun.

He'd left it at the house when Willow had thrown him out. She'd bought it for his protection back when the arsonist had been going after his fellow Hotshots all those months ago, and she'd been so worried about him. But he'd had no interest in the firearm. He didn't even like that she carried one, but at least she knew how to use it.

While he'd gone to the shooting range with her a few times, he wasn't comfortable handling a gun. But maybe he would need to get used to it.

Tonight had proven to him that someone was out to get him. The vehicle hadn't accidentally veered into his lane; it had purposely run him off the road. Just to hurt him?

Or to kill him?

He fisted his hand, getting ready to knock at the door. But before he could raise his arm, something hard jammed between his shoulder blades. And although he hadn't handled one much, he recognized the shape and feel of the gun barrel digging into his flesh.

And he heard the telltale metallic click of it cocking, of the bullet sliding into the chamber...

He'd only just come to the realization earlier that night that he needed to fight. But it had dawned on him too late.

There was nothing he could do now. He couldn't move fast enough to dodge the bullet that was about to be fired into his back.

Chapter 5

The trespasser, with his hoodie pulled up, loomed large in the dark. He was so big Willow had hesitated to confront him before she pressed the gun against his back. Maybe with the barrel between his shoulder blades, he wouldn't dare move—wouldn't try to fight her—because if he did, there was no way she could win. He could easily disarm her because she wasn't sure she could actually pull the trigger.

All she had ever shot at before were targets at the shooting range. Just showing the gun had been enough to scare off the muggers and car jackers that she had encountered in Detroit.

But until tonight she'd never had any threat against her in Northern Lakes. At least no physical threat.

Just emotional…

Tears stung her eyes now as emotion overwhelmed her. She was so scared. Why would someone come after her? What had she done?

"What the hell do you want?" she demanded. "Why did you break into my house?"

"I didn't break in," a deep—and achingly familiar—voice rumbled. "And even if I had, it wouldn't be breaking in since it's still my house, too."

He turned then, even with the gun pressing against his back, and faced her. But she couldn't see much of him, except the faint glimmer of his blue eyes in the darkness and the sheer hulk of his broad shoulders and long, muscled body.

She pointed the gun down at the brick sidewalk now, not wanting to accidently discharge it. Just as her father had taught her how to shoot, he'd also taught her about gun safety.

"What are you doing here?" But she knew, even though he'd just glanced at her in the ER, that he'd noticed she was pregnant.

He gestured at the gun. "Why do you have that out? What's going on?"

She shivered as she remembered that thud she'd heard. She hadn't found anyone inside the house, so she'd shut off the lights and slipped outside. She'd found a chair turned over on the deck. The wind had probably knocked it over.

It was still so breezy that tresses of her hair had slipped out of her ponytail and slapped across her face. She shivered again.

And Luke said, "You're freezing. What are you doing outside?"

"I—I thought I heard something," she said.

"Me driving up?"

She glanced back at his truck. That hadn't been outside when she'd first slipped out the door. He must have driven up after she'd gone around to the back, to the

deck where she'd found that overturned chair. But only
one chair of the four-chair set had flipped over. Why
not all of them, if it really had been the wind that had
toppled it?

"It wasn't a vehicle that I heard," she admitted.

Luke's big body tensed. "What did you hear?"

She shrugged. "A thud or something. I came outside
to check it out but figured it must have been just the
wind until I saw you messing around by the front door."

"I was getting ready to knock."

"Why?" she asked. As he'd pointed out, it was still
his house. She hadn't changed the locks on him, so his
key would work.

"I think you know why," he said.

And she shivered all over again.

Now, after all these months, he finally wanted to
talk again?

There was only one reason why. And she ran the
hand not holding the gun over her belly.

His baby…

He waited until she opened the door and stepped
inside the house. Then after following her inside and
closing the door behind them, Luke asked, "Were you
going to tell me?"

He could think of only one reason why she hadn't.
Because it wasn't his baby she was carrying.

No. That wasn't possible. He and Willow had always been so happy…until they hadn't. Until the miscarriages…

Then nothing had made her happy. At least he hadn't.

Willow didn't answer him. Instead she continued to
shiver. So he walked over to the fireplace. He flinched

as he walked across the rug on which they'd made love so many times.

That was where they'd started that last night. With a fire to ward off the late November chill...

And wine...

And soft, gentle kisses...

Then, as always, the passion had ignited between them just like the fire had. He struck a match and started a fire in the hearth. Flames flickered, throwing off heat. But she didn't come close. It probably wasn't the fire she was avoiding, but him.

He glanced at the mantel and noticed the wedding portrait was gone. Had she removed all signs of him, of their marriage, from the house?

"Why won't you talk to me?" he asked.

A curse slipped through her lips. And as always, it shocked him. Willow didn't swear unless she was really angry, like she'd been that morning, when she'd revealed all her resentment of him, all her accusations that it was his fault that they'd lost their babies. He hadn't been able to argue with her because she was right; he hadn't been there for her when she'd needed him. And the reason why he hadn't—the danger he'd been in—had caused her the stress that had affected her pregnancies.

"You want to talk?" she asked, then snorted. "Yeah, right. You've had months to talk to me, and you never tried."

"I didn't think you wanted to talk to me," he reminded her. That was what she'd told him that morning.

She shrugged. "Maybe not. But I deserved to hear it from you before I heard it from everyone else."

"Hear what?" he asked, but a knot tightened in his gut—a knot of dread and apprehension.

"About you and Louanne..."

He cursed now. "There was never any 'me and Louanne,'" he said. And he couldn't believe that she, of all people, would think that there had been. He hadn't just loved her too much to betray her. He'd loved Dirk too much as well.

But Dirk was gone.

And, for the first time in all of these months, he realized that his marriage was, too. Willow had never really known him if she thought he was capable of cheating on her and his friend. And he wondered how well he really knew her.

"What are you doing?" he asked. "Trying to justify what you've done to me—to us?"

She lifted her free hand to her head and rubbed at her temple. His head was pounding, too, but he was almost getting used to it.

It kept tempo with his madly pounding heart.

"What are you talking about?"

"There are so many things," he said. "Was that you on your way to work—were you the one who drove me off the road?"

She gasped. "What?"

"Your vehicle wasn't at the hospital when I passed it, and if you were coming from here to work, you would have passed me."

Her face paled, and she shook her head. "If I did, I didn't see you."

He wanted to believe her. But he'd been run off the road and had a gun pointed at him all in one night. It was too much. But it was actually nothing compared to learning that she had kept her pregnancy from him.

"I have a right to know about the baby," he murmured, his voice choking with emotion. "I have a right to know…"

She flinched. "That's not…"

"What?" he asked. "You know it's true. I'm still your husband. Even if that baby isn't mine, you should have told me you're pregnant."

She gasped again. "Not yours?" Her face, which had been so pale moments ago, flushed with bright color. Angry color. She cursed again. "How dare you! How dare you break into my home and accuse me of cheating!"

He flinched now, at the volume of her voice, and what she said. "Isn't that what you just did to me? Accused me of cheating on you, and with my best friend's wife? And I didn't break in," he reminded her again. "I came here to ask you a question. And you've done everything you can to avoid answering me." She was all outrage and defensiveness, so maybe she hadn't cheated. Or maybe she had and didn't want to admit it. She'd gotten mad but hadn't actually denied it.

And he could think of one person—from his team—who would have cheated with her. She'd known one of the Hotshots before she'd ever met him. She knew Trent Miles from when she'd worked in Detroit. But they'd both assured him that they'd never dated, even though Trent had obviously tried to get her to go out with him.

They hadn't dated in Detroit. But what about now?

What about after she'd thrown Luke out of their house?

"After all these months, you want to talk now?" she scoffed. "At four in the morning?"

He had no idea what time it was, and he didn't care. He hadn't thought about it when he'd left the firehouse. He'd been thinking only of her.

Of seeing her…

Of talking to her…

Of finding out for certain about the baby. It had to be his. She was showing already, so she must have gotten pregnant when they were still together.

"I don't care what time it is," he said.

"I do," she said. "I'm tired. Too tired to deal with you right now."

She had come home early from her shift. Was that because she was tired or not feeling well?

Was this pregnancy already at risk? They hadn't even known that there had been any issues with her other pregnancies until it was too late.

That knot tightened more in his stomach, threatening to make him double over from the pressure. But he couldn't put that pressure on her, couldn't put any more stress on her. He wasn't going to be responsible for her losing another child.

Not when he knew a baby was all she wanted now.

She obviously didn't want him anymore.

She'd tossed him out months ago and never asked him to come home. Probably because she'd never forgiven him for what he'd cost her. Just as he would never be able to forgive himself for the pain he'd caused her.

He didn't want to cause her any more; he didn't want to upset her again, so he forced himself to walk toward the door. When he passed her, she tensed and sucked in a breath.

His body tingled from her nearness. He wanted to reach out, wanted to touch her...

To slide his fingers along her jaw, to tip up her face to his, so that he could kiss her. He missed her so damn much. Missed her touch...

Her kiss...

But he forced himself to keep walking toward the door. And as he passed her, he heard her exhale a breath in a ragged sigh. He closed his hand around the door-knob, but he hesitated before turning it.

He waited for her to call him back, to tell him to stop, just like he'd waited that morning. And just like that morning, she said nothing.

So he opened the door and walked out. He ached to be inside with her—in their home, in their bed, in her arms...

But while he wanted to fight to prove his innocence, he couldn't fight with Willow—not when she was so fragile, not when it might cost her another child.

He had to do what was best for her. And it wasn't him.

Maybe he had never been what was best for her. She'd refused to date Trent because of his dangerous career as a firefighter, just as she'd refused to date any of her father's law-officer friends. She'd known, from her parents' own failed marriage and the failed marriages of her father's colleagues, that marriage to a man with a dangerous profession was hard. Too hard.

But she'd made an exception to her rule to date him, then marry him. That was an exception she obviously regretted making now.

If only Willow Garrison had shot him...

It would have all been over.

Nobody would ever figure out who'd really had the affair with Louanne Brown. Luke Garrison would have died with everybody believing it was him.

Even his wife...

But did she actually believe it? If she had, she probably would have pulled that trigger. She would have shot him in the back.

But instead she'd lowered her weapon to her side.

She had let him live. She'd only bought her husband a little more time. Luke had to die. And soon.

Before he figured out who was trying to frame him.

Before he got other people believing that he'd been framed.

Had he tried telling his wife that?

If so, she must not have believed him, or he wouldn't have left so quickly.

But then Luke had lingered for quite a while, leaning back against the door he'd pulled closed between them. Maybe he had been more seriously injured in the crash than he'd appeared to have been.

And if Garrison was wounded, then he was weak. Now might be the perfect time to take him out. To finish him off.

And nobody would suspect that he had been murdered. They would believe that he had just succumbed to his injuries from the crash.

Didn't doctors worry about head wounds most of all? About bleeding on the brain or swelling?

Wouldn't it be easy enough to hit him again and cause more damage?

He wouldn't see it coming, just as he hadn't seen his wife sneak up behind him in the dark. Neither of them was wearing night-vision goggles.

The goggles made it easy to keep track of them, easy to see them while remaining undetected. But was now the right time to kill Luke?

Or was it a better time to frame him for another crime, since his car being used in a hit-and-run and Louanne using his gun hadn't been enough for charges to be brought against him? Would people be more likely to accept that he'd been Louanne's accomplice if he was found guilty of something else?

Which was the easier target?

Luke Garrison or his pregnant wife? She was armed but she posed no real threat. Not like Luke. When he'd been staying at Dirk and Louanne's, he might have noticed something, might have caught on to what had really been going on.

Luke was the one who had to die. And soon.

Before he cleared his name. The only way to keep the truth from coming out was for Luke Garrison to go to his grave a guilty man.

Chapter 6

Willow waited, her body tense and aching. He'd been so close—within touching distance. But then he'd walked right past her, just as he had that last morning. He'd walked right out of their home.

Several long moments passed before an engine rumbled, shattering the silence. Lights flashed in the front window as he backed down the driveway.

He was leaving. He wasn't fighting for them. He didn't care enough to fight for them. Sure, she'd told him she was tired.

And she was.

But he could have tried. He could have held her. He could have told her he loved her. But he had just walked away. Maybe he couldn't forgive her for all the things she'd said that awful morning she'd thrown him out. She knew placing all the blame on him wasn't fair, especially when she'd known better than to get involved with a Hotshot. Her mother had told her that it would lead to nothing but fear and heartbreak. But there had been a time that Willow had thought Luke was worth it.

Tears stung Willow's eyes and burned in her nose. Earlier she'd fought them back, but now she let them flow. Seeing him had been so hard. Even harder because all the old feelings had rushed over her, overwhelming her. The desire.

The passion.

The love…

She blinked furiously, trying to clear away the tears. Maybe it was just pregnancy hormones making her overreact. She might have already been pregnant that last morning, when she'd lashed out at him in her guilt.

When she'd pushed him away.

Was it all her fault?

The problems in their marriage? His drinking…

And… What?

What had Luke done?

He claimed he hadn't had an affair with his friend's wife, but then he'd turned around and accused her of cheating on him. Wasn't that kind of defensiveness a sign of guilt?

Or was she only looking for a reason to blame him instead of herself for what had happened? For their marriage blowing up like it had?

Maybe if he'd stayed, maybe if they'd talked…

But they probably wouldn't have talked, just like they hadn't that night. They'd tried that night, too, to share their pain over the loss of their babies. But they'd used passion to distract themselves.

But as always, Willow hadn't been distracted for very long. Then she'd felt guilty, for forgetting even for a moment what she'd lost, and she'd lashed out.

She closed her eyes as a fresh wave of tears threatened to crash over her. Because she felt so guilty again...

But it wasn't about her babies.

It was about Luke.

She'd been so mean to him, so she shouldn't have been surprised he hadn't fought for their marriage. She hadn't given him anything to fight for.

Another engine rumbled to life somewhere in the distance, but not so far away that she hadn't been able to hear it. Had someone else been parked somewhere on their property?

Or was it Luke's truck? Had he stopped and then started it up again?

She hoped that was the case. That it was just Luke.

Because if someone else had been parked out there in the darkness, that meant that someone else could have been inside the house earlier.

That he or she could have left that window open.

Could have moved that wedding portrait.

But that didn't make sense. But neither did Luke cheating or trying to hurt his friends. The Luke she'd known and loved would have never hurt anyone. That was why she'd thought it was worth the risk to fall for him, to marry him, but once she'd had to face the reality of how often his life was at risk, she'd changed her mind. She'd lost her nerve. If only she could lose her love for him, too. If only she could stop worrying about him.

And she was worried because he was clearly in danger again. But she wasn't sure if someone else posed a threat to him or if *he* was the threat to himself.

Walking out had been a mistake. Months ago and now. Luke knew it the minute he'd walked away—both times. But he hadn't wanted to put Willow through any more stress or pain than she had already endured because of the miscarriages. And he certainly didn't want her to miscarry again. He doubted either of them could survive losing another baby.

Even now tears stung his eyes as he thought of the room in their house, the one they'd decorated with little lambs and bunnies. They'd worked so hard painting it and putting up all those cute decals and assembling the creamy white crib and changing table. They'd been all ready for a baby that had never come home. Because Willow had been afraid that Luke would never come home from that California wildfire when they'd lost contact for so long.

And then the second baby had been lost, too…because she'd been so scared that the arsonist was going to target Luke like he'd seemed to target his colleagues, Wyatt, Dawson, Cody and Braden. She'd been right that last morning together to blame him. And now she was probably even more scared that she would lose this baby, too, because of him.

Walking away was the right thing to do. For her.

Even if it killed him.

And he had a horrible feeling that it might—if whoever was framing him didn't kill him first. Why him?

Why frame him?

Had someone wanted him out of the way so he would have another chance with Willow? Someone like Trent Miles? But Trent hadn't acted jealous of them, hadn't seemed to really care that she'd given Luke a chance when she hadn't him.

So maybe he was being framed because he'd been an easy target. He'd been so upset over his marriage falling apart that he hadn't realized what was going on until it was too late.

If only Louanne would have told the truth before that gun had gone off and mortally wounded her…

But she must have been protecting someone. Her real accomplice.

That had to be who'd driven him off the road. That hadn't been any more of an accident than Dirk's death had proven to be. If the car had gone past without stopping or had stopped and tried to help…

But whoever had stopped had doused him with alcohol before Owen and the trooper had arrived. They'd wanted to frame him for his own death. It had to be Louanne's accomplice.

Unless it was somebody who believed he was Louanne's accomplice…

Someone who believed he'd killed Dirk and had tried to kill Owen and Courtney. And maybe that person had decided to punish Luke.

He intended to prove his innocence, but in order to do that he would probably have to prove someone else's guilt.

Who?

It had to be someone close to him—someone close enough to be watching him without arousing suspicion in him or anyone else. So it had to be someone he knew and someone he trusted.

But now he knew that he couldn't really trust anyone.

Owen's heart pounded fast and hard in his chest, and his skin was slick with sweat. As always, he was shaken to his core…from making love with the love of his life. He dropped back onto the mattress with a groan.

Courtney was lying next to him, her body limp. "Wow…" she murmured. "Just wow…"

Owen chuckled.

"If that's how you're going to apologize for being late," Courtney said, "you can be late as often as you want."

He chuckled again.

But she turned toward him, and her brow furrowed with concern. "Why were you late?" she asked. "Bad accident?"

"Bad enough," he said.

"I know you can't tell me because of privacy laws and all of that…"

He grinned. "No. I'm not supposed to tell you." But in the truck on the way back to the firehouse from the hospital, Luke had given him and Braden permission to tell everyone the truth about what had happened that night. At least the truth according to him, that someone had run him off the road and doused him with alcohol. Why would someone do that?

Courtney reached up and touched a finger to the deep crease between his eyebrows. "What's wrong? What's bothering you?"

She knew him so well—better than anyone else ever had.

"I heard you moving around in the store downstairs before you came up here," she said. Her apartment was above her store, which was her baby, stocked with clothing she'd designed. "Were you making sure all the doors were locked?"

He nodded. That was a mistake he didn't intend to make again. Northern Lakes wasn't the safe hometown it had once been for them. People had to lock their doors now—especially people like him.

He didn't want to become the target of a killer again.

And, more importantly, he didn't want to inadvertently put Courtney in danger again.

He hated to admit his fear aloud, but he and Courtney shared everything. And she, after everything she'd been through the last few weeks, deserved to know. "I don't think it's over," he admitted.

She shivered and dragged up the sheets they'd tangled at the foot of the bed. "How can it not be?" she asked. "Louanne Brown is dead."

"Luke Garrison is not," he said. But he had a feeling that someone had tried tonight.

She tucked a strand of glossy black hair behind her ear and focused her wide brown eyes on his face. The short hairstyle accentuated her delicate features and sharp cheekbones. She was so beautiful.

"You believe those rumors?" she asked him. Courtney had never been a fan of the small-town tendency to gossip.

"It was his car that ran us down," he reminded her. "It was his gun that killed Louanne Brown."

"But she was driving the car," Courtney said. "And she pulled the trigger on that gun when she was trying to kill you again. Luke didn't do it."

"So you don't think he had anything to do with it?" Owen asked. Hopefully. He didn't want to believe a man that he'd considered a friend could be involved in murder and attempted murder.

Courtney hesitated for a long moment. "I know how it feels to be suspected of something you haven't done."

Owen flinched. For a brief moment he'd thought she might have had something to do with the attempts on his life. "I was just using that as an excuse to get closer to you," he said.

"To seduce me."

"You seduced me," he reminded her. And she had. She was so damn beautiful and sexy and smart and...

He reached out and touched her face, then slid his fingertips down her cheek to her throat. Her pulse quickened beneath his fingertip.

Her lips curved into a smile. "You're trying to seduce me now," she said.

He grinned, too. "I need a few more minutes of recovery, and I will," he promised.

"And you need more evidence to convince me that Luke Garrison was Louanne's accomplice," Courtney said.

"His car? His gun? That's not enough?" Owen asked.

She shook her head. "It's not even enough for Trooper Gingrich to get an arrest warrant. So, no. It's not enough."

He expelled a ragged breath of relief. He would rather have doubts about Luke's guilt than his innocence.

"You don't want to suspect Luke," she mused.

"No. I always thought he was a good guy."

"Just like you?"

He snorted. "I'm the hometown hero." He was only repeating what she'd said about him, disparagingly, so many times.

She laughed. "Yes, you are."

Owen didn't feel much like a hero. He never had. There were so many people he hadn't been able to save. Fortunately tonight Luke hadn't been beyond help. But if someone really was after him...

"He was the one in the accident tonight," Owen admitted. "He claims he was run off the road."

She shivered again. "Claims?"

Owen shrugged. "Gingrich thought he was drunk and drove off the road on his own."

She nodded. "He does tend to hang out at the Filling Station quite a bit."

"But maybe that's just because he has no place else to go," Owen suggested.

"Since his wife threw him out," Courtney said. "For months everybody has been speculating about why he and Willow split up. And since word got out about Louanne having an affair, everybody now thinks that's why."

"I thought you didn't listen to gossip?"

"Tammy Ingles is my best friend," she said. "Gossip hangs in a cloud around her." Tammy owned the most popular beauty salon in Northern Lakes.

"Since you've heard it, what do you think about it?" he asked.

"I don't really believe it," Courtney said. "Luke's wife is much more attractive than Louanne Brown."

"Looks sometimes has nothing to do with it," Owen said. He touched the scar on his face. "I have this and you're still with me."

She sat up and pressed her lips to the scar. "I think it makes you even sexier."

He didn't need any more time to recover. He wanted her as much as he had when he'd walked in the door earlier. But before he could reach for her, something rattled. Something like glass or wood.

The sound was soft, emanating from the store downstairs. He'd checked the doors. They were locked. But that didn't mean that someone still couldn't get inside—like someone had the night they'd set the store on fire.

The night he could have lost Courtney. The night she'd nearly lost everything she'd been working to build in Northern Lakes.

"Did you…?" Her whisper trailed off as he slipped

out of bed. He pulled on his pants and he wished like hell that he'd bought a gun.

But Courtney handed him her weapon. A bat she'd nearly used on him a few times. It wouldn't be much protection if the intruder had a gun.

But he didn't point that out to her. He grabbed the bat and headed toward the stairs. The fear he'd confessed to her moments ago had been realized: it wasn't over.

Chapter 7

Luke ducked as the bat swung toward his already banged-up head. "Hey, it's me!" he said. But maybe that was why Owen had swung it at him.

Maybe he wanted to finish him off—if he was the one who'd run him off the road earlier. But despite not being able to trust anyone else, Luke really wanted to be able to trust Owen James. He didn't want to think that the town hero would have tried to kill him.

With a curse, Owen pulled back the bat. "I'm sorry. I didn't know it was you."

Luke wasn't so sure about that. "At least you didn't have a gun."

"What the hell are you doing sneaking around the alley?" Owen asked.

"I wasn't sneaking," Luke said. "I parked the truck and then I tried to find a doorbell to ring. But it's dark and I knocked over something that was lying near the dumpster."

Owen peered over his shoulder into the alley. "You shouldn't be driving. You should be in bed. What the hell are you doing here?"

"I'm sorry it's so late," Luke said. But he'd waited long enough to take his life back and clear his name. He couldn't wait any longer, not with someone willing to go as far as they'd gone tonight. He could have been killed, and while he wasn't sure how Willow felt about him anymore, he wanted to be around for that child…wanted to make sure that nothing happened to him or her.

Owen stepped back and gestured him inside the door. Then he flipped on the lights and studied Luke's face in the sudden glare of the fluorescent bulbs. They stood in the back of the store, near a stairwell leading to the second-story apartment where Owen must have been before he'd heard Luke fumbling around in the dark.

"Are you all right?" the paramedic asked him. "Is your head bothering you? Blurred vision? Nausea?"

Luke shook his head and ignored the sudden blurred vision and nausea that overcame him. He wasn't going to let anything stop him now. "No, I'm fine."

"No, you're not," Owen said. "If you were thinking straight, you wouldn't be creeping around the alley at this hour."

A ragged sigh slipped through his lips as he realized how Owen and Courtney must have felt, after all they'd been through, to realize someone was sneaking around their place again. "You're right. I'm sorry I disturbed you. But I really had to talk to you."

"You're sure you're not hurting?" Owen persisted, his eyes narrowed as he continued to study Luke's face.

He was hurting but not just physically. Seeing Willow, being in their home…

All he'd wanted to do was close his arms around her and hold her close. Walking away again had nearly killed him. But he couldn't be responsible for her losing another baby. *He* couldn't lose another baby; just the thought of it intensified that ache in his chest.

"No," Luke said. "I just had to talk to you right away—while it was all fresh in your mind."

"While what was fresh?" Owen asked.

"The *accident* site," Luke said. "Did you see anyone when you drove up?"

Owen shook his head. "Just Marty."

The state trooper.

"Who called for an ambulance?" Luke asked.

"Marty, I guess," Owen replied. "The call came through Dispatch."

Luke cursed. "That's a dead end then." He'd so hoped that Owen had seen something or someone.

"You're not going to ask Marty who reported it?" Owen asked. "If he saw anyone?"

Luke already knew what he'd say. "He's convinced that there was no other vehicle involved. That I drove off the road because I was drinking."

"The blood-alcohol test proves he's wrong," Owen reminded him.

Luke shrugged. "Do you think that's going to matter to him? He wants a Hotshot to be guilty of something, so he can stick it to Braden."

Owen sighed and nodded. "True…" And he was studying Luke's face again.

Luke suspected he wasn't looking for any signs of a concussion right now, though; he was looking for signs of guilt. Luke's…

"It's not me," Luke insisted. "I'm not the Hotshot guilty of anything."

Owen tensed. "But you think a Hotshot is?"

"I hope it's not another Hotshot," Luke said. But now he took his turn to study Owen's face. Because of the scar on the former Marine's cheek, people either stared or wouldn't look directly at him.

"But you think it could be me?" Owen asked. "Remember, I'm the one someone was just trying to kill a few short weeks ago. I had a bunch of *accidents* that weren't *accidents*."

"And I had nothing to do with those," Luke insisted. "So nobody should be trying to get back at me because of what Louanne Brown did."

Owen pressed a hand against his bare chest. It had more scars than his face. The former Marine had obviously been through a lot already in his life, but then in the last few weeks he'd lost another friend and nearly his own life. "You think I ran you off the road tonight?"

Hearing light footsteps overhead, Luke glanced up. Owen wasn't the only one who might have been looking for some payback.

"Hey," Owen cautioned. "Don't even think it…"

"You did," Luke reminded him. "You thought she might have been the one going after you."

"But she nearly lost her store and her life when *your* car ran us over," Owen said.

Which just proved they had motive to go after him. "Exactly," he said.

Owen snorted. "You're not going to blame either of us for what happened to you tonight."

"I don't want to blame you," Luke said. "I want your help to find out who's framing me."

Owen shook his head. "I don't know…"

"You don't know whether or not to believe me," Luke said, and he felt that sickening wave of nausea wash over him again. But it had nothing to do with the concussion. "I swear to you that I never had an affair with Louanne. I would never cheat on my wife."

Owen tilted his head, as if weighing his words. "Does she think that you did?"

Luke was afraid that she did. *Now.* After all the damn rumors had started circulating around town after Willow threw him out. "That's not why she had me leave," he said. "I—I…"

He couldn't share the real reason; it was more painful than being accused of cheating. Being blamed for their babies dying…and knowing that she was probably right. His job put him in dangerous situations, and while he was willing to face those situations, he was putting unnecessary stress on his spouse worrying about him.

"I would never cheat," he repeated.

And he hoped like hell that Willow knew him better than to believe the gossip about him. But just like with Owen and Braden and the rest of his team, he'd seen the doubt and suspicion on her beautiful face. But after Dirk's murder, at the hands of his wife, Luke wondered how well anyone really knew anyone else.

"I can't believe that Louanne was…" He shook his head and winced at the pain that jabbed his temple. "I spent so much time over there, but I never noticed that they were having problems."

Of course, he'd been preoccupied with his own problems. So maybe that was why Dirk hadn't burdened him with what had been going on with his marriage.

Despite feeling a flash of guilt that he was gossiping about the dead, Luke added, "But they always seemed more like friends than lovers…"

While he and Willow had always been more lovers than friends…

Maybe that was why instead of turning to him when they were grieving, she'd turned *on* him. They'd always had more passion than friendship.

"She wasn't his friend," Owen remarked bitterly. He'd been with Dirk when he died; he could have been killed as well. But it had probably been almost as bad to see how much Dirk had suffered in his final moments.

"I was his friend," Luke said. "I would have never hurt him. He was a good man. A good friend."

Owen nodded in agreement with his jaw clenched so tightly a muscle twitched in his cheek.

"I thought you were a good friend, too," Luke said.

"I am," Owen said.

"Then why didn't you tell me that Willow's pregnant?" Since Owen worked at the hospital, too, he had to have noticed. Especially since Willow also worked in the ER.

Owen sucked in a breath, clearly shocked. "You didn't know?"

Luke clenched his jaw now, so tightly that his teeth ached, and shook his head.

"Why didn't she tell you?" Owen asked.

Luke couldn't answer that. Before they got married, they had promised to always be honest with each other. To never lie.

That was why he'd believed what she'd told him that morning, that she wanted him to leave. That she hated him.

She hadn't kept her resentment from him. So he would have never suspected that Willow would keep her pregnancy from him. Did she hate him that much that she didn't even want him to be part of their child's life? Or had she been afraid that Luke would cost her this pregnancy, too?

"Even if I'd known you didn't know, I wouldn't have said anything," Owen admitted. "It's Willow's news to share...not mine."

"And your allegiance is to her, not me? Not a team member?" Luke asked.

Owen said nothing, but that muscle twitched just above his clenched jaw.

What the hell had happened to the Hotshots? Dirk's death had turned them all against each other. Or at least against him, although no one was a fan of the man who'd taken Dirk's place on the team either. Trick McRooney.

Coming here had been a mistake—not just because of the hour, but also because he would get no help from Owen. Disappointment added to the weariness weighing on him. Owen had been his only hope, since he really couldn't trust anyone else on his team—not when one of them could have been having the affair with Dirk's wife.

Or maybe even with Luke's wife.

Had Willow finally given Trent Miles the chance he'd wanted with her so long ago? Or was Trent the one trying to get Luke out of the way so that Willow would give him that chance?

Whisper-soft kisses pressed against her cheek before trailing down her neck to her shoulder and then her breasts...

Soft hair brushed across her skin like those kisses, making her tingle everywhere as tension built inside her. He knew just where to touch her, where to kiss her...

Luke...

She reached out, wanting to touch him, wanting to kiss him...just wanting to feel him close to her. But her fingers skimmed across empty sheets, and she jerked awake to find herself alone.

Like she'd been for the last few months.

But then the baby fluttered around inside her, reminding her that she was not alone. And for the baby especially, Willow could not get all stressed out...like she'd been the night before.

After she'd heard that second engine, she'd heard another noise. But instead of going outside to investigate again, she'd made certain all the doors were locked and retired to the main bedroom. When she rolled over, she saw the gun lying on the nightstand. She'd been ready if anyone had tried to come through the bedroom door.

But nobody had tried.

The last noise she'd heard must have been the wind. It wasn't Luke. He hadn't returned after she'd thrown him out. Would he ever come back? Did he even want to?

He hadn't made any effort these last months to reconcile. Didn't he miss her the way she missed him, so much that she physically ached for him?

She glanced from the gun to the clock on the nightstand and groaned. She had a hair appointment this morning that she'd had to schedule weeks ago. If she missed it, she wasn't likely to get another appointment for several more weeks. Tammy Ingles's salon was so popular that the schedule rarely had open slots.

And even more than she wanted her hair done, Willow wanted to talk to the savvy salon owner. Tammy always knew what was *really* going on in Northern Lakes. Maybe she could put Willow's worries about Luke to rest.

Or make them worse.

Ignoring her doubts and fears, Willow hustled to get

ready. She didn't even have time to eat, and her stomach— or maybe the baby—growled in protest. But she bypassed the kitchen to head through the living room since she'd parked nearer the front door. As she walked through the room, she felt that strange chill again.

But she'd shut and locked that window the night before. The curtains were lying flat against the panes, so it hadn't been opened again. But then she noticed the pewter picture frame facedown on that side table. She reached out to right it and cursed as broken glass nipped at one fingertip.

Cracks ran across the wedding portrait—just like the cracks that had broken her marriage. The grief, the guilt, the blame...

Tears stung her eyes, but she blinked them back. The frame could be fixed. Could her marriage?

Maybe Tammy would have some information that could help Willow determine if that was possible—if she could forgive Luke or if she had anything to forgive...

Maybe she was the one who owed Luke the apology. And not just for placing all the blame of the miscarriages on him, but for thinking—even for a moment— that he could have betrayed her and his best friend.

She put the frame back down and grabbed her keys and purse. The minute she opened the door, she noticed that there was something off about her vehicle—that the SUV seemed to be sitting lower to the ground.

Then she noticed why: all four tires were flat—so flat that the rims sat on the asphalt driveway. The tires had been slashed.

She gasped.

Who would have done something like that?

Luke?

Was he that furious with her over not telling him about the baby? Did he really believe that it might be someone else's child?

The baby fluttered again inside her. Because of all the movement and how much she was showing, she was probably even further along than she'd thought, than that last night they'd shared. She'd finally pushed aside her fear about losing this baby and had scheduled an appointment for an ultrasound next week. Soon she would know how far along she was, hopefully far enough that this baby could survive if she went into early labor again. Because of stress.

And staring at those flattened tires had her pulse quickening, and her heart beating heavy with dread and fear. Who would have done something so vicious? She didn't want to believe it was Luke, that he was capable of such petty anger.

She had to report it. Not just because the insurance company would probably require a report but also because of the baby. She needed to protect herself so that she could protect her child, too.

But was the person she needed protecting from the person she loved the most?

"So he was with you last night?" Braden asked Owen, his voice pitched to a low whisper. He didn't want the other Hotshots filing into the conference room on the third floor of the firehouse to overhear their conversation. Usually the group talked boisterously until he started the meeting, but they were all curiously quiet.

Since Dirk's death, there had been a pall over the team. They weren't as close as they'd once been. Maybe Dirk's death wasn't the only reason for that, though.

Maybe someone else had begun to realize what Braden had been told in a note: one of them was not who they all thought he or she was.

"Last night?" Owen grumbled. Dark circles rimmed his blue eyes. "More like this morning. But, yeah, he showed up at the store."

That was where Luke had told Braden he'd been when he'd questioned him after Garrison had returned to the bunkroom at the firehouse. But Braden had had a niggling feeling that his team member had left something out. "Luke told me that he'd wanted to question you about the crash…about what you'd seen."

Owen nodded. "Yeah." He sighed. "I wish I saw something that would help him."

"You want to help him?" Braden asked, and his heart lifted. He'd been wondering if calling all the Hotshots together for this meeting had been the right call. He intended to remind them all that they were a family, and that there was no real evidence against Luke, or Gingrich would have happily arrested him before now. This meeting was about rebuilding the camaraderie they'd once shared.

As he glanced around the room, he could see the curiosity on the faces of his team. They were obviously wondering why the hell he'd called the meeting. He hadn't told anyone—not Trick and not even Luke.

Luke stumbled into the conference room, his hair mussed as if he'd just woken up. But the circles around his eyes were even darker than Owen's. He looked like hell—like he hadn't even slept at all the night before. And between his trip to Owen's place and Braden waking him up every hour the rest of the morning, he probably hadn't.

The way everyone else stopped talking and stared at

Luke confirmed to Braden that he was doing the right thing. He could have suspended Luke until the investigation proved his innocence. But that wouldn't send the message he wanted to send. He wanted to bring his team back together as a family again and that meant supporting each other during tough times, not turning on each other.

He turned his attention to Owen, who had yet to answer his question. And the paramedic Hotshot nodded. "Yes, I want to help him."

"So do I," Braden said. But before he could call the meeting to order, sirens wailed so loudly that the windows rattled.

Instead of being alarmed, the Hotshots chuckled.

"Stanley must have hit the sirens again," Cody Mallehan said with a grin. Stanley was Cody's former foster brother, and Cody had talked Braden into hiring the teenager to maintain the trucks and clean up around the firehouse.

"Or Annie," Braden grumbled. Annie was the enormous mix of sheepdog and bullmastiff that had somehow become the firehouse mascot.

But Owen was shaking his head. "That's not the engine sirens."

And Braden agreed. He moved toward the rattling windows. On the street three stories below sat a state police cruiser with lights flashing and sirens blaring.

"What the hell…?" he murmured.

Trooper Gingrich burst into the room seconds later. But he didn't speak right away—instead he panted for breath. The former high-school jock was obviously too out of shape to climb three stories. Once he could breathe, he headed toward Luke. "Turn around!" he ordered him. "I told you last night that you needed to get used to the feeling of these handcuffs." And he snapped the metal around Luke's wrists.

"There was no alcohol in his system last night," Owen said, stepping in to help Luke just as he'd said he'd wanted.

Unfortunately the rest of the Hotshots just stared at Luke getting arrested. Not in horror, but almost in acceptance. As if they'd been expecting it.

"Why are you arresting him?" Braden asked.

Despite his efforts over the last few weeks, the dimwitted trooper hadn't been able to make a credible case against Luke. The prosecutor had refused to press charges based on circumstantial evidence.

So what had changed?

If the trooper had finally found evidence where Braden had found none, maybe Marty wasn't the dimwitted one. Maybe Braden had been for wanting to believe in Luke's innocence.

Chapter 8

Luke hadn't had a clue why the superintendent had called the meeting of all the Hotshots. But maybe now he knew.

Maybe Gingrich had given him a heads-up and Braden had wanted everyone to see the arrest—to have whatever closure they needed to move on from Dirk's death. The only problem was that Luke wasn't guilty.

He turned to his boss and shook his head. "How could you?" he murmured.

As those cuffs snapped tightly around his wrists, he was beyond humiliated. He'd been betrayed. And for a few moments the night before, he'd started to hope that Braden and Owen believed him. That they, too, had realized he'd been framed.

Sure, Braden was asking why he was being arrested, but it was probably just because he wanted the trooper to announce it for him. Why else would he have called the entire team together? Wildfire season wasn't projected to begin for a few more weeks, and they'd nearly finished the fire break they'd been working on when Dirk died.

"This is bullshit," Luke said as he strained against the cuffs. He wasn't just protesting the arrest, though. He was protesting his guilt and all the suspicion he saw on the faces of his team members. That concussion had finally knocked the fight back into him; he only hoped it wasn't too late.

"I have not done anything wrong," he shouted to the room as Gingrich began pulling him back toward the door. "I loved Dirk like a brother. I never would have betrayed him. And I sure as hell would have never betrayed my own wife."

Gingrich snorted. "I'm arresting you because of your wife's report."

He tensed but stopped struggling. "What? What the hell are you talking about?"

She must really hate him, even more than he'd thought, that she would lie and press charges against him.

"I'm arresting you for trespassing—"

"On my own property?" Luke scoffed. And he hadn't even let himself inside; he'd been about to knock when she'd pulled the gun on him.

"And malicious vandalism," Gingrich added.

Luke's already pounding head pounded harder with confusion and pain. "Vandalism?" he asked. "I didn't touch anything." Not even Willow. And it had killed him to not reach out to her, to not pull her into his arms and hold her close—so close that he would never let her go again.

But she obviously didn't want that. She didn't want

him with her. She wanted him behind bars...for something he hadn't done.

Gingrich snorted again. "Save it for your lawyer..."

Luke didn't have one—not even a divorce lawyer—because he didn't want one. He didn't want a divorce, but he'd been waiting for months for Willow to file. He had no doubt that she intended to do that now. If she could file false charges against him...

Then he didn't know her at all.

And the looks on the faces of his team members as Gingrich led him away echoed his sentiment. They didn't know him at all, because they all obviously believed he was guilty. Or had one of them set him up to look that way?

He studied their faces as Gingrich pulled him through the doorway. Some looked away from him, as if disgusted or embarrassed for him. Like the female Hotshots, Henrietta "Hank" Rollins and Michaela Momber. Others were harder to read, like Ethan Sommerly, but his bushy beard and long hair made it difficult to see his face at all. And Trent...

The Detroit firefighter was reputed to have seen and done it all, especially if he was the former gang member some speculated he was. But he shook his head before turning away.

Maybe it was just Luke's imagination but he thought a smirk might have crossed Trent's lips. He was the only one who looked remotely amused, though.

The others looked angry, as if they figured he was guilty of all the rumors. That he'd betrayed their friend.

Luke had to prove his innocence, or he was going to lose even more than he already had. He was going to lose his job and his freedom.

But then he remembered how that vehicle had come

straight at him last night. Someone had deliberately run him off the road, and they couldn't have known that he would survive the crash.

Maybe he needed to be worried about his life as well.

Maybe it was the pregnancy hormones. Maybe it was the ordeal she'd already endured that morning, after the trauma of seeing Luke the night before. Whatever the reason, a simple act of kindness had reduced Willow to tears. Her shoulders shook with sobs she tried to muffle as Tammy Ingles pulled her car into a parking space in front of her salon on the main street of Northern Lakes, Willow in the passenger seat.

She had learned at a young age to hide her tears because crying had made her father so uncomfortable. A stoic man who had never shown his own emotions, he hadn't known how to deal with hers. So she'd worked hard to hide them on the weekends she'd spent with him and eventually that ability had spilled over into her weeks with her mother and into the rest of her life.

"Are you okay?" the hairdresser asked.

Willow nodded. "I'm sorry," she said, managing to gasp the apology she'd always wound up giving her father whenever she'd given in to the weakness. "I'm so sorry."

"Why are you sorry?" Tammy asked. "You have nothing to be sorry about."

"I'm hysterical," Willow pointed out—probably needlessly since her voice cracked with that hysteria and she couldn't stem the flow of tears down her face.

What the hell was the matter with her? Usually she was stronger than this—better able to cope.

Tammy reached out and curled her arm around Willow's shoulders. "You're entitled. Cry your heart out…"

Her heart was already out. It had left with Luke. Or so she'd thought until she'd learned she was pregnant. Then her heart had found its way to her baby, where it beat steadily every time she listened for it. And she listened often when she was at work, needing that steady reassurance that this child was alive. It hadn't slipped away without her noticing like her last baby had, dying inside her sometime before she'd gone into labor. The first had just tried to come too early—way too early.

She dragged in a deep breath and attempted to pull herself together. "You are so kind," Willow told Tammy. "You didn't need to come out and pick me up."

But that was exactly what the salon owner had done after Willow had called to cancel the appointment. Tammy had shown up at the house, after the flatbed had taken away the SUV, and she'd insisted on bringing Willow to town.

Tammy squeezed her shoulders again. "I was happy to do it."

And the tears bubbled up and over again. Willow shook her head. "That's going above and beyond…"

"I run a full-service salon," Tammy said with a little chuckle. "I also consider us friends."

The admission overwhelmed Willow. She had work friends and she had befriended other significant others of the Hotshots. But Tammy…

Tammy Ingles was everyone's friend and known for being a damn good one. That she would consider Willow a friend as well…

The tears flowed again. And Willow fought to blink and wipe them away. "I'm sorry," she said.

Her father would have been horrified. But he would be in Florida for a few more weeks before returning to his fishing cabin on one of the many lakes of Northern Lakes.

Even though he wasn't here to witness her tears, Willow was horrified that she was crying on Tammy. "I just can't seem to stop."

"It's okay," Tammy said. "You can blame the hormones. I'm not even pregnant and I blame hormones." She blinked herself, fluttering her thick black lashes, as if fighting back tears—probably of sympathy.

The stylist was a walking advertisement for her salon with her movie-star-perfect looks. Her tawny hair was thick and wavy. Her makeup expertly highlighted her delicate features and full lips. But her beauty was not just external; it ran deep inside her big heart.

"Thank you," Willow said. "I don't think I deserve your friendship."

Tammy waved a hand dismissively. "Hey, you've been there for me every time I imagine I have some disease I've read about online."

Willow laughed, probably exactly as Tammy had intended. Too bad her father hadn't used humor to stop her tears instead of silent disapproval. Then maybe Willow would not have worked so hard bottling up her emotions that they eventually exploded out of her, like her anger and resentment had exploded that morning she'd thrown Luke out of their home.

"And you've helped my business," Tammy continued.

Willow furrowed her brow with confusion. Tammy's business had been thriving before Willow had even moved to Northern Lakes. "How?"

"Everybody thinks I have something to do with what's just your natural beauty."

Willow laughed again. "I am a mess right now."

"I can fix you up," Tammy promised her.

"A haircut can't fix me," Willow warned her. "You really should have just put someone else in my slot."

"I think you needed to get out of that house for more than work," Tammy said. "We don't have to go into the salon either. We can go upstairs to my apartment. I can trim your hair up there."

Willow breathed a ragged sigh of relief. "Good."

"Of course, it's not going to stop everybody from gossiping about you," Tammy said. "But at least you don't have to listen to it."

Willow grimaced. She really hated to be the subject of gossip. But she knew she was definitely being talked about and appreciated Tammy's honesty. As she followed her up the stairs on the side of the building to the apartment over the salon, she asked, "Do you believe all the rumors?"

Tammy shrugged. "I don't believe anything I haven't witnessed with my own eyes."

Willow waited until the stylist unlocked the door and escorted her into the apartment, which was, with its light and airy furnishings, as stylish as the woman who owned it. Then she asked, "Have you witnessed any of what's being said about Luke?"

Tammy shrugged again. "I saw him hanging out at the Filling Station more over the past few months than he ever has. I've seen him drinking more than he ever has. But the rest of it…" She shook her head.

And the tightness in Willow's chest eased somewhat. "But everybody's saying…"

Terrible things. Trooper Gingrich had told her terrible things this morning. He'd had no doubt that Luke was the one who'd slashed her tires even though he'd had no proof. Willow had made it clear that she hadn't witnessed anything, like Tammy had said, with her own eyes.

Tammy sighed. "That's the problem. Once a person gets a reputation in this town, it's hard to shake…" For a second, sadness dimmed her pretty green eyes. But then she blinked it away and forced a smile.

Tammy had a reputation for being a man-eater, but Willow had actually rarely seen her with anyone but her friends.

If the rumors about the stylist were wrong, they could be wrong about Luke, too. The trooper could be wrong. Luke could still be the man Willow had fallen in love with when he'd come into the ER with a deep cut on his hand just those few short years ago.

It had definitely been attraction at first sight…for both of them. But she'd fallen for him, too, despite her resolve to never date anyone with a dangerous profession like her father's. She'd known the problems it had caused in her parents' marriage, eventually leading to their divorce. After Willow's first miscarriage, her mother had confided that Willow was an only child because her mother had had many miscarriages. She'd blamed those miscarriages on Willow's dad's job, and at the time, Willow had thought her mom had over-reacted and been unfair. But then Willow had had her second miscarriage, and even before her mother had said "I told you so," Willow had known she was right. That she would have been smarter to marry a man with a safe career, one who worked nine to five and came home every night.

Falling for a firefighter, a Hotshot, no less, had probably been an even bigger mistake than falling for a cop like her dad. Luke was in every bit as much danger as her father had ever been on the police force. Maybe more, if he'd been telling the truth, if he hadn't caused that accident the night before.

* * *

The plan was going to work perfectly. Everyone in Northern Lakes had had a front-row seat to Luke Garrison's fall from grace—especially after every member of the Huron Hotshots had witnessed his arrest. His crimes were piling up, and although there probably wasn't enough evidence to convict him in a criminal court, he'd already been found guilty in the court of public opinion.

Firefighters, especially, believed that if there was enough smoke, there had to be a fire. And this one was going to burn Luke Garrison alive.

Everybody would believe he'd taken his own life because he hadn't been able to deal with his guilt and mental instability. Nobody would realize who had really struck the match that had started the fire that was burning Garrison's life out of control.

Chapter 9

Maybe leaving the hospital the night before had been a mistake. Pain reverberated inside Luke's head, and his entire body ached with it, but that pain wasn't really physical.

Willow should have just pulled the trigger the night before. Her shooting him in the back would have been easier to handle than her stabbing him there. He had no idea why she would have sworn out a complaint against him.

He hadn't trespassed. And he definitely hadn't damaged anything. He'd even left, without an argument, when she'd told him to—just like he had last time.

Maybe that was the real mistake. That he kept doing what she wanted him to do—that he kept leaving. Maybe he should have forced her to deal with him.

But he suspected she would have pulled the trigger then. Or called the police even earlier than she had.

Why did she hate him so much? Because of the children they'd lost? He hated himself for that, hated the worry he'd caused her, hated even more that he hadn't been there for her while she'd miscarried. He blamed himself, but now he knew for certain she also hated him because of their losses.

And that broke his heart even more than her throwing him out had, almost as much as losing those babies had hurt. He'd wanted them, too, had wanted so badly to be a father. Not that he'd had any idea how to be one; he'd lost his own when he was young and there'd only been him and his mom for so many years. Until he'd disappointed her, too, like he had Willow. And his mother had stopped loving him just as easily as his wife had.

He lay down on the bunk and closed his eyes, hoping to dull that throbbing pain in his head and in his heart. But a sudden clatter against the thick steel bars echoed throughout the cell, the loud noise threatening to shatter his skull. He flinched and groaned.

After booking him, Gingrich had escorted him to an empty cell. Either he was getting company or the trooper had come by to gloat.

Neither prospect compelled Luke to open his eyes. Ignoring the doctor's order the night before had been a mistake. That and not even bothering to fill the prescription the doctor had given him for pain relievers for his concussion.

But Luke knew no matter how many pills he took, there would be no relief from this pain. Only proving his innocence would make him feel better.

And having Willow forgive him.

"I thought you would jump at the chance to get outta here, Garrison," the trooper griped.

Luke opened one eye and peered up at Marty Gingrich, who was standing in the open cell door. Luke's heart lifted a bit. "Did someone bail me out?" And more importantly, who?

Braden? He doubted it. He was pretty damn certain his boss had known he was about to be arrested and had decided to have the whole damn team witness it. Why else had he called that meeting when he had? Maybe he'd wanted the rest of the team to finally feel safe again because, thanks to the arsonist and all the accidents they'd been having for over a year, they'd been on edge even before Dirk's death. And after Dirk's death had been proven to be a murder, they'd become even more distrustful of each other. And with good reason...

If Braden hadn't bailed him out, who had?

Willow? Luke's heart warmed with hope. He wanted it to be her that had gotten him released. That she had dropped the charges.

But it had most likely been Owen. Last night he had seemed to want to believe Luke. Of course, his arrest could have changed that, too. The guy had all but admitted that his allegiance was with Willow.

Gingrich's gaze dropped to the concrete floor of the cell. "No..."

Luke opened both eyes and sat up. "Then why are you letting me out?"

Gingrich grimaced then begrudgingly admitted, "The county prosecutor doesn't think there's enough evidence for this charge yet either."

"There isn't *any* evidence," Luke said. "Because I didn't do it. I haven't done anything."

And maybe that was the problem. He hadn't been fighting for his marriage or to prove his innocence.

Gingrich snorted. "Don't get too cocky," he warned Luke. "I am going to prove you were working with Dirk

Brown's widow. And you better stay away from your wife."

"She is still my wife," Luke reminded him. In case Gingrich got any ideas…

Rumor had it the trooper had had a fling with Braden's first wife even though Gingrich was married himself. Of course, the lawman's affair was just a rumor, and Luke had recently learned—painfully— how wrong gossip could be.

"I wouldn't count on her staying your wife much longer," Gingrich advised him.

Luke figured the trooper was right about that. If Willow could think he would try to hurt her…

Or even inadvertently hurt her…

Then she didn't know him at all.

At the moment, he felt like no one did. Instead of wallowing in self-pity, though, he intended to show everybody who he really was.

A good man.

And the best way to prove that was to find out who really had betrayed Dirk. He couldn't do that from a jail cell, so he jumped up and headed toward that open cell door.

Gingrich stood yet in the way, his thick body blocking the exit.

"I thought you didn't have any grounds to hold me," Luke reminded the trooper.

The guy glared at him. "Not yet. But I will. So you better not go too far, Garrison, because you'll be back here very soon and probably for good."

The pain in Luke's head dulled to an ache. Gingrich's threats were like a toothache—naggingly persistent. He uttered a ragged sigh and advised the trooper, "You need to find someone else to harass. I'm not your man."

But he intended to find out who the guilty party was. And he wouldn't rest until that person was where he'd just been—behind bars.

A hand closed over Willow's shoulder, startling her so much that she nearly dropped the tray of sutures and bandages she'd been carrying to stock the ER.

"I'm sorry," Cheryl said. "I didn't mean to scare you."

"It's not your fault," Willow assured her. Her friend wasn't the reason she was on edge. "Did you need my help with something?" she asked hopefully.

She hated nights like this—that were so slow she had too much time to think. But then she would prefer that to having Luke show up again...hurt.

"You have a visitor," Cheryl said.

And Willow's pulse quickened. Had Luke come to see her? But she wasn't certain if she should be happy or upset if he had. Either way, she was excited.

She missed him so much, so damn much...

"It's that sleazy state trooper," Cheryl said with a sniffle of distaste.

And Willow swallowed a groan. There was already enough gossip about her and Luke flying around town; the last thing she needed was the loudmouthed trooper spewing more fuel on the fire.

Before she could make an excuse not to see him, he barreled down the hall toward them. "There she is," he said, as if Cheryl had been hiding her from him.

Cheryl gave her a pitying glance before leaving them alone. She didn't go too far, though, and other coworkers seemed to move closer, some probably protectively. Although, she was cynical enough to suspect that some probably just wanted to overhear something they could add to the gossip mill. Those rumors had to have started somewhere.

"I wanted to give you a heads-up that I had to release him," Gingrich said.

Willow tensed. "What are you talking about?"

"Your ex—"

"We're not divorced," she said.

"You should get that wrapped up soon," Gingrich advised. "And while you're at it, you need to have your lawyer file a personal protection order against him. That way I can arrest him the next time he shows up at your house."

"Did you arrest him?" she asked, horrified at the thought of Luke in jail.

"After what he did to your vehicle, hell, yes," Gingrich replied. "Unfortunately the prosecutor didn't think there was enough evidence to press charges against him. I'm sorry."

No. Willow was sorry that she had even filed the report. "I told you that I don't think he did that," she said, loud enough that her coworkers would overhear. "That's not something Luke would do." He had never intentionally hurt her. And if she asked, he might even quit his job for her. But she hadn't wanted to ask, hadn't wanted to make him give up something he'd loved. And she hadn't been entirely convinced that he would have. He hadn't given it up when his mom had asked him to choose another profession all those years ago.

"Well, he's been doing a lot of stuff people didn't think a Hotshot would do," Gingrich said. "He's one of *those* guys, so you better be careful."

"Those guys?" she asked. "A Hotshot?" She knew that the trooper held a grudge against the superintendent of the Huron Hotshots. But she hadn't realized that grudge extended to the entire team.

"A hot*head*," Gingrich said.

"No…" Luke didn't even have a temper. Whenever she yelled, he usually just walked away; he never yelled back. But maybe that was just because he didn't care.

"I've seen a lot of domestic situations like this," Trooper Gingrich said. "Husband goes crazy when the wife files for divorce. Gets all, if he can't have her, nobody else can."

From working in emergency rooms in Detroit and even here in Northern Lakes, Willow had seen evidence of Gingrich's claim. The bruises. The broken bones. And worse…

She shivered. But that wasn't Luke. He was not a violent man. She was the one who'd physically shoved him out the door that day she'd told him to leave, that she could never forgive him for what he'd cost her.

"You need to file that protection order," Gingrich persisted as he glanced down at her swelling belly. "If not for your safety, at least for the safety of your baby."

That was why she'd called him when she'd found her tires slashed. But she should have realized then that he would automatically blame Luke. The estranged husband was the most likely suspect. But Willow struggled to see Luke doing something so vicious and vindictive. That wasn't the man she knew.

When Gingrich walked away, Willow hurried off, too. She didn't want her coworkers interrogating her about what had happened. About Luke…

She knew talking to them would only elicit more opinions similar to Trooper Gingrich's. None of them knew Luke like she did. They would think the worst of him more easily than she could.

But even she had had her doubts about him. Had that been because of the gossip, or because she'd wanted to think the worst? That way she wouldn't feel so bad over how she'd treated him.

She felt terrible now—that he'd been arrested. She could imagine how Gingrich must have made it sound, like she'd sworn out a complaint against him, and she'd refused to do any such thing. Like Tammy had said, unless she'd seen him slash those tires herself, she couldn't believe that he had done something so petty and malicious.

Once she stepped into the employee locker room, she opened her locker and took her cell phone from her purse. Her finger shook slightly as she punched in his contact. But her call went directly to Luke's voice mail.

Was he too furious with her to talk to her? Or wasn't he able to talk to her?

Someone had slashed her tires last night. Did they mean her harm? Or was this about her husband? To make Luke look guilty of another crime? He had claimed someone had forced him off the road and poured that alcohol on him. Was someone out to get him? And had that person caught up with him?

"Come on, Marty," Braden chided his old rival. "That was a dick move and you know it."

Arresting Luke in front of the entire Hotshot team…

Marty glanced up from his almost empty beer mug, beads of condensation rolling down its sides to pool on the bar at the Filling Station. "You're the one who had called that meeting," Marty reminded him. "Not me. I didn't know everybody would be there."

Braden grimaced at what had to be the truth. "You still could have waited. You could have called him outside."

Marty snorted disparagingly. "When are you gonna realize that you and your Hotshots are nothing special and you're not gonna get special treatment from me or anybody else in this town?"

"What can I get you, Superintendent Zimmer?" the bar owner, Charlie Tillerman, interrupted, with a wink at Braden. The owner often tended the bar himself, especially since he'd rebuilt the place after the arsonist had burned it down all those months ago. If he didn't hold a grudge against them for that happening, why did Gingrich? Or was Gingrich's grudge just against Braden for being more athletic and more popular than him in high school all those years ago?

Braden shook his head. "Thanks, Charlie, nothing right now…"

Not until he found Luke.

Once Charlie walked away, Braden addressed a disgusted-looking Marty. "I tried to post bail to get Luke out, but I was told it wasn't possible. How the hell did you get bail denied?"

What evidence did he have against Luke?

Gingrich chuckled. "I guess, despite what you think, you don't know everything, Zimmer."

Braden had no doubt that there was a lot he didn't know—like who the hell on his team wasn't whom he or she seemed to be. And if Luke was guilty of conspiring with Louanne Brown.

He didn't know that. He hoped like hell Luke wasn't. But he didn't know for certain.

"So tell me, Marty, what do you know that I don't?" he asked, figuring the guy would relish the opportunity to gloat about his superior knowledge.

Marty snorted. "I'm leaving after this beer, so I don't have time to cover everything."

Braden clenched his jaw and his fists. But he knew better than to swing. Last time he'd let Marty goad him into a reaction, he'd struck a beautiful woman instead of the belligerent trooper. Fortunately that woman hadn't pressed charges against him, despite Marty urging her to, and ultimately she'd become Braden's wife.

"I want to know what's going on with Luke Garrison," Braden clarified. Not that he expected an honest or unbiased answer from his nemesis.

But Marty must have had to leave soon, so he sighed and replied, "He wasn't denied bail. He wasn't officially charged with anything, so he was released."

The admission must have nearly killed Marty because he gulped down the rest of his beer. Before he could slide off his bar stool, Braden blocked his escape.

"How long ago?"

Marty shrugged. "Hours…"

"Then where is he?"

"It's not my job to keep track of him…yet," Marty said. "But I'm sure I'll have him back behind bars soon enough."

Braden clenched his arms against his sides, so he wouldn't give in to temptation and swing again. "How many times do you have to be told that he's innocent?"

"I haven't been told that," Marty said. "I just need more evidence to prove how guilty he really is. And I will get it."

Braden snorted now. "I wouldn't hold your breath…" Unless he held it so long that he passed out, so he would finally stop spewing nonsense. But Gingrich was the least of his concerns at the moment. "Who picked up Luke?"

Marty shook his head. "Nobody."

"He didn't call anyone?"

He shook his head again. "Didn't use his one call while he was in custody and didn't use his phone after I handed it back to him."

"So you drove him there, but you didn't give him a ride back?" Braden persisted. The jail for the state-police post was miles outside of town.

"I'm not a taxi service," Marty said. "He had his phone. He could have called for a ride if he'd wanted one. He could have called you."

He could have. But he hadn't. And Braden remembered the look on Luke's face when Marty had slapped the cuffs on him. He'd thought Braden had betrayed him, that he'd known the arrest was going to happen and had called the meeting so that everybody could witness it. Braden's reason for calling the meeting had been exactly the opposite. He'd wanted everyone to give Luke the benefit of the doubt, to trust him and each other again. But now Luke was the one who wouldn't be able to trust Braden again.

Braden had to find him—had to set him straight. He hadn't betrayed him. Luke had to feel right now like there was no one on his side. Willow had called the police on him. All his team members had acted as though he deserved to be arrested.

And Braden hadn't stepped up as quickly as he should have. He hadn't defended Luke or reached out to help him. Now he could only hope that he hadn't already lost him.

For good...

Chapter 10

Until that cell door had opened and Luke had walked out, he hadn't realized how alone he was. Even though Gingrich had handed him back his phone, he'd had no one to call. At least no one he could have called to pick him up from jail. And Gingrich had refused to release Luke's truck from the impound lot yet, claiming it was still being processed for evidence in his crash.

Luke had wanted to call Willow. But he hadn't trusted himself at that moment. He'd been too furious, that she could have thought he would hurt her, to confront her. He hadn't wanted to upset her—not at the risk of her pregnancy. She needed this baby to survive, and so did Luke.

He wanted to be a father, to have a child call him "Daddy" and look up to him—the way Luke had wished he'd had a dad to love and protect and guide him.

Luke hadn't had anyone like that in his life until

he'd joined the Huron Hotshots, and then he'd had a lot of men to look up to, until now. Until they'd all begun to look down on him. Except for Stanley. While Stanley hadn't remembered enough about the night of the hit-and-run to provide Luke with an ironclad alibi, the teenager had once been falsely accused of a crime himself.

Stanley had been accused of being the Northern Lakes arsonist. But like Luke, Stanley had been set up to take the blame for somebody else—a young man he'd considered a friend. Luke had been more than a mile away from the jail when he'd finally remembered Stanley and called the nineteen-year-old to pick him up. Stanley was always happy to be helpful, so he'd quickly obliged.

Fortunately, by the time they'd returned to the firehouse, everybody had left. So Luke didn't have to greet anyone but Annie, who'd jumped all over him in her delight.

If only people were as trusting as dogs...

But maybe it was a good thing that not everybody was. Luke had obviously been too trusting himself. He had never suspected Louanne of wanting to kill her husband and wanting to place the blame for that murder on Luke.

Stanley had had to rush home for dinner, so he'd left Annie with Luke. Or maybe he'd felt sorry for just how alone Luke was and had figured the dog was better company than nobody at all.

Stanley had offered to bring him back leftovers from dinner, but Luke had assured him he would be fine. Feeling sick over nearly being arrested, he hadn't felt hungry. But he'd been thirsty enough to grab his water bottle from the fridge. He knew it was his because he'd scrawled his name across the plastic. Willow had gotten him hooked on infused water a while ago, so he didn't want anyone surprised with the cucumbers and mint leaves in the bottle.

He took a deep swallow of it before he noticed the odd flavor. What the hell was that...?

Had the cucumbers gone bad? He'd put them in the bottle just that morning before he'd headed up to the meeting. They should have been good yet.

Unless...

His vision began to blur, Annie growing even fuzzier as she stared quizzically up at him. She cocked her big head and whined, as if she sensed that something was wrong, too.

Luke's knees began to weaken, threatening to fold beneath him. He reached out and grasped the edge of the tall table in the middle of the kitchen, and as he did, a small, plastic bottle toppled and rolled off it.

Then Luke toppled, too, falling onto the concrete floor. His knees struck hard, and he flinched. He automatically reached out to break his fall with his hands, so his head hit his arms instead of the floor. But the movement jarred him, sending pain reverberating throughout his skull.

Annie stood over him now, licking and pawing at him as she continued to whine with concern. He turned his face to the side and saw the bottle that had rolled off the table was a prescription bottle.

His name was on the label. It was the prescription he hadn't filled the night before. But someone had, and now all the pills were gone, the bottle empty.

As his vision blurred and consciousness slipped away

from him, he realized where those pills were now. In his water bottle and now in him...

Had he swallowed too much? Had he drunk enough to kill him? That must have been the intent of whoever had filled that prescription and dissolved those pills in his water.

Somebody wasn't just trying to frame him for conspiring to take Dirk's life. They were trying to make it look like he'd taken his own.

Willow cursed as Luke's voice mail answered her call. He sounded so mechanical—so polite—in his greeting. And every time that recorded voice answered her, instead of his real one, she grew more and more frustrated.

And concerned...

Was he so furious with her over his arrest that he wouldn't pick up? Or was it more than that? Was he unable to pick up?

The door to the locker room opened and a female voice called out, "Are you all right?"

Guilt flashed through her over Cheryl's concern. She didn't deserve it since she'd taken much too long a break from the floor.

"I'm sorry," she apologized. Cheryl was her friend as well as her supervisor. But she didn't want to take advantage of her friendship with the older nurse. "I know I'm distracted—"

"You have every reason to be," Cheryl said. "Don't worry. I just wanted to make sure you're okay. You keep coming back here to the locker room."

"I'm sorry," Willow said again. "I'll stay on the floor from now on."

"It's not busy," Cheryl reminded her. "Or it wasn't. We do have a unit bringing in an accident victim."

Her breath caught. "Is it…?" Luke? Was that why he wasn't answering? Had he been hurt again?

Cheryl shook her head. "Owen James is bringing in a patient who fell using Rollerblades for the first time. Possible concussion and broken wrist."

"The kid wasn't wearing a helmet?"

"The sixty-year-old grandmother wasn't," Cheryl corrected her with a smile. "She was showing off in front of her grandkids and fell. Hopefully she's fine."

She was—completely alert and chagrined when Owen and his partner brought her in moments later. While Cheryl took her to Radiology for a head CT and a wrist X-ray, Willow caught Owen before he climbed back into his rig.

"Have you seen Luke?" she asked him.

Owen glanced around then lowered his voice to a rumbly whisper. "Not since the trooper arrested him."

"He shouldn't have done that," she said.

"He said you swore out the complaint against Luke," Owen said.

She swallowed a curse. That was what she'd suspected the trooper had claimed. "I refused to swear out a complaint," she informed him. "I don't think Luke's the one who slashed my tires. I told Gingrich I heard another vehicle after Luke left the house last night. But he insisted that it was Luke coming back."

"Luke stopped by Courtney's store last night," Owen said. "He came by to talk to me, to see if I saw anything at his *accident* site…"

"You don't think it was an accident?" she asked, and her pulse quickened even more with concern.

"Whatever it was," Owen replied, "the blood-alcohol test proves that it wasn't like it was supposed to look."

"Like Luke was drunk…"

Owen nodded. "He had no alcohol in his system even though he smelled like it for some reason."

"Do you think somebody is trying to frame him?" she asked.

Owen opened his mouth, but no words came out. He obviously wasn't certain enough to give her a definitive answer.

"That's why I'm so worried," she said. And she couldn't afford to be worried, not when she was carrying another child she didn't want to lose. "I can't get a hold of him. His phone keeps going straight to voice mail."

"He's in jail," Owen said.

She shook her head. "No. The prosecutor told Gingrich there wasn't enough evidence to hold Luke. I didn't see him do it…" And she desperately wanted to believe that he hadn't, that he was the honest and kind man she'd thought he was when she married him.

"He was calm when he came to the store," Owen told her. "Not like he'd just been in some rage or something. In fact he seemed more focused and clearer than he's been in weeks."

"Focused on proving his innocence," she mused.

Owen nodded.

So why would he have slashed her tires? It didn't make any sense. None of it did. He'd been so close to Dirk that she couldn't imagine him betraying the man or any other member of his team. After his mom had disowned him, they were his only family now.

"Can you try to call him?" she asked. "He might just not want to talk to me." And she fully understood why he wouldn't—after the way she'd doubted him and especially after she'd kept her pregnancy from him.

Owen pulled out his cell and punched in a contact. His brow furrowed as he listened to the voice mail. "He might just not want to talk to me either."

Owen's partner called out to him from the driver's seat. "Hey, James, we need to get back on the road."

Owen nodded and began to close the rear doors of the paramedic rig. But when he started around to the passenger side, Willow grabbed his arm.

"Can you keep trying to reach him?" she asked.

"You're worried?" he asked, his voice gruff.

She nodded. "I just have this strange feeling…"

Like something bad had happened.

Like Luke needed help.

But everybody had turned their backs on him—even she, who had sworn to love him in sickness and health, in good times and bad…

But instead she'd pushed him away. She'd blamed him for their losses. She'd thought then it was better to end their relationship than to worry about him being in danger so often. But it didn't matter that she'd thrown him out; she was still worried. Too worried…

That he could die…

Willow's worry ignited Owen's. As he settled into the passenger seat of the rig, an uneasy feeling gnawed at him.

"What's wrong?" Chris asked from the driver's seat.

Owen shrugged. "Hopefully nothing, but let's head back to the firehouse."

They often parked in the lot so they were available and close in case of an emergency call. But Owen didn't just want to sit in the lot. He wanted to go inside the house and check for Luke.

Maybe the injured Hotshot had just come back and

crashed on a bunk. He hadn't had much sleep the night before. And he did have a concussion.

His head and his bruised ribs had to be killing him. And he'd been too damn stubborn to stop the night before to fill his prescription. Maybe he'd done that now, taken a couple of pain relievers and conked out.

That was what Owen hoped.

But he fished his cell from his pocket. Before he could hit the redial for Luke's contact, his phone buzzed with an incoming call. "Hey, Braden—"

"Have you seen Luke?" his boss interrupted.

And that bad feeling intensified so much that he groaned.

"What?" Braden asked.

"His wife just asked me the same thing," Owen admitted. He gestured at Chris to speed up.

"And what did you tell her?" Braden asked.

"I thought he was still in jail," Owen admitted.

"Marty had to release him."

"Marty never should have arrested him in the first place," Owen said. "Willow didn't tell him that she thought it was Luke who slashed her tires."

Braden's breath rattled the phone as he audibly sucked in a deep one. "Someone slashed her tires…"

"The malicious vandalism," Owen reminded him of the charges Gingrich had listed as he'd led Luke off in handcuffs.

"But why?" Braden asked.

"To frame Luke," Owen offered. It was beginning to look more and more like his friend might have been telling the truth all along.

"We have to find him," Braden said.

"I'm on my way to the firehouse," Owen asked. "But I'm sure you already looked there."

"Hours ago," Braden said. "Since then I've been to the Filling Station, where I ran into Marty. After he admitted to releasing Owen, I drove out by the jail—to see if he's walking..." Braden's voice trailed off, gruff with guilt.

And a pang of it struck Owen's heart. Luke had come to him for help the night before and he hadn't offered it. He hoped it wasn't too late to help him now.

Chris pulled the rig up to the firehouse, and Owen was out the door before it came to a complete stop. He hurried into the three-story building. Only the engines filled the bays. The place looked deserted, but then he heard a faint whine.

"Annie!"

She barked in reply, but she didn't rush out to greet him. She kept barking with a sudden urgency, an urgency that drove Owen to run up the steps to the second story.

This was where the bunkroom was. But it was empty—of the team and the dog. But she peeked her head out of the doorway to the kitchen and the overgrown puppy let out the most serious bark Owen had ever heard from her. It was deep and compelling, and made Owen run those last few feet to meet her.

She darted back into the room. And Owen joined her.

The dog stood, her body trembling, over Luke, who was lying on the floor. His body was still—his chest not even rising, as if he'd stopped breathing.

As if he'd stopped living...

"Damn it!" Owen yelled.

"What?" Chris asked from the doorway, and even though the other man was a few years younger than Owen, he panted from running up the stairs.

"Grab the gear," Owen told him. And he wished like

hell he'd thought to grab his bag before he'd come up-stairs. "We need oxygen and maybe the defibrillator."

But if Luke had been out a long time, it might be too late to bring him back—to save him…

Chapter 11

Willow stood out in the ambulance bay of the ER, her arms wrapped around herself. "Go inside," Cheryl told her. "You're cold."

She was chilled right to the bone, but that had nothing to do with the early spring weather and everything to do with the call that had just come in.

Owen had found Luke.

But had he found him in time?

"You can't work *this*, anyway," Cheryl reminded her, her dark eyes warm with concern and glistening with a sheen of tears. Cheryl and her husband had hung out with Willow and Luke many times. "I'm not sure *I* should work this…"

Cheryl had stepped aside the night before, too, but because they'd been slow tonight she'd already let the extra nurses go. She and the resident on duty were all Luke had.

And Owen...

Thank God that Owen had found him. She shivered as she remembered the call: probable OD...

Luke had overdosed?

The Luke she'd known and loved hadn't even liked to take aspirin. But that Luke had never drank more than a couple of beers at a time either. That Luke had hung on to his control even when they'd made love, making sure she'd experienced climax a few times before giving in to his own needs. She missed that Luke...so much.

Tears stung her eyes and burned the back of her throat. She swallowed hard, trying to choke them down, so she wouldn't break down as she had earlier. Her eyes were probably still puffy from how hard she'd cried on Tammy Ingles.

She needed to maintain her control. She couldn't cry anymore. But the moment the paramedic rig pulled in and the back doors opened, panic rushed over her, pressing down hard on her lungs. She could barely draw a breath...because Luke, lying motionless on the stretcher, didn't look as if he was breathing either.

"Oh, my God!" she exclaimed.

Cheryl grabbed her by the shoulders. "Go. Sit down."

She hadn't realized she was shaking until she tried to move and her legs threatened to fold beneath her. As an ER nurse, she'd learned to handle her emotions so that she could do her job. Of course, her father had taught her that long before she had become a nurse.

But Luke was more than her job.

He was her everything. And because of that, she'd worried so much about him that she'd lost their babies. The two she'd carried before. And...

She clasped her hand over her stomach. She could

not lose this baby. Not when she might have already lost Luke.

"What was it?" Cheryl asked Owen, who guided the stretcher from the back. "Heroin? Cocaine?"

Owen shook his head and handed over a prescription bottle. "I found this empty on the floor next to him."

Pain lanced through Willow's heart like she'd been stabbed in the chest. Had Luke taken all those pills? Had he tried to kill himself?

And how successful had his attempt been?

"We need to pump his stomach and get a charcoal treatment in him," the resident chimed in as he, Owen and Cheryl rolled the stretcher past Willow. She wanted to reach out—wanted to grab the side of the stretcher and stop them from moving him away.

Luke looked so limp, his face as pale as the white sheet on which he was lying. He couldn't be gone.

She couldn't have lost him forever.

Instead of reaching for the stretcher, she pressed both hands against her belly now. The baby fluttered inside her. No. The move was more than a flutter; it was a kick.

The baby was moving now, was fighting inside Willow—just like Luke needed to fight. For his life…

For their life…

For their child.

Luke's head had already been hurting, but now it felt like it was full of cotton. Swollen. Dry. Achy…

And he was so damn tired. He could barely summon the energy to lift his eyelids, but he was afraid that Annie might keep licking his face, so he blinked until he opened his eyes. It wasn't Annie's ugly mug staring down at him, though.

Willow stood over his bed, her green eyes damp

with tears. "Did I die?" he murmured, his voice gruff. His throat was dry, and his tongue felt twice its normal size.

She was so heartbreakingly beautiful. Like an angel…

She shook her head and brushed away the tears. "No." She studied his face intently, hers tight with concern and something that looked almost like guilt. "I'm so sorry that you wanted to, that you felt like you had nothing to live for."

"What are you talking about?" he asked. "I don't want to die." Especially not now, with a child on the way. Because he knew that baby was his, and Luke wanted to be a dad almost as much as he wanted to be Willow's husband.

"The pills you took—the prescription bottle was empty," she said. "You had to know how dangerous it was to take all of them."

"I didn't take *any* of them," Luke said. "I didn't even fill the prescription." He noticed Owen standing behind her. "Ask him. I told him and Braden not to stop at the pharmacy."

Owen nodded. But then, his blue eyes glistening with something that almost looked like tears of his own, he added, "You had all day today to have filled it, and after this morning, after how Gingrich arrested you in front of the whole team, I can understand why you might think you had no other option…"

Luke snorted. "I can't believe either of you think I would take those pills. You both know I have no use for drugs." Because his father had used them too much, so much that he'd died before Luke had been old enough to remember him. "I had no option or opportunity to fill that prescription. I had a pretty full day—what with being arrested and all. And I didn't waste my one call on the pharmacy." He actually hadn't called anyone at all until after he'd started walking back to the firehouse. Stanley was the only one who'd been willing to help him. "I didn't fill that prescription."

"But you must have filled it," Owen said, his brow furrowing with confusion. "Your name is on the bottle."

"It's probably my prescription," Luke agreed. "But I didn't fill it and I certainly didn't take any."

"The bottle was empty, and you were passed out on the kitchen floor when I found you at the firehouse," Owen said, his voice cracking before he continued, "Barely breathing…"

Frustrated that they didn't seem to believe him, Luke cursed. "I swear I didn't knowingly take anything. But I think somebody put something in my water bottle. It tasted funny, and the next thing I knew, I was falling down with Annie fawning all over me."

Willow sucked in a breath. "Annie?"

"The firehouse dog," he reminded her. But his heart lifted at the look of jealousy that briefly crossed her beautiful face. While it was better than the guilt and dread he'd seen on her face, he still didn't want her upset. "You have no more to worry about with her than you have with Louanne. I would never cheat on you with anyone. And I would *never* try to kill myself."

As if he was beginning to believe Luke, Owen chuckled. "It looked like Annie was trying to give you mouth-to-muzzle when I showed up."

Remembering how much she'd licked him, Luke rubbed his hand over his face. His skin felt dry but cool.

"We washed you up after the resident pumped your stomach," Willow said.

"Couldn't have been much to pump out," he mused. The last thing he'd eaten had been just part of that hamburger at the Filling Station the night he'd been run off the road. He hadn't even taken a sip of the beer Charlie had put on the bar in front of him. He hadn't ordered it, and he doubted anyone had actually bought it for him. Had Charlie given it to him out of pity? Or had someone bought him that beer with the intent of slipping something into it like the night that his vehicle had been used to run down Owen and Courtney? He needed to talk to Charlie.

But Willow gasped and drew his attention back to her. She shook her head. "There wasn't…" Then she turned to Owen, and her voice vibrated with something like relief when she added, "There wasn't any trace of the capsules from the pills."

"Couldn't they have dissolved already?" Owen asked.

Luke groaned. "No, because I didn't take them."

Hopefully Willow was beginning to believe him and that was why she sounded relieved; she was relieved that he hadn't tried to kill himself. "There would have been some trace of them," she persisted. "At least the dye used to color the capsules…"

Owen's blue eyes narrowed as he studied Luke's face. "You really didn't, did you?"

"No, I didn't," Luke insisted. "Why the hell would I?"

"I can think of one reason," Owen murmured with a sideways glance at Willow.

Luke's gaze ran over her, too—over her belly. "That's the reason not to," he pointed out.

Her, the baby…

It had to be his. She was too far along for it to be anyone else's. And while rumors had been going around town about him, he hadn't heard anything about Willow with anyone.

"Then there's this whole thing with Dirk," Owen added.

Luke groaned again. "That's another reason not to. I intend to prove that I had nothing to do with Louanne and definitely nothing to do with Dirk's death or those attempts on your life."

Owen and Willow just continued to stare at him, doubt and concern furrowing both their brows. Despite his efforts to convince them, they obviously didn't entirely believe him.

But could he blame them?

Luke knew how it looked—that he'd tried killing himself. But that was because it was supposed to look that way, just like all the other things that had been done to frame him. Why? So that no one looked any deeper into Dirk's murder? So that no one found Louanne's real accomplice?

To convince them, Luke added, "A dead man can't prove his innocence."

"No, he can't," Owen agreed. "So you need to be careful."

"I was taking a drink of water," he said. "I wasn't fighting a fire."

"The accident the night before—"

"I wasn't the one who came into the wrong lane," he added. He was sick of taking it—sick of taking all the doubts and suspicion. He was damn well going to defend himself now.

"If what you're saying is true—"

"It is!" he interjected, interrupting Owen.

"Then you're in danger," Owen said. "If you were run off the road and poisoned…"

It wasn't just his reputation or his freedom that was in danger. Somebody was trying to kill him.

Hadn't it been enough to destroy his life? Now some-body wanted to take it, too.

What the hell was the deal with Luke Garrison? How did the man keep surviving?

Owen James had been the same way. Louanne had tried and tried to get rid of him with *accident* after *accident*. But nothing had worked. And in the end, she was the one who'd wound up dead.

That wouldn't happen this time—not with Luke. He wasn't as lucky as Owen James was. He had already come closer to dying than Owen had.

And he was a hell of a lot more vulnerable.

Luke Garrison was like a wounded animal separated from the rest of the herd—weak and easily overtaken. Or so it had seemed. But somehow he kept surviving—both the attempts to frame him and the attempts to kill him.

And unfortunately each attempt seemed to have made him stronger rather than weaker. He was more alert and determined now—to prove his innocence and to survive.

How else was he still alive?

The next attempt had to be more carefully orches-trated. Had to be foolproof, so that there was no way he could escape death again.

Luke Garrison had to die. And soon…before he or anyone else started digging deeper into Louanne's life and figured out the truth. Before they figured out who was really framing him…

Chapter 12

Luke must have died. Waking up with Willow standing over him, her face wet with tears that she'd cried with concern for him, had been unreal enough. But now she'd left work early and had brought him home with her.

Home.

He'd given up on ever calling it that again. But at the moment it didn't feel like home either. He felt like a visitor in the house he co-owned. And Willow felt like a stranger to him.

He didn't really understand her anymore.

"Why did you bring me back here?" he asked. "So you can call the trooper and get me arrested again?"

Color flushed her face. "I didn't call him to get you arrested in the first place."

"You accused me of breaking and entering, and malicious vandalism," he reminded her. And himself. He couldn't let himself hope that anything had changed—that they could go back to what they once were. Too much had happened since then to them. "You probably took out a restraining order against me now, too."

"I didn't accuse *you*," she said. "Trooper Gingrich just assumed it was you."

He tensed as realization dawned. He'd thought she'd known it was him when she'd put that gun in his back the night before. But she must have just been scared, and apparently with good reason. "Did someone break into the house last night?" he asked with alarm. He glanced around the cozy living room, looking for broken windows. "Are you all right?"

He stepped closer now and stared down at her face. All the color that had been in it moments ago drained away, leaving her pale except for the dark circles rimming her beautiful green eyes. His heart ached with fear and with love. He loved her so damn much…and that was why he had to be careful, had to make sure he put no stress on her.

Her throat moved as she swallowed. Then she nodded. "Yes, I'm fine…"

He glanced down at her belly, where her hands rested protectively, as if she was determined to hold this baby inside her—to keep him or her alive.

"I would never do anything to hurt you," he vowed. And because of that, he knew he should leave. Just being around him must have put her in danger the night before. "What happened last night?"

"Gingrich didn't tell you?"

"I didn't know what to believe," he admitted.

She stared at him, her green eyes speculative. "I know how that feels…"

"I didn't try to kill myself tonight," he insisted. "I didn't have an affair. I wouldn't hurt you or anyone else. You know that. You know *me*."

She was the one who'd become a mystery to him. After the miscarriages, she had been so upset that he hadn't known what to do or say—how to comfort her. She'd been so angry with him.

"I didn't tell the trooper that you broke in," she said. "And I certainly didn't say that you'd slashed my tires."

"Your tires were slashed?"

She nodded. "That's why I had to call the police. For a report for the insurance company."

"Of course, you did," he wholeheartedly agreed. "And not just for insurance." Someone was obviously messing with her. But why…?

Because of him? Had just his coming here the night before made her a target now, too?

"You didn't call the police tonight," she said. "Owen wanted you to call—to report what happened at the firehouse—about the pills…" Her voice cracked with concern.

Because he hadn't filed a report or because she had doubts again that he might have taken those pills himself? "I didn't take them," he reminded her. "You know that because you didn't find any of the capsules in my stomach." Even if she hadn't believed him, she'd eventually been satisfied with the proof she'd discovered herself. Fortunately Owen had been satisfied, too. "You really think Gingrich would have believed that I didn't take them myself?" he asked. "He probably would have arrested me for attempted murder…of myself. Or worse yet…"

Gingrich might have tried to have him committed. But Luke didn't want to mention that to her. As his wife, she must have been able to request that he have a psychiatric evaluation. He'd overheard her friend Cheryl recommending it.

When Willow had told him to come with her, he would have been less surprised if she'd brought him to a psychiatric hospital than her bringing him home.

But it probably would have been safer for her if she had. "Somebody really slashed your tires…" Why? Why would anyone go after Willow?

But he doubted she'd been the intended target. The slasher had to be the same person framing him. Because framing him for an involvement in Dirk's death and the attacks on Owen hadn't worked, he or she had decided to frame him for harassing his wife. The husband was always the prime suspect in cases like this—when the spouses were estranged.

He groaned. "I really should leave." Although he ached with the desire to stay, with desire for her…he couldn't put her in danger or cause her any more stress. But he hesitated because he'd missed her so badly. So very, very badly…

"I didn't take out a restraining order against you," she reiterated, as if she thought that was why he wanted to go, because he was afraid he might be arrested again.

"The trooper suggested it, though," he said, taking a guess.

She sighed and nodded.

"You won't need it," he assured her. "I'll stay away from you." Even though it was killing him…

But he would rather suffer himself than put her or the baby in danger. He had to get the hell out of there.

He could walk back to the firehouse. Or he could call Stanley again once he was outside.

If he could force himself to turn away from her.

If he could force himself to walk away again.

He stared down into her beautiful face, and he ached to close the distance between them, to brush his lips across hers. Her lashes fluttered as if she was waiting for his kiss.

But if he kissed her, he wouldn't leave. He wouldn't ever want to leave. So he drew in a deep, shaky breath, turned and walked toward the door. His hand shook as he reached for the knob, but he forced himself to close his fingers around it. He had to open the door. He had to go.

For her sake.

For the baby's.

And even for his, because if something happened to her or that unborn child…

Unlike the previous attempts on his life, it would kill him for certain.

In disbelief, Willow stared at Luke's back. She'd thought he'd been about to kiss her. Instead he'd turned and walked away. The disbelief turned to anger. And when the door creaked open, her control on her temper snapped.

"You son of a bitch!" she yelled at him.

He jerked in surprise, and so did the baby inside her. And she wondered which of them really had the bitch for a mother. She'd never met her mother-in-law. The woman had disowned Luke when he'd gone against her wishes and followed his passion to become a Hotshot firefighter.

Ironically his mother had done it because she hadn't wanted to lose him. But then she'd willingly given him up.

Willow felt the sharp bite of irony herself. Hadn't she done the same damn thing?

But he hadn't had to leave. Sure, she'd told him to, but she'd been a mess back then. She hadn't really known what she wanted. She'd just been so overwhelmed with emotions that she hadn't been equipped to handle. And she was nearly as overwhelmed now as she'd been then.

"You're just going to walk away again?" she asked.

He turned then, and he was the one in disbelief, his brow furrowed with confusion. "What are you talking about? I didn't walk away. You threw me out. I didn't want to leave."

"You didn't tell me that," she said. "You just packed up a bag and left."

"Because you said that was what you wanted," he reminded her. He rubbed one of his hands across his forehead, as if it was pounding. And it probably was. He had a concussion, and she was shouting at him.

Only Luke had ever made her feel this way—had ever made her lose control. She loved him so much. That was why she'd been so afraid of losing him. She admitted as much now. "I always thought I would lose you…"

That was why she'd fought so hard not to fall for him, because on some level she'd known her mother was right, that loving a man with a career like his would lead to heartbreak. But it had been too late; the minute she'd met Luke Garrison, she'd loved him. She doubted she would ever stop.

"Like Dirk?" he asked.

Remembering the Hotshot's gruesome injury, she shuddered. "Not necessarily like that, but to the job." She released a bitter chuckle. "I resisted all my dad's attempts to set me up with cops, thinking their lives were too dangerous. Then I go and fall for a firefighter."

He rubbed his hand across his forehead again. "This concussion, the poisoning—those things didn't happen to me because of the job."

She wondered about that. "No. I didn't lose you to the job," she said. "I lost you to another woman."

His eyes widened with shock, and his mouth fell open. Then his face flushed as his temper flared. "Never! I told you that—I've told everyone that. I would never cheat on you. I would never betray you or hurt *you*!"

But she heard the pain in the gruffness of his voice. She was the one who'd hurt him—with her accusations, with her doubts.

She closed the distance between them and reached up, cupping his handsome face in her hands. "I'm sorry," she said. "I'm sorry..."

She'd been in so much pain over the miscarriages that she'd needed someone to blame, so she'd lashed out at him and pushed him away. She'd been so self-centered and selfish that she hadn't considered how badly he must have been hurting, too. And then she'd been so stubborn, waiting for him to come back to her, when she should have been the one reaching out to him, begging for his forgiveness.

If he had taken those pills, it would have been her fault. But she believed him; she believed that someone was after him. But why? Why Luke?

She reached out now, as she rose up on tiptoe and pressed her lips to his mouth. "I'm sorry," she murmured again. She needed to say more—to tell him that she'd didn't blame him, that she loved him...

But when he kissed her back, the rush of passion overwhelmed her. She slid her hands down his face, over his broad shoulders and down his arms until she caught his hands in hers. Then she tugged him across the living room and down the short hall to their bedroom.

Luke tensed the minute he stepped over the threshold into their room. Was it possible that he didn't want her anymore? That she'd pushed him away so hard that he never wanted to come back?

"Are you sure?" he asked, and his voice was so gruff she could barely understand him. She must have looked confused because he cleared his throat and repeated, "Are you sure? Because I don't know if I'll be able to stop. I want you so badly…" His voice cracked with his need.

And it intensified her own. Her body throbbed already for his. She pulled off her scrub top and dropped her pants, standing before him in only her underwear. It wasn't anything sexy—just a cotton bra and bikini underwear, the same green as her scrubs.

But his breath caught, and his eyes burned with passion, as if she was wearing fancy lingerie. He'd always told her that lingerie was a waste of money, though, because he preferred her in nothing at all.

So she reached behind herself and unclasped the bra before pushing down the panties.

And his breath escaped in a ragged groan of desire. "You're killing me, Willow…"

She didn't want that. But it was possible that someone did—that someone had tried to kill him. More than once. She could have lost Luke forever.

That fear urged her forward, to hold on to him. Forever. She dragged his shirt up over his head, mussing up the thick black strands. She tossed the shirt onto the floor atop her scrubs. And she sucked in a breath now.

He was so damn handsome. So muscular and sexy…

Hotshots had to be in top physical shape for the jobs they performed. And Luke took his job seriously. His body was all sculpted muscles under a soft dusting of black hair.

She ran her palms over his chest, and his heart thudded heavily beneath her hand. But still, he didn't touch her. Did he not want her?

Her belly was swollen, but he hadn't been turned off during her previous pregnancies. He'd loved the changes to her body as much as she had.

Her breasts were fuller and even more sensitive. When she stepped closer and rubbed them against his chest, she moaned at the sensations streaking through her—from her nipples straight to her core.

And he groaned. But before he touched her, he asked again, "Are you sure?"

"Yes!" she yelled at him again, then winced at the tone of her voice.

But he chuckled. And finally, he touched her.

He touched her like he had the first time—with wonder, with reverence…

He touched her like he was learning every curve of her body, every inch of her skin. He laid her on their bed and he kissed her everywhere—her lips, her neck, the curve of her shoulder, the bend of her elbow…

She giggled and shifted against the mattress as the tension inside her wound so tight. She needed release. She needed him. While she'd taken off his shirt, he was still wearing his jeans. But she could feel his erection straining the fly. She rubbed her fingers over it.

And he groaned again.

Then she unbuttoned his jeans and tugged down the zipper, freeing him. He was so hard, so hot…

"Luke…" she implored him.

But instead of joining their bodies, he pulled away.

Was this his revenge for her throwing him out? He intended to make her crazy with passion, but stopped before giving her the release? She hadn't thought he could be cruel.

But he only moved down her body, tenderly kissing her belly before moving lower. And with his lips and his tongue, he released that tension that had wound tightly inside her body. She sobbed from the intensity of the orgasm.

But it wasn't enough. She still felt empty. She needed him inside her, filling her. She clasped his shoulders, trying to drag him up. But he moved slowly, his lips again pressing against her belly, then moving over her breasts. He gently kissed a nipple before pulling it into his mouth and teasing the tip with his tongue.

And the tension wound back inside her.

She was not too stubborn to admit her feelings. "I need you. I need you inside me…"

He must have kicked off his jeans and boxers at some point, because he was as naked as she was. And then he was inside her, gently sliding in and out.

She arched and lifted her legs, wrapping them around his lean waist. Then she wrapped her arms around him, too, around his tautly muscled back. And she met his thrusts, urging him to find a faster pace.

But he hesitated. Sweat beaded on his brow and his upper lip. "I don't want to hurt you or the baby," he murmured.

She shook her head. "You won't…" He hadn't. She needed to tell him that, too—that it hadn't been his fault she'd lost the babies. But he started moving faster, and the pressure inside her broke.

She screamed his name just as his body tensed and he joined in her release, a low growl emanating from his throat. He sounded like he was in pain. And when he stared down at her, he looked like he was. His blue eyes darkened with so many conflicting emotions.

Making love had changed nothing. There was still so much pain between them. And with someone clearly intent on framing him for crimes and trying to kill him, there was bound to be more pain in their lives. Too much for her to risk asking him to come home, too much for her to risk this pregnancy with more stress.

But she wanted to savor this moment, so when he flopped onto his back next to her and slid his arm around her, she rolled against him, and laid her head on his chest. Then she pressed her palm against it, against the soft hair and taut muscle over his heart that pounded hard against her hand. She wanted to relax, wanted to sleep, but she couldn't stop thinking about how close she'd come to losing him. Forever.

Knowing that he wasn't safe, that someone was trying to kill him, was causing her more than stress. She was in fear for his life and felt helpless to do anything to protect him. Unless...

She lifted her head and stared up at him. "Let's investigate."

Luke tensed and stared down at her. "What are you talking about?"

"You've said that you didn't take the pills, that someone must have put them in your water bottle—"

"You know that's what happened," he interjected.

"So someone drugged you today and last night forced you off the road," she said.

"They've done more than that," he reminded her. "They've made it look like I was involved with Louanne, like I was the one who ran down Owen and Courtney..."

She heard the frustration in his voice, the aggravation, and assured him, "I don't think Owen believes you did that."

Luke released a ragged breath. "He might be the only one."

Willow drew in a deep breath, bracing herself for what she was about to admit. "He's not the only one…"

Hope brightened Luke's eyes. "You believe me?"

"I wouldn't have brought you home if I didn't," she said.

"I thought you just did that so I wouldn't off myself, and you'd feel guilty about it," he said.

Heat rushed to her face that he'd pegged how she'd felt in those first moments when she'd thought he'd purposely taken those pills. But she'd felt more than guilt; she'd felt despair.

And stress…

Knowing what stress caused, she reached protectively for her stomach, sliding her palm over the swell of it. Of their baby.

He covered her hands with his. "How far along do you think you are?" he asked, his voice gruff with emotion.

She tensed. "Why? Are you still wondering if it's yours?"

His face flushed then with bright color. "I'm sorry. I shouldn't have ever doubted you…"

"Like I doubted you?" she asked.

"That's not why you threw me out," he reminded her. "There was no talk of Louanne before then. You were so angry with me. Why would you help me now?"

"This baby is yours," she said. "And I want to carry this one to term."

"Then you need to stay far away from me," he said, and he pulled his hands away from hers and climbed out of bed. "I need to leave."

He stood beside her, gloriously naked, his skin slick over his taut muscles. He was so perfect in every way, except for what he did for a living. And that was so much a part of who he was that she couldn't ask him to give it up. "Luke—"

"Do you want me to stay, Willow?" he asked, almost hopefully. "Do you want me to move home?"

Her breath caught in her lungs, and she couldn't reply. She could only shake her head. Then she murmured, "No…" Nothing had changed. She couldn't risk her pregnancy for him—not again. She wouldn't survive another miscarriage.

"Then I need to leave," he repeated.

She felt a pang of disappointment that he wasn't trying to argue with her, that he wasn't trying to convince her to let him stay. But she'd made up her mind, so it didn't matter…much. He still mattered, though. "I don't want you hurt." Or worse…

"And I don't want you hurt," he said. "That's why you need to stay out of it."

"Who else is going to investigate?" she asked. "Gingrich?"

He groaned. "I'm the only one he wants to investigate."

"Then who?"

"Me."

"You're a firefighter, not a cop," she said.

"And you're a nurse, not a cop," he retorted.

She snorted. "I grew up with a cop," she reminded him.

"So now you want to play Nancy Drew?"

"I want to find out who's been framing you, don't you?"

"Hell, yes," he said. "But I don't want to put you in danger to do that." He reached out then and touched her

belly. "And I don't want to put another baby in danger…"
His voice cracked as he trailed off and his blue eyes glistened. He blinked and shook his head. "No, you were
right to throw me out, Willow. I've already cost you too
much. I already cost *us* too much. I won't take anything
else from you."

Tears stung her eyes now, and her heart ached for
the pain and regret in his voice. If she'd had any doubts
or second thoughts before, she had none now. Clearly
he had accepted what she was just now realizing: they
were really over.

Chapter 13

Luke's head was whirling. Maybe it was from the concussion the night before. Or the drug overdose earlier today.

Or maybe it was because of Willow and what they'd done back at their house. They'd made love. For him that was always what it would be. For her...

She cared about him.

He was grateful for that. But he was also worried because she was still determined to help him. Even though they'd both seemed to agree that they were over and that he needed to stay away from her, she'd dressed as quickly as he had and had insisted on driving him back to town. But on the way she'd pulled into the drugstore.

"Do you need something?" he asked with concern.

"The truth," she said. "Owen brought the pill bottle to the hospital with you, and this is the pharmacy that filled it."

"You are serious about this investigation," he murmured. He was still surprised and touched that she wanted to help him, but he couldn't get her any more involved than she already was. "It's not safe, Willow. Last night someone slashed your tires—"

"And I'd like to find out who did that," she said.

"So would I," he murmured. It was bad enough that he'd been targeted, but Willow had nothing to do with this and nothing to do with him. At least she'd been able to get new tires on her vehicle, so that she had transportation. He wondered when, or if, Trooper Gingrich was ever going to release his truck from evidence. As for the car that had run down Owen and Courtney, he never wanted to see that again.

"Then let's go inside," she said as she pulled her SUV into a parking spot.

Luke pointed toward the dark windows. "It's already closed."

Willow groaned with frustration and then a sound from her stomach echoed it.

"Did you eat?" he asked with concern.

She shook her head. "I left work tonight before my lunch break."

He glanced at the clock on the dash of her SUV. "If we hurry, we can get to the Filling Station before the kitchen closes." Like the pharmacy, everything else had probably closed already. There weren't major chains of anything here in the small town of Northern Lakes, and the businesses that were here closed early until the tourist season in the summer. When she hesitated to move the vehicle, Luke reminded her, "You want to investigate. There will be a lot of suspects at the bar."

Specifically, they were in their usual corner booth.

When Luke and Willow walked into the bar moments later, that was where Luke noticed most of his team squeezed in close together. Braden wasn't with them or his assistant superintendents, and Owen was absent as well. While the new team member was in the bar, like always, Trick McRooney sat at a table by himself. Nobody had accepted him as Dirk's replacement because nobody thought he'd earned it; being Braden's brother-in-law hadn't been his only qualification for the job, though. He had experience as a Hotshot, and his father had worked for years as a smoke jumper and now trained the best of the best. Trick was the only one who greeted him with a nod. But like the rest of the team, Luke didn't trust him either.

There was something about him, something too watchful. Was he investigating them? Or was he worried that they would investigate him?

In the past, Luke's team would have greeted him with a shout or a wave. But now they just stared at him…like everyone else in the bar.

No. There was even more judgment and distrust coming from them than from anyone else. A jab of pain that they could think so little of him made him flinch.

A small hand gripped his forearm and squeezed. "Let's sit at the bar," she suggested.

He'd already been heading there. "That's usually where I sit," he said.

Like Trick, Charlie greeted him with a brief nod and then slid a beer across the counter toward them. Then the bar owner turned toward Willow and asked, "What would you like?"

"Just water," she said.

"Me, too," Luke said.

And Charlie arched a dark eyebrow as if surprised, which was odd given that Luke hadn't touched the last beer that he'd served him without Luke requesting it. That had been last night...when someone had driven Luke off the road. Luke hadn't had a drink for a few weeks before that, since the night someone had used his vehicle to run down Owen and Courtney in the street outside the bar. He reached out to help Willow onto the stool and as she sat down, she dropped her keys and her purse onto the bar top.

Just as Luke always dropped his keys onto the counter...

His brow furrowed as doubts began to niggle at him. The person with the easiest access to slipping something into his drink was the person who served it to him.

"I'd really like something to eat," Willow told Charlie. "Is your kitchen still open?"

"For you, of course," he replied with a quick grin. With thick dark hair and chiseled features, the bar owner was a good-looking guy.

Luke had overheard some of the customers admitting they came into the Filling Station just to flirt with Charlie Tillerman. Louanne had certainly spent a lot of time at the bar. Luke had figured she'd just been there to spend time with her husband, since Hotshots were gone from home so often.

But had she come into the bar when they were gone?

"What would you like?" Charlie asked Willow as he slid a menu and a glass of water onto the bar in front of her. The menu covered her keys.

How many times had one covered Luke's keys? How easily could Charlie have slipped them out from underneath and run out to copy them at the hardware store across the street?

Being suspicious like this, of a man Luke had once considered a friend, had dread churning sourly in his stomach. Or maybe that was whatever he'd been given in the ER to counteract the overdose.

"You want anything?" Charlie asked Luke.

Luke shook his head. "Just that water…"

"Still not feeling well?" Willow asked once Charlie headed into the kitchen.

"No," he said. "I hate feeling this suspicious of everyone." He shared his supposition with her about Charlie possibly copying his keys and drugging his drinks.

Instead of reacting with shock, she nodded as if those doubts had crossed her mind, too. "Good," she said. "You need to be suspicious of everyone."

He sighed. "Yeah, to catch the real guilty person."

"Most importantly, to stay alive," she said, and she reached out again, covered his hand on the bar and squeezed.

His skin tingled in reaction to her touch as he always reacted to her, but never more than now. They'd made love…but had it been for the last time?

Would she ever let him that close to her again?

"What are you doing with him?" a deep voice asked. "Did you bail him out?"

Willow jerked her hand from Luke's as if she'd been caught cheating with someone else, someone who wasn't her husband. And she twirled toward the man who'd so easily snuck up on them.

Trent Miles stood behind Luke, but his total focus was on Willow. His topaz eyes stared intently at her with concern and something else.

Obsession?

Trent hadn't applied to join the Huron Hotshot team until after Willow had left Detroit for Northern Lakes to be closer to her retired dad. Or that was what Luke had always believed. Or had she left Detroit to get away from an obsessive old boyfriend?

Luke had always assumed they'd just been friends, since Willow had told Luke that he was the only firefighter she'd ever dated, the only man with a dangerous career for whom she'd made an exception to her rule.

She had come to regret that, as she'd told him that morning that she'd tossed him out. She'd said she never should have gotten involved with Luke and wouldn't make a mistake like that again, one that had cost her too much.

So she wasn't likely to ever give Trent the chance he clearly wanted with her. Even if Trent got rid of him.

And if some of the rumors about Trent were true, if he had once belonged to a gang, then he knew how to commit a crime, maybe even one as serious as murder.

"I'm her husband," Luke reminded the other man. Though Luke doubted that it would be the case for much longer.

"You haven't filed for divorce yet?" Trent asked her, his brow furrowing with confusion and disapproval. "After everything that he's done?"

Luke sucked in a breath, feeling that he'd been punched. "So you've already tried and convicted me?"

Trent finally spared him a glance, one filled with disgust. "Gingrich arrested you this morning, so it's only a matter of time before a jury convicts you, too."

"Gingrich had to drop the charges and release me," Luke said.

Trent shook his head. "Gingrich is an idiot. Somebody else should take over that investigation."

"I agree," Luke said. "Then they'll find out who was really having the affair with Louanne." And he gave

Trent the same look of disgust that Trent had been giving him.

Trent snorted. "It wasn't me, and you damn well know that since it was you. How could you do that to your best friend? And Willow? You never deserved her."

Luke couldn't argue with that. Knowing how she'd felt about men with dangerous careers, he never should have asked her out. Or he should have given up his job.

Hell, he might soon not have a choice about that. With how the rest of the team felt about him, it was only a matter of time before Braden had to let him go. They couldn't do the kind of work they did if they didn't trust each other.

It was damn clear that none of them trusted Luke anymore. But he didn't trust them either.

With a clatter, a plate dropped onto the bar top, drawing everyone's attention to Charlie. "Is there a problem here?" he asked.

"Yeah," Trent said. "Your clientele is going downhill, Charlie. You should toss him out."

"After the fire, a lot of people said I should toss out all the Hotshots," Charlie admitted. And he acted as if he was considering it.

The Hotshots had been the target of the arsonist, and Charlie's bar had burned down as collateral damage. He'd rebuilt, but did he resent them over that?

Did he resent them enough to have an affair with the wife of one of them while trying to frame another for murder? But what about Willow?

Why would anyone go after Willow?

To hurt him? Because nothing hurt him more than her being hurt—that was why he needed to stay away from her. He didn't want to be the cause of any more pain for her.

"Don't worry, Charlie," Luke said as he slid off his stool. "I'll leave. I don't want to cause any trouble for anyone."

Least of all, his wife...

"Too late for that," Trent remarked bitterly.

"Luke," Willow said, and she reached out to grasp his arm.

He shook his head. "I'll walk back to the firehouse. You stay and finish your food." He tossed down some bills on the bar and headed toward the door.

And as he walked out, he could feel all the stares— all the disapproval and maybe hatred... Because whoever had framed him and tried to kill him definitely hated him.

It was worse—so much worse than even Willow had imagined. They had all really turned their backs on him—Trent literally, as he turned away from where Luke walked out the door to slide onto the bar stool he'd vacated.

"What are you doing?" she asked.

"I'm joining you," Trent said.

"I didn't invite you," she pointed out. And she didn't want to talk to him. But she had to...if she was going to find out the truth.

And she needed to know the truth. She wasn't the only one, though. Everybody needed to know or they would continue blaming Luke for Dirk's death, for the hit-and-run involving Owen and Courtney.

And they were all he had now that she'd thrown him out. Guilt churned in her stomach as the baby moved within her womb. She pressed her hand over it protectively. While she'd been afraid to go to her obstetrician yet, afraid of finding out something was wrong with this pregnancy, she had been taking prenatal vitamins. She'd been taking care of herself and him or her, except for the stress. And that was what had cost her those other babies. She could not lose this one.

Maybe Luke was right. Maybe she needed to stay out of this and away from him. That was obviously what he'd intended when he'd walked out and left her alone in the bar. He'd made the message as clear to everyone else as it had been to her earlier at their home: they were done.

They had no future.

But she still wanted Luke to have one, doing the job he'd once loved so much. Probably more than he'd ever loved her...

But how could he love her after what she'd done? After how she'd blamed him for their losses, for their pain?

Sure, she had been stressed over his job, when his crew had gone missing and when the arsonist had been after all of them. But she should have been able to cope better, to protect her babies herself.

But she was no stronger than her mother had been, no more able to handle the stress of being married to a man with a dangerous career.

"I thought you and I were friends, Willow," Trent said.

She knew he'd always wanted more than friendship from her. How badly had he wanted it? How badly had he wanted her?

Enough to try to get her husband out of the way?

Dread lurched in her stomach now, and she pushed away the plate of food Charlie had given her. She understood what Luke had meant, about hating having to suspect everyone. But it really was the only way to stay safe.

For him…

Was she in danger as well?

Someone had slashed her tires. She lifted her purse from the counter and felt reassured with the weight of the gun inside it. She had protection.

What did Luke have, as he walked back to the firehouse alone? What if someone tried to run him down like they'd run down Owen and Courtney? She glanced around the bar to see if anyone might have followed Luke out. The new guy was gone.

Now her dread and suspicion turned to fear.

Fear that Trent must have seen because he reached out and touched her arm. "I'm sorry, Willow. I know this much be hard for you, especially now." He glanced down at her stomach. "I want to be your friend. I want to be there for you." There was such sincerity in his deep voice and in the depths of his topaz eyes.

Trent Miles was a good man. Or so she'd always thought. She'd just never been attracted to him like she was to Luke. She'd never wanted more than friendship from him.

"I'm fine," she insisted, but her voice was hollow with the lie.

"I know your dad is in Florida for a few more weeks," he said. It was common knowledge that her dad was what was called a snowbird. He lived in his place in Florida when there was a chance of snow in Michigan. And this far north in Michigan, there was a chance of snow for a few more weeks yet. "So if you need anything let me know, and I'll be there."

"You're staying in Northern Lakes?" she asked. "Don't you have to go back to Detroit until the Hotshot team is called up?"

Color flushed his face, but she wasn't sure if it was from anger or embarrassment. "I'm not leaving until we know for certain what happened to Dirk."

"His wife killed him," she said.

"But I want to know who helped her," Trent said.

"How do you know for sure that anyone did?" Charlie asked.

Willow glanced up to see that he was standing over them at the bar. She hadn't even noticed him approach. Just like Luke might not have noticed him slip something into his drink.

"What do you mean?" Trent asked.

"How do you know she didn't act alone?" Charlie asked. "Louanne Brown was a capable woman. She could have rigged that cable that killed Dirk by herself. She could have lifted Luke's keys off him and taken his gun and his car."

"Sounds like you knew her well..." Willow mused.

Charlie shrugged. "Everybody knows everyone in small towns."

"No," Trent said. "I don't think anyone knew she was capable of murder. No matter how close you are to someone you might not know what they're capable of doing..." He gave Willow a pointed stare. He was obviously talking about Luke.

But Willow didn't think her husband had had an affair with Louanne Brown any more than she thought the woman had acted alone. Because if Louanne had acted alone, Luke wouldn't be in danger. Someone wouldn't have tried twice to kill him.

When would they try again?

Because she had no doubt that they would…

That they would keep trying until they were caught.
Or until they succeeded.

Chapter 14

Feeling like he had during the overdose, Luke fought to rouse himself from the deep slumber that gripped him. His head ached, and his eyes were so heavy that he could barely open them. But then something big and wet swiped across his face, and he groaned and pushed off Annie's furry head. She sat next to his bunk, her tongue lolling out of her mouth, dripping saliva onto the floor.

He groaned again.

And Stanley chuckled. "She wakes me up like that, too." The teenager, with his curly blond hair all tousled, looked like he'd just woken up, too. He leaned against the open door to the bunkroom, a Tupperware container in his hand. "I brought you some leftovers from last night's dinner. Serena always cooks like she's still feeding everybody at the boardinghouse." Serena was Cody Mallehan's fiancée, so she'd gotten to know Stanley well, as he was Cody's foster brother. She was also Courtney Beaumont's sister. Stanley's smile slid away, probably as he remembered what had happened to the boardinghouse that Serena used to own and operate. Stanley and Serena had nearly died in a fire the arsonist had set there.

But Annie and Cody had saved them, just like Annie had tried to save Luke the night before.

The teenager obviously hadn't heard about what had happened to Luke yet, about the overdose. But eventually the gossip would reach even Stanley and since Luke needed the kid's help, he climbed out of bed and filled in Stanley on what had happened—about how Annie had tried to be a hero again.

"She kept you awake?" Stanley asked.

Eventually he had lost consciousness entirely, but he nodded. "Yes, she did. And she led Owen to me."

"Just like she led Cody to me and Serena during the fire…" Stanley had been betrayed and nearly killed by someone he'd thought was his friend. That *friend* had been setting up Stanley to take the fall for his crimes… just like someone was setting up Luke.

"She's a good dog," Luke said, praising the overgrown puppy. She was certainly more loyal than some other friends of theirs.

"Annie deserves a medal," Stanley said.

She definitely should have received one for saving him and Serena. But Luke had just gotten lucky. He hadn't drunk enough of the drugged water for it to kill him. While Luke appreciated Annie's efforts to help him, he needed human help right now. He needed a witness.

"Before you came to get me from jail yesterday, did you see anyone hanging around the firehouse?" Luke asked.

Stanley's eyebrows disappeared into the curls hanging over his forehead. "Like who? Braden was here when I left."

Braden. He'd known about the prescription. But why would he want to kill Luke?

It didn't make sense.

"He wasn't at the firehouse when we came back," Luke reminded him.

Stanley shrugged. "He must have left."

"Did you see anyone besides Braden?" he asked.

"Most of the team was in and out all day," he said. But then his eyes widened with shock as he must have realized what Luke was really asking, and Stanley shook his head vehemently, tumbling his curls around his face. "Braden wouldn't put those pills in your water," he said. "Nobody would."

But somebody had. It didn't necessarily have to be a member of the team. Anybody could have snuck into the firehouse while Stanley had been gone. Driving to pick up Luke from jail would have given someone enough time to get into the firehouse and dissolve the contents of those capsules into his water. And since the firehouse was rarely locked up, anyone could have gotten in.

Like Charlie Tillerman.

"Are you in trouble again?" Stanley asked.

"Again?" *Still* was a better word to describe his situation. Ever since Louanne Brown had died.

No. His life had gone to hell the minute Willow had thrown him out. He could have survived losing the babies if she hadn't pushed him away. But then the pain of losing them *and* her...

It had all been too much. But not so bad that he would have considered ending it. Or hurting anyone else.

"Like that night that your car ran over Owen and

Courtney," Stanley said. "I'm so sorry I didn't see anything that night either."

Luke sighed. "I just wish you'd seen me that night." But Stanley had already been sleeping in one bunk when Luke had shown up and climbed into another. Only Annie had seen him that night.

"I'm sorry," Stanley said, his voice thick with regret. "I wish I could help you."

Luke reached out and squeezed his thin shoulder. "I know. I know you would if you could."

"I would lie," Stanley murmured. "If I could."

Luke grinned and ruffled the teenager's curls. "I don't want you to lie for me," he assured him. Not that he thought the kid was even capable of that.

He was too honest. That was why he'd been so hurt when people had begun to think he was the arsonist. Stanley, more than anyone else, knew how it felt to be framed for something you weren't capable of doing, and hurting people you cared about.

"If only Annie could talk," Stanley murmured. "She could have vouched for you that night."

And she could have told him who'd put those pills in his water bottle because Annie had probably seen whoever it was. Had she known them? Since everybody in town knew that Annie wouldn't bite, anyone could have walked right past her into the firehouse.

Luke wanted to think it was someone else, someone outside the team. It was bad enough that they had all turned their backs on him. But if one had framed and tried to kill him…

He wasn't sure how he would deal with that kind of betrayal. A memory flashed through his mind, of that morning he'd been arrested, of the slight smirk that had crossed Trent's mouth as he'd turned away. Then last night Trent had been all but begging Willow to divorce Luke.

Did Trent think he would finally have a shot with her if he got Luke out of the way? And since framing him for the hit-and-run and an involvement with Louanne hadn't been enough to make her file for divorce, did he intend to make Willow a widow instead?

Was the man willing to kill Luke to get to his wife? Trent was a fool; all he had to do was wait. Because Luke had no doubt that Willow wasn't going to give him another chance.

Willow shouldn't have let Luke leave the bar alone last night. She would never forgive herself if something had happened to him. But when she'd left, shortly after he had, she'd driven past the firehouse and had seen a shadow in the window to the bunkroom. It had looked like his. But that night she'd shoved a gun in his back in the dark, she hadn't recognized him. So she couldn't be sure. And all morning he hadn't answered any of her calls.

So, early in the afternoon she drove to the firehouse to make certain that he was all right. After she pulled her SUV to the curb outside it, she hesitated before opening her door. She'd never felt awkward about stopping by before. But last night, and how everyone had stared when she'd walked into the bar with Luke, flashed through her mind again. Everyone really was speculating about them, about their separation. Probably only Cheryl at the hospital and Willow's mother knew the truth.

She hadn't been able to bring herself to share it with anyone else. Not even Tammy.

The beauty parlor was down the street from the firehouse. Close enough that she could see as a customer stepped out of the building. The woman turned and headed toward the firehouse. She'd probably parked in the lot since she was one of the Hotshots. Usually Henrietta Rollins's long black hair was bound in a braid, not curling down around her shoulders as it was now. Hank, as everyone called her, was one of the two female Hotshots on the team of twenty, but she was every bit as tough as the guys.

Willow had always admired her and appreciated that the woman had no time for bullshit and always told it like it was. Willow stepped out of her SUV and greeted the woman on the curb outside the firehouse. "Hello, Hank."

"Willow..." Hank murmured. She'd been in the bar last night, so she didn't seem particularly surprised to see her at the firehouse.

"Are you going inside?" Willow asked. She wasn't comfortable going up to the bunkroom alone, just in case Luke wasn't the only one sleeping in it. And if he was alone, the temptation to join him in bed might be too great to resist...like it had been the night before.

Hank shook her head. "Are you?" she asked, and she sounded a little like Trent now—disapproving.

"I want to make sure that Luke's okay," she said.

"He's not," Hank replied. "He's a mess. He's been a mess for months."

Willow flinched. At least one person seemed to have taken Luke's side in their separation. "So you don't believe he had an affair with Louanne?"

"Do you?" Hank asked.

Willow shook her head. "That's not why we separated."

"Everybody started speculating the minute you threw

him out," Hank said, and she glanced back at the beauty parlor, where she must have just heard plenty of gossip. "I suspect you already know what everyone's saying."

Willow nodded. "They're repeating rumors, but has anyone actually seen anything to prove these claims?"

"No," Hank replied. "Luke had only been around Louanne when he'd been with Dirk at their house along with a lot of other Hotshots, playing cards or working on that truck in Dirk's garage. And then, after you threw him out, he crashed at their place. Dirk was worried about him with good reason. He was devastated."

Willow hadn't been wrong about the accusation in Hank's voice. She had definitely taken his side.

The other woman continued, "I *never* saw Luke alone with Louanne."

"What about Louanne?" Willow asked. "Did you see her with anyone else?"

Hank shrugged. "Louanne and I weren't friends. I only saw her when Dirk was around. What's with the questions? Are you playing detective?"

Maybe because she'd grown up with a lawman father, it was in her DNA. "I just want to know the truth."

"Then maybe you should talk to your husband," Hank suggested, and as she said it, she looked over Willow's shoulder.

And she knew, even before she turned, that he was standing behind her. She whirled toward him, happy that he was all right. But he didn't look all right.

With big dark circles under his blue eyes, he looked exhausted. And wounded. With his jaw tightly clenched, he also looked angry. He nodded at Hank, who passed them to walk around the back of the three-story firehouse, probably to the lot behind it, where she must have parked her vehicle.

"What are you doing here?" Luke asked.

She felt a little jab of pain strike her heart that he wasn't happy to see her, like she'd been happy to see him. "I came to check on you."

"You're not trying to play detective like Hank asked?" His blue eyes narrowed with suspicion as he studied her face.

Her face, which probably flushed with color as she guiltily blushed. "Well…"

"Willow, I told you it's too dangerous," he said.

"No, what's dangerous is not knowing who's been doing these things," she said. "Gingrich isn't going to find out."

"Not when he has his heart set on pinning it on me," Luke said before emitting a ragged sigh.

"So what are you going to do?" she asked. "Wait around for him to slap the cuffs on you?"

"Again," he said. "He's already tried arresting me twice."

Just as many times as someone had tried to kill him. "We can't wait for the third time," she said.

"*I* can't," he said. "*You* need to worry about yourself." He reached out then and pressed his hand over her belly, where her red sweater was stretched tight. "And the baby…" His blue eyes glistened.

Tears stung her eyes, too, as she thought of those other babies. The ones she felt like she'd failed. "I know, but… I think I'm more stressed waiting around, worrying about what's going to happen next. Being proactive makes me feel less stressed."

"Maybe it makes *you* feel less stressed," he said. Then he drew in a shaky breath and continued, "But it makes me more stressed. I don't want to put you or the baby in danger. Not again…" His shoulders slumped with the guilt she'd piled on him.

She wanted to relieve it, wanted to assure him he'd done nothing wrong. But she didn't want to give him false hope for a future together. Because once his name was cleared, his team would support him again, would be the family he hadn't had since his mom disowned him. Since she'd thrown him out.

Being back with his team was better for him than giving up a job he loved for her. She blinked hard, fighting back those threatening tears, and focused on his face. "I won't be in danger," she said. "We'll just go to the pharmacy—"

"I already went," he said. And from the sound of defeat in his deep voice, it hadn't been a successful trip.

"What happened?" she asked.

His jaw clenched so tightly a muscle twisted in his cheek. Then he sighed and said, "They insisted I came through the drive-thru and picked it up myself."

"But you didn't…" she murmured, but now a doubt crept back in.

"No, Willow, I didn't, but I had no way of proving it. The pharmacy tech admitted to never checking IDs in the drive-thru when the person pays cash, like I supposedly did. She also said the person was wearing a hat and dark glasses, and through the window, she couldn't really tell what they were driving. I asked to see the security footage, but the pharmacist intervened then and refused. The tech must have been afraid of getting in trouble because then she accused me of lying, of drug seeking…"

And Willow knew how much he hated drugs and why, because of his dad.

"Then let's go back to the crime scene," she suggested.

His brow furrowed as he stared at her in disbelief.

"What crime scene? Gingrich towed my truck and won't release it from the impound lot yet."

She shook her head. "Not that one. We want to know who Louanne was having the affair with," she reminded him. "We need to go back to her house." To where she'd died.

Luke shuddered. "It's not safe," he murmured.

"She's dead," Willow said. And so was Dirk. "Nobody's there. Nothing bad can happen."

He snorted. "We both know better than that. Something bad can happen anywhere."

He was right. While he'd been lost in that wildfire in California, she was the one who'd been in real danger. Her and their child.

While Luke had survived unscathed, she'd lost her baby and a part of herself. The part that had once been strong enough to face challenges head-on.

She wanted to find that person again. Maybe that missing Willow was at the crime scene, too. "I have my gun," she assured him. "We'll be safe."

Luke's long body tensed, and she nearly smiled. She'd had to force him to take the gun that she'd bought him when the arsonist had been going after Hotshots. Luke hated guns. He hadn't been raised around them like she had.

"Louanne had my gun," he reminded her. "It didn't keep her safe."

"She wasn't using it for protection," Willow pointed out. She'd tried to use it to take out Owen James because she'd thought Dirk had told him something or he'd seen something that would lead back to her. And just like the person trying to kill Luke, she'd made her first attempts on his life look like accidents.

So clearly, whoever was after Luke had been her accomplice since they operated the same way and maybe for the same reason. Maybe Luke had seen or heard something that he shouldn't have and just hadn't realized it yet.

"There must be something back at the house that will reveal who she was having the affair with," Willow insisted. "A diary or letters or a card—something."

Maybe a memory. And once she got Luke in the house, she could try to get him to recall it.

Luke shrugged. He clearly wasn't as convinced as she was. "The state police must have already searched the place," he said.

"But how hard did they look?" Willow asked. "They probably thought the case was closed when Louanne died. But we both know that's not true."

He shuddered now. "No, it's not over. It won't be over until we find out the truth."

Where were they going? Luke Garrison had climbed into the passenger side of his wife's SUV, and she pulled away from the curb, turning to head out of town.

The frame-up should have ended their marriage, not reunited them. What was she doing? Why was she reaching out to him?

Could she still have feelings for him, even though it had been made to look like Luke had been cheating on her with his best friend's wife?

She'd tossed him out before that, though. So they'd already had problems before the frame-up. She should have been happy to get rid of Luke; it would save her the expense of a divorce and the hardship of splitting up assets. That had been Louanne's reasoning for killing Dirk. Then she'd taken out that life-insurance policy on him for an even bigger payout. She'd never been able to enjoy it, though.

She hadn't lived long enough to even benefit from his death. And she'd left behind a mess.

A mess that needed to be cleaned up. Gloved hands gripped the wheel, steering the vehicle around the curves in the road the Garrisons were taking out of town as it followed at a great enough distance that it wouldn't be noticed but not far enough to get lost.

Even when they took an abrupt turn down a long driveway—a familiar driveway, the one leading down to the house where Dirk and Louanne Brown had lived. And where Louanne had died.

What the hell were they doing here? And what might they find?

Anything that would lead them to the truth? Luke Garrison needed to die to protect that truth, but now he wasn't the only one. His wife might have to die with him. Right now.

Chapter 15

Luke shouldn't have agreed to come out here with Willow, but she'd been so determined that she would have headed out by herself. And he would have wound up here, anyway, since everything else had proved to be a dead end. He'd struck out with Stanley, who hadn't seen any more than Luke had yesterday. And the pharmacy had been a dead end, too. As if he'd ever go seeking drugs…

The last thing he wanted was any more drugs. No. All he wanted now was the truth.

And Willow.

He always wanted Willow—even more after last night. Despite being with her, his body ached for hers. His heart ached even more, feeling empty and lost even though she sat in the seat next to him. She'd shut off the SUV and just stared through the windshield at the Browns' ranch house. Yellow tape that was still strung across the front porch fluttered in the breeze. The crime scene had probably been released, the case closed when Louanne admitted to killing Dirk right before she died from the gunshot she'd gotten when she and Owen struggled over the gun she'd aimed at him. The estate would be in probate for a while. Unlike Dirk, Louanne hadn't had a will with an executor. She'd made sure Dirk had had one, along with that hefty life-insurance policy. But then she'd known he was going to die. She hadn't realized that killing him would wind up killing her as well.

So maybe, because she'd been so arrogantly certain that she would get away with making his death look like an accident, she hadn't been too careful with what she'd left around her house. Maybe they would find some love letters or pictures or...something that revealed the identity of her real accomplice, her true lover.

"How long did you stay here?" Willow asked, her voice barely more than a whisper.

He sighed. "Long enough that it started to feel strange, like I was causing issues..."

"Sounds like Louanne was who caused the issues," Willow remarked.

"But Louanne and who?" Luke mused.

"You don't remember anything?" she asked. "Don't remember hearing anything?"

He shook his head.

Willow pushed open her door and stepped out. "Let's go inside. Let's see if we can find anything. Or if you can remember anything..."

He couldn't think about anything but last night, about making love with her again. About how wonderful she'd felt in his arms, how like sliding into her body had felt like coming home...and how for that brief moment in time, he'd actually felt whole again. Instead of hollow and empty and so damn alone…

He pushed open his door and stepped out, rushing around to join her as she headed toward the porch. She moved quickly, as if she was hopeful that they would find something. Luke wasn't as hopeful. The house had already been searched as the scene of a crime, where Louanne had tried to kill Owen and had wound up shooting herself instead.

With Luke's gun…

The gun he hadn't even wanted. Since he'd left it at his house with Willow, how the hell had Louanne gotten it? Had she stolen it while Willow was home? Had that killer been that close to his wife and their unborn baby? The thought made his stomach heavy with dread.

No. Louanne had been smart. She would have made sure nobody would see her taking that gun. She was probably too smart to have left any evidence lying around either.

Of course, the only evidence Gingrich had probably been looking for was something to implicate Luke as her accomplice. The resentful trooper would have disregarded anything that pointed to someone else like, hopefully, someone outside the Hotshot team. Gingrich certainly would have missed that. Hell, he might have even destroyed it since it wouldn't have supported his mission to take down Braden.

As Luke joined Willow on the porch, he snapped the yellow tape between the posts. It reminded him of the cable that Louanne had rigged to snap on her husband, and he shuddered. Maybe she hadn't known the damage it would do to Dirk. Or maybe she had…

How could anyone think Luke would have cheated

on his wife, who'd dedicated her life to helping other people, with a mercenary woman like Louanne Brown?

What was worse was that even Willow had thought that he might have. The first night he'd come home since their separation, she accused him of cheating with Louanne. His heart ached with pain over her thinking so little of him.

"Are you okay?" Willow asked with concern. For whatever reason, she believed him now.

He nodded. "Just makes me think of Dirk…" And how horribly and senselessly he'd died.

"If this is too hard for you, I can go in alone," she offered.

He shook his head at the thought of her being anywhere around here on her own. Even though it was only late afternoon, it was already dark back here in the trees—the house and outbuilding were cast in deep shadows.

He used to love coming here; he had loved hanging out with Dirk. After Willow had thrown him out, it had been a soft place to land, where neither Dirk nor Louanne had pried him for details about the trouble in his marriage. They hadn't made him talk. They'd just offered him a couch on which to flop.

Despite all the time he'd spent on that couch, in this house, he'd had no idea they were having problems in their own marriage. Of course, he'd been preoccupied with his—with Willow.

"No," Luke said. "I'll go in with you." There was no threat here. Everybody was gone. Only ghosts lived in the Brown residence now. Too bad Luke didn't really believe in ghosts. If he did, he might be able to make one of them talk to him and tell him where to find what he was looking for. He crossed the porch to the front door.

Thick, sticky tape sealed it shut, but the knob turned easily. Either the lock was broken or hadn't been engaged. With a shove, he was able to push it open, the tape making a sucking sound as it released the door from the jamb.

It was even darker inside the house. He automatically reached for the switch, having been there so many times that he knew where it was. The overhead light came on, as well as a lamp that was lying on the floor, its shade crumpled. Its glow illuminated the chalk outline of a body and the dark stain on the hardwood floor.

Willow followed him inside and gasped at the sight of that outline. She gripped his arm then, either offering comfort or seeking it. She'd said she'd moved away from Detroit to get away from scenes like this, from this kind of danger and violence. Or had she moved to get away from Trent Miles?

Before Luke could ask, Willow murmured, "That's where she died..."

If only Louanne had lived long enough to say more, to clear his name, to identify her real accomplice...

But she'd died too soon.

Like Dirk...

His heart ached for the loss of his friend just as it ached for Willow. Luke might have the chance to get his wife back, but Dirk was gone forever. He deserved real justice, to have all his killers held accountable. With renewed purpose, Luke stepped over that chalk outline in the foyer and headed inside the house.

Willow followed him closely, as if she was worried about him. Or watching him.

Instead of looking around the family room, she stared at him. He turned toward her, his eyes narrowed.

"What is it?" he asked. "Do you think I've been lying to you about anything?"

She shook her head. "No, but I still wonder if you overheard something, or saw something, while you were staying here…"

He nodded as comprehension dawned at what she was getting at. Owen had mistaken Dirk's last word as a call for his wife, but he'd been naming his killer.

"You said you stayed here for a while," she reminded him.

It had felt like forever. Every minute he'd been away from her had seemed like hours. Even now, with her in the same room with him, he felt a distance between them. A distance that had only been bridged last night, in their bedroom, in their bed…

His body tensed with desire to be that close to her again. But he suspected last night had been a moment of weakness for her that she didn't intend to repeat.

He shrugged. "I don't know. I was so out of it…"

"Drunk?" she asked.

He cursed. "No. No matter what you've heard. No. I just…" He'd been so broken, so full of guilt and remorse for causing her so much pain, so much loss. Tears stung his eyes, but he blinked them back and focused on her beautiful face. "No, I was just wallowing in my own self-pity," he admitted. "And I was totally unaware of what Louanne was planning." He cursed again. "If I'd only paid more attention, if I'd caught on to what she was up to…" His voice cracked as guilt overwhelmed him. "I might have been able to save him."

Willow closed the distance between them now and slid her arms around his waist, holding him like she'd held him last night. With concern…

And probably pity.

"It wasn't your fault that she killed him."

"But even you think I must I have heard something—"

"Only because I think that might be why her accomplice is trying to frame and now kill you," she said. "Just like she tried to kill Owen."

He sucked in a breath and closed his eyes, trying to remember what had happened while he'd been staying there. Sleeping on that couch...

But he'd never been able to sleep that deeply that he hadn't heard the low murmur of voices.

I can't talk now...because he's here again... We'll meet up later to discuss the plan.

He hadn't thought anything of the comments at the time, believing she'd been making plans with a friend. But now he gasped at what could have been the real context of those comments. He shared the snippets of conversation with Willow. "She could have just been talking to a friend about the plan to go to lunch or a movie or..."

"Or her lover about their plan to murder her husband," Willow said. "That was all you remember?"

He nodded. "There were other variations of that. I didn't know what she was talking about for sure, half thought that she might have had some plan about me, getting me out of her house..." Once he'd surfaced enough from his misery, he'd realized he hadn't been all that welcome.

"There has to be something here," Willow insisted as she began pulling open the doors on the entertainment center. They discovered that Louanne hadn't been the sentimental type. She had no scrapbooks or journals. Only a few framed pictures of her and Dirk's wedding, and some of the entire Hotshot crew. Had she kept those because of her husband or because of her lover?

Was he in those photos? The man who'd betrayed Dirk? Who was betraying Luke? Luke felt a sharp pang as he stared at that photo; he and Dirk had had their arms around each other, leaning against each other with that absolute trust that if one faltered, the other would catch him. Luke had faltered, and Dirk had caught him. But Luke hadn't been there for him...

"Are you okay?" Willow asked. "Is this too hard for you?"

He shook his head even as tears stung his eyes again. He furiously blinked them back and focused on another photo, one of a bunch of them hanging out in Dirk's detached garage. Louanne was in the photo as well, although it was hard to see since she was wearing a welder's helmet while operating a torch. His finger shaking, Luke pointed out the torch. "That's probably what she used to sabotage that cable on the winch truck..." They'd been removing a fallen tree, and when the cable Dirk had been winding around the tree had snapped, the sharp metal fibers had mortally wounded him.

Willow shuddered. "I was there when Owen brought him in. There was no way he could have survived... nothing anyone could have done..."

"If he hadn't died then, she would have tried again," Luke said, and now fury bubbled up inside him. "She had her plan..." And he might have realized that if he hadn't been so distracted. "I didn't even know Dirk was intending to divorce her until Owen and Braden found out after he died. He didn't tell me anything that was going on." And his heart ached that his best friend hadn't felt as if he could confide him in.

"I'm sorry," Willow murmured, and she reached out and squeezed his arm.

Despite his jacket and shirt separating her skin from his, he felt her touch deep inside him, where it made him tense with longing for what he knew they could never have again. They'd suffered too much loss and pain for their marriage to survive. He directed his thoughts back to Dirk's marriage. "According to Braden and Owen, Dirk already had an appointment with a divorce lawyer. He never made it…" His voice cracked with pain—for Dirk and for himself. He had to know, so he asked, "Do you already have an appointment?"

She jerked her hand away from him, and her face flushed. Was that embarrassment that she'd started the proceedings? Or embarrassment that she hadn't, especially after Trent had seemed so appalled yesterday to see them together.

"Maybe Miles called a divorce lawyer for you last night," he added, and then he flinched at the obvious jealousy in his voice and churning in his stomach.

Willow tensed and narrowed her eyes in a glare. "We're here to find out who's trying to kill you."

"Maybe it has nothing to do with Louanne and Dirk," he suggested. "Maybe it's someone else who has a grudge against me for another reason…like I wound up with the woman he wanted."

"You're stuck on Trent," she said and shook her head.

"I don't want it to be him," Luke admitted. "I don't want it to be any member of our team. Hell, I don't even want it to be Charlie. We've all hung out at that bar for years. That's why the arsonist burned it down, to get to us."

"And maybe Charlie resents you all for it," Willow suggested.

Luke nodded. "Maybe…"

Willow gazed around the house. "But I can't help but think that the answer's here somewhere."

"Maybe we're looking in the wrong place," Luke mused, and he glanced out the window at the outbuilding. "Dirk was divorcing Louanne for a reason. Maybe he found out about the affair. And Dirk wouldn't have listened to rumors. He would have had to have proof."

Luke had an idea where he would have kept it—in the place where he'd spent the most time when he was home. "I'm going to look outside."

"I still think there could be something in here, too," Willow said. "If Louanne had a diary, she wouldn't have left it where it would be easy to find."

"You search here, and I'll go out to the garage," Luke said. He needed some distance from her. It had been so hard on him all these months that they'd been separated with no contact. But being physically close to her and knowing there was no way to bridge that emotional distance... That was even harder.

Willow reached inside her purse. "Do you want the gun?"

Luke shuddered. "No. You keep it." She'd be more likely to use it than he would. And it was bad enough that she'd insisted on investigating with him, he wanted to make sure she had protection for her and their baby. But the gun couldn't protect her from the stress he caused her. Only he could. Or maybe it was like she'd claimed, maybe being proactive helped her because she seemed almost excited, or maybe just determined, as she peeked under the couch and checked inside DVD covers.

She was amazing. He'd been lucky to have her as long as he had. She hadn't been lucky, though, not with all she'd lost. For the first time since the miscarriages, she actually seemed more like the woman he'd met and married. Fearless and strong…

She glanced up from her search and asked, "Are you going to check the garage?"

He smiled at her impatience and nodded. He needed that distance, but it probably wasn't going to be enough for him to stop falling for his wife all over again.

With a ragged sigh, Luke stepped out of the house and pulled the door shut behind himself. It was even darker now, so dark that he stumbled over gravel as he headed across the driveway to the garage. There was no tape around it. But the door wasn't locked, and Dirk had always locked it to secure his tools.

A strange feeling settled heavily on Luke—more than dread, more than loss…

Fear.

Which was weird since nobody had died inside the garage. He should have felt that way entering the house instead. But the chill sank deep inside him, and he shivered as he pushed open that door.

The darkness inside the garage was complete. But like the house, Luke knew the place well, so he reached for the switch. It was already flipped up, but none of the shop lights had come on.

Had the power been shut off?

But the house had electricity. Why wouldn't the garage? It had its own breaker box, near the back of it, so Luke headed toward it. One of the breakers might have blown. It had happened often when they'd been working on stuff.

The darkness was so complete that he couldn't see well. He stumbled into tools and vehicle parts, cursing as his knee struck hard metal. A few more steps had his foot hitting something that rolled beneath him, sending him sprawling onto the concrete.

He cursed. But before he could do more than sit up, his curse was choked off as something wrapped tightly around his throat. Rough fibers bit into his skin, and he realized it was rope, or rather a noose, that was drawing tighter and tighter. He clutched at it, fighting against it even as consciousness began to slip away from him. But then Luke thought of Willow and the baby she carried. Once the killer finished with him, he might go into the house. Luke had to make sure they would be safe.

So even though he clawed at his own skin, he slid his fingers beneath the rope. Now it bit into his hands more than his throat. He could draw a breath. He could fight off the oblivion threatening to claim his consciousness. He needed to fight off whoever the hell was standing behind him in the darkness, pulling up on the rope looped around his neck.

The assailant was strong—damn strong.

Using both his hands, Luke jerked down on the rope, making it a little looser, loose enough that he was able to slip the palm of one hand between it and his throat. Then he moved his other hand to the ground, feeling around for a weapon—for something to strike out at his assailant.

His hand skimmed across something smooth and supple like leather. Probably a shoe. It jerked from beneath his touch. He pawed at the concrete for a bit longer until his fingers touched something cold and hard. Some kind of tool. Probably whatever he'd tripped over earlier. He clutched his hand around the metal object and swung out with it.

And he struck something, his effort rewarded with a grunt from the assailant. The rope loosened a bit more before a quick jerk pulled it tight again, so tight that his hand pressed against his throat now and threatened to shut off his airway. And it didn't feel as if someone was holding it now, but that it was tied to something as tightly as it was tied around his neck. And the more he pulled, the more it tightened.

While he was tethered here, his killer could slip away—slip into the house to attack Willow, too. He raised the tool, but before he could swing again, he heard the pounding of footsteps across the concrete, and the side door swinging open and shut. And Luke was left tethered with that rope, stuck inside the garage, unable to run after his attacker, to stop the son of a bitch from going after Willow. He'd already failed her in the past; he had to make sure that this time he protected her and their unborn child. But the more he fought, the more the rope seemed to tighten, cutting off his oxygen, his life…

The minute Luke had stepped outside Willow had paused her search. She should have been straight with him when he'd asked if she had an appointment with a divorce lawyer. She should have told him that she intended to follow through, for her peace of mind, for her pregnancy. She couldn't lose another baby, and she couldn't live with the fear that she might lose Luke someday to his dangerous job. But at the moment she was more worried that she was going to lose him to whoever wanted him to die with everyone thinking he was Louanne's accomplice.

Clearly he wasn't. All the pictures in the house that included Luke showed him with his arm around Dirk. They truly had been best friends. Guilt overwhelmed her that she'd let him go through that loss, that funeral, without her support. But she hadn't wanted him to see her and discover she was pregnant then. She hadn't been ready yet for anyone to know because she'd been so scared that she would miscarry again. That was why she'd avoided Luke, avoided the pain he'd been going through.

That hadn't been fair to him. And her not answering his question hadn't been fair either. She needed to tell him outright that she couldn't see how to make their marriage work. It would be better for them both to know for certain, rather than live like they had for the last few months, in this strange, silent limbo. It reminded her of the childhood game of statue, where kids froze in place, moving neither forward nor backward while being unable to speak.

That was how she and Luke had lived.

And she knew neither of them could continue that way.

She glanced out the family-room window and saw that night had fallen, and the Browns had no yard lights, nothing to illuminate the property. No lights even shone from the outbuilding. How was Luke searching it in the dark?

The outbuilding probably was the better place to search. To have that appointment with a divorce lawyer, Dirk might have known about his wife's affair, and if he'd had evidence, he more than likely would have hidden it in his garage.

Willow had found nothing in the house to clear Luke's reputation. Nothing to implicate anyone else. Had Louanne destroyed the evidence? Or had her accomplice done it?

If her accomplice had been a fellow Hotshot, he would have known Dirk well enough to have already searched the garage, too. So what was taking Luke so long?

Fear quickened Willow's pulse. Had something happened to him? She shouldn't have let him go outside alone without the gun. He was in more danger than she was. Anxious now to find him and make sure he was all right, she rushed out of the house, but as she crossed the porch, she reached inside her purse. Hopefully she didn't need the gun, but it was inside her big bag. She skimmed her fingers across it and pulled out her flashlight instead.

Her dad had always insisted she carry one of those as well. And his advice had come in handy, especially after they'd moved to Northern Lakes, where the only streetlamps were just inside the village.

She flipped it on and directed the beam toward the ground. It was even, so she didn't need to worry about tripping. She tipped up the flashlight and directed the beam around, then caught a flash of something moving between the trees.

Maybe it was a deer. Or some other animal. Bears had recently been spotted in the area. But she didn't reach for her gun. The shadow was moving away from her, not toward her.

She was safe.

Probably. But she listened intently to the sound of it crashing through the trees, making sure that it didn't circle around to come up behind her. Would an animal be that sneaky, though?

Two-legged ones might be.

"Luke?" she called out, concern making her voice raspy. "Luke?" Had that shadow been him? She doubted he would have been running away from the area unless he was chasing someone…

She directed the beam back toward the shadow she'd

seen. But there was no movement now, not even a gust of wind. Still, she shivered.

What the hell was she doing?

She had no business being out here, alone in the dark. But she wasn't alone. And that was the problem.

The baby moved inside her belly, as if trying to run after whatever had been crashing through the trees. She felt the baby flip and kick. And she pressed her hand against her womb, trying to soothe her child.

But the baby must have felt her heart pounding madly, her pulse racing, and had picked up the anxiety.

She'd already lost two babies. And nothing had seemed precarious about those pregnancies. She'd been healthy and happy, overjoyed at the prospect of becoming a mother, of she and Luke starting their family. Until he'd been in danger...

And then she'd gone into early labor for that first baby...

And the second had just slipped away...like she'd felt happiness slipping away from her. Hope...

Now Luke was in danger again, so much that even their child seemed to sense it, stirring so restlessly inside her. Willow couldn't risk losing this baby, too, not even for Luke. She'd been a fool to think she could investigate the attempts on his life without putting her and her baby in danger, too, just like he'd feared.

"Luke?" she called out, louder and with more urgency. Would he have gone chasing after someone without a weapon? Without anything to defend himself?

Then she heard another noise. It wasn't something crashing through the trees this time, but something tumbling over inside the garage. The side door swung open, and she grabbed for her purse, for her gun.

But the door must have just creaked open on its own

because nobody was there. Nothing moved—not even the shadows. Yet she felt some kind of presence, as if she could feel a heart beating aside from her own, which was madly pounding in her chest. Maybe she just felt the baby's heartbeat as she felt his or her movements more and more. The baby was growing, was getting stronger and stronger.

And because of that, Willow felt stronger and stronger. She had to be—for her baby and for Luke. Was he inside the garage? Gravel crunching under the soles of her shoes, she closed the distance between her and that open side door to the garage. Before she stepped inside, she pulled the gun from her bag, so she had that in one hand, the flashlight in the other.

She was strong. Not stupid.

She swung the beam around the garage, following it with her gun barrel—just as her father had taught her. Her dad had joined the police department because his father had been a cop. Maybe he'd expected her to do the same, although he'd never pressured her. And he'd seemed proud when she'd become a nurse, just protective…as always.

He'd never approved of any boy she'd dated until Luke. Despite the often territorial rivalries between cops and firefighters, he'd respected Luke for the dangerous job he'd chosen. Fortunately her dad only lived in Northern Lakes for the summer months, or he might have heard the gossip about Luke and changed his mind. But then her father was a good detective; he would have immediately investigated to learn the truth, instead of relying on rumors.

Maybe she should have acted more like her father sooner. But it wasn't too late to investigate now. She stepped farther into the garage but stumbled over some hard tool. As she regained her footing, she cast the flashlight beam across the floor.

The beam illuminated the body lying on the concrete. Unlike whatever she'd seen running through the trees, this person wasn't moving. She dropped to her knees beside him. She didn't need to roll him over to know that it was Luke.

His body...

His hair...

She knew them better than she knew her own. She slid the gun into her purse and reached for his neck. Something streaked over his skin, which felt swollen and hot beneath her touch. She focused the beam of light on him and noticed the blood trailing from his forehead, over his neck. And his neck was red and chafed. That was when she noticed the rope clutched in one of his hands.

A cry slipped through her lips. And she moved her fingertips more gently across his throat. He could have a broken neck. Or a crushed airway...

And depending on how long he'd been deprived of oxygen, brain damage...

Or maybe it was already too late. Maybe she'd chosen to investigate too late. Maybe Luke was already gone.

"Where the hell could Luke be?" Braden asked his brother-in-law.

Despite the late hour, they were still at the firehouse—in Braden's office. Too bad Sam was working out of town on her arson investigation. He needed her help now. But the two of them had worked for months trying to figure out who was behind the accidents that had been happening to the Hotshots. And they'd gotten no closer to learning the truth.

Louanne had only been behind the *accident* that had killed Dirk and the attempts on Owen's life. But there had been many more incidents before that—small things that damaged equipment and caused only minimal injuries.

Dirk must have told his wife about those accidents and she'd used them to stage an accident of her own— the one that had killed him. The opening his death had given the team had given Braden the opportunity to take his wife's advice and bring in her brother to help him investigate.

Trick shook his head. "I don't know. I looked everywhere you suggested. His house. The Filling Station. Hell, even the jail and the hospital. He's nowhere."

"He's somewhere," Braden said. He just hoped like hell that nothing happened to him wherever he was.

"I can't protect him if I can't find him," Trick said.

Braden nodded. "I know. I know…" Usually he just had a sixth sense about fires, about when one was about to start. But now he had another sensation, a sense that Luke needed protection more now than ever.

The attempts on his life had escalated, just as they had with Owen when he'd been targeted. Someone was determined to kill him. And Braden's feeling was that another attempt was happening now and that it might have proved successful this time. Braden might soon have another opening on his team.

Chapter 16

Luke awoke to soft lips moving over his, to warm breath blowing inside his mouth, sliding down his throat. And he gasped as the air hit his lungs, and he opened his eyes. He could see nothing in the darkness, but he knew that touch, that kiss...

"Willow?" His voice was just a rasp from his throat, and it burned. He lifted his hand to his neck, which was hot and swollen. "What happened?"

"Are you okay?" she asked, her voice cracking with fear.

Then he remembered his fear...for her. He jolted upright and reached for her in the dark. "We need to get out of here, before he comes back."

"Who?" she asked. "Did you see anybody?"

"I can't see anything," he said. "It's so damn dark in here."

A beam flashed on then, illuminating a small circle

of the blackness. "Where are the overhead lights?" she asked as she swung her flashlight around the garage.

"By the door," he said, his voice still just a rasp. "But they didn't come on. So I was heading back toward the breaker box, tripped over something and when I was down…" He'd been attacked, just like before. Someone kept hitting him when he was most vulnerable. And he was vulnerable now, worried about Willow and their baby. "We need to get out of here." He scrambled to his feet but swayed and leaned back against the vehicle behind him.

Willow got up too, but the beam of her flashlight moved toward the back of the garage instead of the front. The overheard fluorescents came on, the lights buzzing and flickering before burning so bright that Luke had to squint.

"We need to call 911," Willow said, and she pulled a cell phone from her purse.

Luke scrambled over to her and closed his hand over hers. "No!"

"You're injured," she said, and she stared at him with tears pooling in her beautiful green eyes. "You need medical attention."

"You gave it to me," he said. "I'm fine." And he was. His throat hurt, but he was breathing fine. He was conscious now. Very conscious of what might happen if the authorities showed up.

"Someone tried to kill you," she said.

"And you think Gingrich is going to believe that?" he challenged her. He didn't think anyone would believe it. But he needed to make sure that she did. "You know that I didn't…"

"Try to hang yourself from a car bumper?" She gestured toward where fibers from a rope dangled from the grill of one of Dirk's old cars. "No. I know you didn't."

He tensed. "Did you see who did it?" he asked. And now he thought about not just calling the cops, but reaching for her gun as well as her phone.

She shook her head. "I saw something moving through the trees." She released a shaky sigh. "But I wasn't even sure it was human."

Luke touched his aching throat. "I don't think it was." Because whoever could kill someone so viciously was more like an animal than a person. No. That was an insult to animals; they had more empathy than this killer. Annie seemed to actually have more empathy than most humans.

Than him...

He noticed then how badly Willow was shaking, and alarm coursed through him. "Are you all right?"

She jerked her head in a quick nod, sending her hair swirling around her tear-streaked face. She was obviously afraid...for him.

For the baby?

"We need to get out of here," he said. But when he turned toward the door, she grabbed his arm.

"No."

"What? You want to give him a chance to try for me again?" he asked.

"No, I want to see what must be out here," she said. "What he must have been trying to make sure you didn't get a chance to find."

He released a shaky breath now. "I thought the breaker was off so the son of a bitch could attack me in the dark."

"Maybe he didn't want you to see what's in here."

Luke was torn between wanting to hustle Willow

off the Brown property, to somewhere safe—if there was any such place—and wanting to see what the killer might have been worried Luke would find in the garage.

Was there something here? Was that the reason the breaker had been off? Or had it just been another trap to get Luke out of the way? If there'd been anything in here, Luke doubted his assailant would have left it behind.

"I don't think this is a good idea," he murmured, and he swayed a bit on his feet.

Willow reached out then, clasping his arm, holding him steady. "No, you're right. I should get you to the hospital."

He groaned with dread. "No."

"You're obviously hurting," she said.

"I'll be fine." He probably needed some ice and pain-killers, but he wasn't worried about that now. He was worried about this killer setting another trap, not just for him, but for Willow as well. "I'm more worried about you," he admitted. "You and the baby…"

She reached for her stomach then, and her face turned pale.

"What?" he asked. "Is there a problem?" He hadn't been there during her last two miscarriages. He hadn't been there to support her, so she'd gone through those losses alone. He wanted to be here for her now, but he sure as hell didn't want her to miscarry.

Again, it would be his fault if she did. "I knew I shouldn't have come here with you. It's too dangerous."

"Nobody tried to strangle me," she pointed out.

"That doesn't mean that you're not in danger, too." What if, instead of running away, the person had turned around to come back? To finish them both off?

"We do need to get out of here," he insisted. And now he had her arm, and was tugging her toward that open side door. Before they got close to it, it slammed shut on them.

Willow let out a small squeak of alarm.

And Luke was reminded of how Louanne had tried to kill Owen, by setting fire to Courtney Beaumont's store with Owen and Courtney trapped in the upstairs apartment.

With all the gas cans and tanks for the torches scattered around the garage, this building would explode if a fire started. He and Willow wouldn't have time to escape like Owen and Courtney had.

"We have to get out of here," he said again.

Willow must have heard the urgency in his voice, because she moved closer to him and pulled the gun from her purse.

And he realized what she had. That just opening that door and stepping outside made them targets, if whoever had tried to kill him was waiting outside…with a gun.

But if the person had been armed, why try to strangle him instead of just shooting him? Had he still been trying to make Luke's death look like his own doing?

Like he'd tried to kill himself?

That wasn't going to work anymore. Not with Willow being here.

So what would the killer try next?

Would he or she try to take them both out the minute they stepped outside the door? Or would they start that fire instead, like Louanne had started at Courtney's store?

Luke sniffed the air, and he couldn't be sure but he thought he smelled smoke.

Willow could feel the fear in Luke. After what had happened, after someone had nearly strangled him to death, she could understand why. She felt fear for herself, too, and for their child. But the baby wasn't quietly slipping away, like her second baby had.

This one was somersaulting inside Willow's womb. Maybe she or he felt their father's fear, too. And hers.

She wanted to stay in the garage and search it for whatever Louanne's accomplice probably didn't want them to find. But the longer they stayed here, the more danger they might be in…unless they called the police.

But instead of reaching for her phone, Willow tightened her grasp on her gun. "Open the door," she told him. And she tried to step between him and that small side door.

But instead of pushing that one open, the overhead door rumbled as Luke pushed the button for it. Then he grasped her arm and tugged her toward the bigger opening. "Run for the SUV," he said. "Are the keys in it?"

She nodded.

"Then once we get there, I'm driving. We need to get the hell out of here."

And just as he said it, all hell broke loose. Bullets pinged off tools and equipment inside the garage. And somewhere outside a fire sparked and kindled…

A scream burned the back of Willow's throat, and she nearly froze. But then she remembered Luke and the baby. She wasn't going to fail her child this time.

So she gauged from which direction the shots were coming, and fired back. And as she fired, she ran beside Luke, who was guiding her toward her vehicle. He pulled open the passenger door and shoved her inside. Then he ran around the front of the vehicle and pulled open the driver's door. He started the ignition and threw the vehicle into Reverse. "Get down!" he yelled as loudly as his raspy voice could manage.

She ducked as she grappled for the seat belt. Her SUV bumped along the ruts in the driveway as Luke sped away from the crime scene. And as he drove away, a blast filled the night like the sound of gunshots had.

And the garage exploded into a fireball that rose above the trees. "Oh, my God..."

If she'd insisted on looking for evidence...

If she hadn't left with Luke when he'd wanted...

They would have been in that garage. They would have gone up in that fireball, too. She shuddered in reaction and glanced across the console at him. "Thank you," she murmured.

He'd saved her life. Saved their lives...

But then she noticed the blood streaking down the side of his face. He hadn't escaped unscathed this time. He'd been hit. How badly?

Luke Garrison might be as lucky as Owen James was. He had, unbelievably, survived yet another attempt on his life. Or had he? Had any of the bullets struck him as they'd run away from the garage?

They'd gotten out too quickly, had escaped before the fire could have killed them both. But hopefully it had consumed anything else that Dirk Brown might have hidden in his garage.

Before they'd gotten away, had either of them seen anything?

Had Luke, during their encounter? Or had the garage been too dark for him to identify his assailant? Without the night-vision goggles, it undoubtedly would have been. And Luke's back had been turned when the rope wrapped around his neck. After that, Garrison had been fighting too hard to stay alive to be able to see who had wound that rope around his neck.

But what about Willow Garrison?

She'd had that flashlight that she'd been swinging around, along with a gun in her hand. Had she seen what had been running through the trees? Or had she thought it was an animal? Once she'd gone inside the garage, doubling back had been easy. Setting the fire.

Setting the trap. But it hadn't gone according to plan. Luke had recovered enough to run away. And Willow had had that gun… Some of her shots had come close. Too damn close.

Her dad had taught her well how to use a weapon. Too well. But she hadn't had on a bulletproof vest. Neither of them had. And a lot of shots had been fired.

At least one bullet must have hit them.

Chapter 17

Fury gripped Luke, making his entire body shake. He gripped the steering wheel tightly, his knuckles turning white. Somebody hadn't just tried to kill him, they'd tried to kill Willow, too. Was that just because she was with him? Or had she also become a target?

"You shouldn't have been there," he said. He pressed harder on the accelerator, speeding away from the scene. While the Browns' house was outside town, someone must have been close enough to hear the blast, to call the fire department.

Willow was pulling her phone from her purse. He reached across the console and grabbed it. "I'm sure someone else called it in."

And now he could hear sirens in the distance…

Hell, maybe Braden's sixth sense had predicted the fire. Maybe they'd already been on their way. Or maybe whoever the hell had set it had called.

"I'm calling the ER, letting them know we're on our way," she said.

"For you?" he asked with alarm. "Are you having pain?" Was she losing this baby, too, because of him?

"For *you*," she said. "You're bleeding."

He shook his head and droplets fell from his face and spattered the console between them.

"You must have been hit!" she exclaimed, her voice rising with panic.

"I probably hit my head when I was fighting to get that rope loose...or when I first tripped over whatever was on the ground."

"You're not in pain?" she asked.

He couldn't feel anything now but that anger. Anger with whoever had tried to kill them. And anger with her...

She just wasn't getting it.

"You had no business running around that crime scene with me," he said.

"You're my husband," she murmured.

Luke's anger drained away with the break in her voice. She still cared.

He hadn't dared to believe that all these months. He'd thought that whatever they'd had had been lost with their dead babies. That she blamed him for their deaths and couldn't love him anymore.

But now he wondered...

"For how much longer?" he asked. "We both know it's over. You're never going to forgive me for what we lost."

"Luke..." she whispered. But she didn't argue with him anymore. She remained curiously quiet even as he pulled into the driveway of their house.

The headlights glinted off the back bumper of his pickup truck, the one he'd inherited from Dirk. "What's it doing here?" he asked. And who the hell had dropped it off?

Gingrich?

He hadn't thought the guy would even release it from the impound lot, let alone drop it at his house. Maybe Braden had arranged it. But why would any of them think that he would be staying here?

They all knew he'd been staying at the firehouse. That he couldn't go home again. Not even now.

Willow must have had just as many suspicions about it being here because she pulled her gun from her purse and reloaded it. She might have saved their lives back at the Brown place with that weapon. If she hadn't been firing at whoever had been shooting at them, they probably would have been hit.

Luke raised his hand to his head, where blood trickled from a wound on his forehead. And he wondered...

Had he been hit?

"Let's get in the house," she said. "Let me treat that wound." But she hesitated before reaching for the door handle.

They both knew they might have to run another gauntlet, like they had from the outbuilding to the SUV. Luke drew in a deep breath and opened his door. But as he stepped out on the driveway, he heard nothing but the faint whine of those sirens far in the distance.

Back at the Browns'...

The Browns were gone. And now Dirk's outbuilding was, too.

"It's clear," he told Willow as she came around the front of the truck. It was clear what he needed to do. He needed to get into Dirk's old truck and get as far away from his wife as he could get.

It was the only way to keep her safe.

* * *

"Where are you going?" Willow asked when Luke headed toward that battered truck instead of the house.

"I need to get out of here."

Away from her. She suspected that was really what he wanted to do. He seemed angry with her. And she wasn't exactly sure why. She wasn't the one who'd tried to strangle and shoot him. She was the one who'd tried to save him. She just wasn't certain how successful she'd been.

She shook her head. "No. You're coming into that house and letting me treat your wound," she insisted. That wasn't all she wanted to do; she wanted to call the police, or at least Braden. Surely, they could trust Braden Zimmer.

But Braden was probably at that fire along with the other Hotshots. Would they realize that she and Luke had been there when the fire started? At least one person had seen them.

Whoever had set the fire.

Whoever had fired those shots at them...

She shuddered in horror over how close they'd come to dying.

And Luke reached for her then, sliding his arm around her to guide her toward the house. "I'm sorry," he said. "You must be cold."

It was still early enough in the spring that the nights got below freezing. But Willow didn't feel the cold. She only felt the fear and the realization of how close a call they'd had. Luke's even closer than hers...

She needed to get him into the house. So she pulled out her key and slid it into the lock. And as she pushed open the door, Luke stepped in front of her, as if shielding her body with his.

He cursed, and she peered around him to see if any-one was inside, if anyone had disrupted the place. But when he flipped on the lights, it looked like it had when she'd left earlier that day.

"What's wrong?" she asked.

"I just realized that whoever copied my keys prob-ably still has them," he said. "The key that got them in-side here before, that got them my gun…"

She shuddered again as she remembered. "I found a window open that night you went in the ditch with the truck."

The truck that sat in the driveway outside. Who'd brought it here?

"You need to get out of here," he said. "Go stay at your dad's, or—"

"I'll change the locks," she assured him. "And when-ever I'm home, I use the slide bolt on the doors." They could only be opened from inside.

"But what if someone's already in here, waiting for you?" he asked.

She raised her weapon. "Then I'll make sure I check for them first." She did that now, quickly moving from room to room, but the house was empty except for their furniture and their memories.

She slid the gun into her purse and gathered up her first-aid kit from the bathroom. When she walked back into the living room, Luke was already heading toward the door. But he must have started a fire in the hearth first.

"Don't go!" she said.

"I can't stay. I'm only putting you in danger," he said. "And you already hate me."

She wished she did. But she didn't. She couldn't. Even

if she couldn't live with him again, she would always care about him. Too much...

That was the problem, really. If she didn't love him, she wouldn't worry about him so much that she risked her own health, her babies...

She pressed her free hand over her stomach, which moved beneath her palm. This baby hadn't slipped away. Not yet.

But it couldn't try to come too soon.

"Let me treat your wound," she said. "And then you can go."

Because he was right—that probably would be for the best.

He turned then and settled onto a chair. The wound was deep enough that it probably wouldn't stop bleeding without a couple of stitches.

"You need to go to the hospital," she insisted.

He shook his head. "I can't." And instead of touching his head, he touched his throat, which was swollen and scraped from that rope and probably his own fingers digging at it. "They'll think I tried to hang myself. They'll have me committed."

"Maybe I should," she murmured. "It would keep you safe."

"For seventy-two hours," he said. "But it would keep me away from you, so maybe you'd be safe then, too."

"I will be safe," she assured him.

He shook his head. "Not if you keep thinking you can figure out who's behind this," he warned her. "He'll come for you then. If he hasn't already."

She shivered at the prospect but was then compelled to point out something. "You don't know it's a man. It could be a woman."

He shrugged. "I hadn't thought about that, but..."

"But what?"

He shrugged again. "Whoever had that rope wrapped around my neck was strong—really strong."

"So was Louanne. So are Hank and Michaela." The two women wouldn't have made it onto the Hotshot team if they weren't as strong as they were, physically and mentally. Since he'd refused to go to the ER, Willow cleaned his wound, put a liquid bandage onto it and a butterfly patch over that.

Luke cursed, and for a second she'd thought she'd hurt him until he murmured, "It keeps coming back to that, to the team."

"And you want it to be anyone else."

"I want it to be nobody," he said. "I want this to be over."

"The only way for that to happen is to find out who's really behind it and stop them," she pointed out.

"*I* will find out," he said. "Not *you*. I don't want you involved in this anymore. You could have been killed tonight."

She didn't have a scratch on her, though. Because of him. He was the one who'd gotten hurt. Who kept getting hurt, and that hurt her.

"You're my husband." She clasped her stomach. "The father of this baby."

He focused on her belly then, and the look on his face, the longing…reached deep inside her. Clearly he'd wanted those babies as much as she had, and when she'd lost them, she'd refused to grieve with him. Instead she'd lashed out at him.

His broad shoulders slumped as if bearing a terrible burden, and he uttered a ragged sigh. "That's why I have to leave, Willow. You were right all those months ago. Being with me has already cost you more than you could stand losing. You can't lose this baby, too. And you can't lose your life. Not for me."

He jumped up from the chair then and headed toward the door.

Willow knew that she should let him go. That he was right. She could have died tonight, in that garage or during that mad dash to the vehicle. She could have been burned up or shot, and she would have lost the baby and any chance of ever being a mother again.

But she could have lost Luke, too.

Tears stung her eyes and trailed down her face as pain gripped her. It wasn't the baby. He or she moved restlessly in her stomach. This was her heart.

Staying would put her in danger, so Luke had to go. But he couldn't close his hand around the knob. He couldn't pull open that door and leave her. He knew that he should, that he had to…but then he turned back and saw her tears.

He quickly closed the distance between them.

Her nearness had his body tensing and aching with need. But he couldn't give in to his desire, for his overwhelming need for her. It would be selfish of him to stay, to put her in any more danger.

She closed her eyes, but tears slipped from beneath her closed lids and trailed down her cheeks. And his heart broke…

He had never been able to handle her tears. She was always so strong, so stoic—like her old man. She fought showing any emotion, so when she cried—which was rarely—she was really hurting.

And that made him hurt—so badly.

Helpless to fight his feelings anymore, he reached out and pulled her into his arms.

A shaky sigh slipped through her lips and she clutched at him. "I'm sorry," she murmured.

He wasn't sure what she was apologizing for—putting herself in danger, or for admitting all those months ago to how badly she resented him for her miscarriages.

They needed to talk. Really talk…

But that was so hard for her to do. And he wasn't going to push her when she was already upset. So he just held her, his arms and heart aching.

She, as always, quickly sniffled away her tears. Then she tensed in his arms, as if just realizing that he held her. But she didn't push him away—instead, she pulled him closer, melding her soft body against his hard one.

And he was so hard, overcome with desire for her.

He didn't want to fight with her and he didn't want to fight his feelings any longer. He let her pull him farther into the house—over to the stone fireplace, where flames burned low in the hearth.

She pulled him down onto the hardwood floor—onto the brightly patterned rug where they'd made love so many times. She pulled off his clothes, jerking his shirt over his head before unbuttoning and unzipping his jeans and pushing them down over his hips.

He groaned as she pressed kisses against his chest. Then she moved her lips higher, over the swollen and chafed skin on his throat. And he heard a catch in her breathing again.

She tensed, and he felt her fear. For him… "You could have died," she murmured.

"You could have, too," he reminded her, and now tears burned his eyes, at the thought of losing her. Of losing another child as well.

He couldn't put her in danger again, so he had to leave. But not yet…

Not when she'd pushed down his boxers and freed his erection. Her hands slid over it, then her lips. And he nearly came undone.

But he wanted her as ready as he was. So he pulled off her knit pants and the heavy sweater she wore. She was braless beneath it, her breasts so full and beautiful. He made love to them with his lips and his fingers.

She moaned and threw back her head. Then he skimmed his mouth up her throat, where her pulse pounded madly for him. And he kissed her deeply. And as he kissed her, he moved his hand lower—from her breast to her core. Pushing aside her panties, he found her ready for him—so ready.

She shifted against his hand and moaned in her throat…or maybe in his. He moved his fingers over her, stroking her, until her moan turned into a cry of pleasure.

Then he tugged off her panties before joining their bodies. He slid his erection inside her slowly. But she arched up, meeting his thrusts. And she moved her hands over him, stroking his skin as she kept kissing him so passionately.

The tension inside him wound tightly, but he denied himself his release until she came again. This time she screamed his name. At the sound of it on her lips, his control snapped. He thrust hard and deep, and an orgasm overtook him, making his body shudder with the sheer power of it. He yelled her name, even though his voice was still raspy from the swelling in his throat.

He wanted to say more. He wanted to declare his love and promise that if she gave their marriage another chance—if she gave him another chance—that he would do everything within his power to make her happy this time.

But he couldn't make good on that promise if he was dead. Until he found out whoever was after him, he had no business even being near her. It only put her—and their child—in danger.

"This was a mistake," he murmured as a feeling of panic overcame him.

Being with her...

He shouldn't have done that—shouldn't have put her in danger.

She didn't argue with him. She must have known that it was, too. That they're being together would never work. And just as he had the last time they'd made love, he realized how over they were. No matter what promises he made, he wouldn't be able to keep them. He had no control over what happened in life, over what other people did. But he could control his own actions and could make sure he didn't put her in danger anymore himself.

He jerked on his clothes with hands that shook slightly. He had to get away from her. From their baby...

From the home.

He didn't know who'd gotten the truck out of impound and dropped it off, but hopefully they'd left the keys in it. Without another word to Willow, he headed out the door and straight to the truck. Fortunately the ditch hadn't done much damage to the vehicle he and Dirk had worked so hard to restore. One light was out and the fender and bumper were a bit crumpled, but when he jumped inside and turned the key dangling from the ignition, it started right up.

But as soon as he turned out of the driveway onto the road, he felt something off. The steering was way too loose, the wheel swinging widely beneath his hands. He'd been in such a hurry to get away from Willow, so that he didn't put her in any more danger, that he'd pressed too hard on the accelerator.

A sharp curve loomed ahead, so he moved his foot to the brake pedal now. But like the steering wheel, it felt loose. The pedal pressed tightly against the floor and nothing happened. The truck didn't stop. He tried to jerk the wheel but it spun loosely beneath his hands.

He had no way of stopping or controlling the truck. No way of steering around the curve. And there was no ditch on the side of this curve—nothing to slow the truck as it headed straight toward a thick stand of trees.

He cursed with the impact, his body slamming into the steering wheel as the truck crashed into a thick tree trunk. And everything went black...

Chapter 18

Where the hell was Luke? Why hadn't he responded to the fire call at Dirk's? When Owen had reported to the firehouse to go out on the call, he hadn't seen Luke. And he hadn't shown up at Dirk's on his own, like a lot of the other team members had. Trent Miles had been late. And Trick, and even Hank.

It wouldn't have mattered how many firefighters had come. The garage was a total loss. What the hell had started it? And why? Had there been something here—something that would have led back to Louanne's real accomplice? Because Owen didn't believe anymore that it was Luke.

"So this was it…" Braden murmured.

"What?" Owen asked his boss.

"I had that feeling earlier…"

Owen smiled. His boss's sixth sense for knowing a fire was about to start was legendary. "Of course, you knew it was coming." But with all the gas cans and the tanks in the building to fuel the fire, it wouldn't have mattered how much advance notice they'd had. There would have been no stopping it. A firefighter would have known that…would have known that the heat of the fire would have destroyed any evidence.

"No, I thought it was about Luke," Braden admitted. "I thought something was going to happen to him."

Owen glanced around at the few other firefighters who remained at the scene, making sure nobody was close enough to overhear him before he asked, "You don't have Trick following him like you had him following me?"

Owen had once suspected that the man might have been the one behind Dirk's death, to make sure a spot opened up on his brother-in-law's team that he could fill. But now he knew that Braden had planned to bring him aboard all along to help investigate the little accidents that the team had been having even before Dirk's death.

Braden glanced around, too, before grimly shaking his head as he admitted, "Trick couldn't find him."

Owen cursed. "Want me to go out to Willow's and check to see if he's there?"

"Trick drove out there earlier, but nobody was home," Braden said. "She must be working."

Owen shook his head. "She wasn't at the hospital earlier. She's taking some time off." Because of the baby or because of Luke? "Mind if I take your truck and drive out there?" he asked his boss.

"I'd appreciate it," Braden said. So it was clear that even though there'd been a fire, that he still suspected his premonition had been about Luke.

Owen worried that he might be right. He rushed off

without another word, jumping in the truck to head out toward Luke and Willow's house. He didn't make it very far before he saw the red taillights of the truck that had gone off the road—not into a ditch, but into a thick stand of trees. There were no skid marks on the road— no indication at all that the driver had tried to stop.

He cursed as he steered his own truck onto the narrow shoulder of the road. After throwing it into Park, he scrambled out of the driver's side. His heart thudding heavily in his chest, he rushed over to the crash site. The front of the truck was smashed against a few wide tree trunks, the engine nearly pushed back into the cab—into Luke.

Was he crushed?

Was he conscious?

Owen peered through the smashed side window. Then he knocked out the shattered glass and reached inside. And as he reached, he prayed he found a pulse. He prayed that he wasn't too late.

A bright light bored into Luke's eye. Was this the way to the afterlife? With no brakes and no steering, it would have been a miracle that he survived this last crash. But he recognized the deep voice speaking to him.

"Good, you're regaining consciousness," Owen James murmured approvingly. "I would have figured this last concussion might have put you down for the final count."

Luke was still down, lying on his back, staring up at Owen. He turned his head slightly to the side and saw the truck crumpled up against the trees. How the hell had he gotten out of it?

Then he turned his head toward the other side and

saw the fire truck that Owen must have called out. Luke had used the Jaws of Life before, but he'd never had them used on his behalf—to extricate himself from anything. Two tall men crouched beside the truck as they shone flashlights underneath it.

Hopefully they would find evidence of what Luke suspected had happened. Someone must have cut the lines for the brakes and the steering. That was the only explanation for what had happened to the truck.

"N-not me," Luke stammered, his already swollen throat making his voice so raspy. "I—I didn't..."

"I know," Owen said, and he reached down and squeezed his shoulder. "But we've got to stop meeting like this."

Luke's head pounded with pain and with the sudden doubts bombarding him. He'd once thought that Owen could have been involved—that, thinking Luke was behind those attempts on his life and Courtney's, he was after revenge. "Why—why is it that we keep meeting like this?" he asked.

Owen was usually the first one on the scene.

Owen's lips curved into a slight grin. "I'm a paramedic, remember?"

"But you weren't on duty tonight."

Owen sighed. "No, but I responded to the fire call at Dirk's garage. You didn't, so Braden asked me to look for you."

"Look for me?" Luke repeated. "Why?"

Had Braden somehow figured out that he and Willow had been at Dirk's earlier? Was he being framed for that fire? Because Willow had been with him, she might be implicated as well. He'd been such a damn fool to let her go along, to have her help him investigate. But she'd seemed like the old Willow then, the determined one...

"I think you're in danger," Owen said. "But I think it's because whoever framed you is now trying to kill you."

To have one of the team support him—the team member who actually had the most reason to doubt him—humbled Luke.

"And now we need to get you to the hospital for X-rays," Owen said. "We need to find out if anything's broken besides your head."

"Nothing's broken," Luke said. Except for his heart—that had been broken when Willow had thrown him out all those months ago.

"You don't know that," Owen said.

"I feel the same as I did the last time that truck went off the road," Luke said. Like hell.

"Your body has taken a beating the past few days," Owen said. "You need to be checked out."

"I need to make sure Willow is okay," he said. "Somebody sabotaged that truck." And he had no idea where it had happened. At the house or before. It had made it to the house somehow, so probably not before. "They must have done it while it was parked in the driveway at her house. It might not have been the only thing that was sabotaged there. We need to go check on her."

"You'd be no help right now," Owen said. And he raised his arm and waved over Braden and Trick. "They can go check on Willow while we get you checked out at the hospital."

Before Luke could protest anymore, Owen was lifting the stretcher he was lying on and carrying him, along with the help of another paramedic, toward the ambulance.

* * *

Willow was so used to the sound of sirens that at first they hadn't awakened her. But as they continued wailing, she pried open her eyes. The fire had died in the hearth, and she felt chilled even though she'd pulled her clothes back on and dragged a blanket down onto the floor, where she was lying. She tilted her head and listened to the noise.

It was closer than the ones they'd heard earlier going to Dirk's house. The emergency vehicle had to be just down the road. But when she awakened fully and listened for it, the sound began to recede, as if the vehicle was heading away from her. And panic gripped her.

Where was it going? Hospital? Jail? Firehouse?

She didn't know where it was going, but she had a pretty damn good idea who was inside it.

Luke.

Had Trooper Gingrich arrested him for something? Or was Luke lying in the back of an ambulance again?

Her heart pounding furiously with fear, she jumped up from the floor, but as she did, a cramp struck her, making her double over with the pain as she gripped her belly.

"Oh, no!"

Not the baby. Not again. But after today, after nearly being killed, she shouldn't have been surprised that the stress would affect her and would affect the pregnancy.

She sucked in a deep breath, trying to calm herself. Trying to breathe through the panic.

And the fear…

Now she wasn't just afraid for Luke. She was afraid for their baby, too. She could not lose this one—not like she had the others.

"Please…" She prayed and prayed until the pain subsided. Then she started walking toward the door just as lights struck the front of the house. A vehicle had pulled into the driveway. It wasn't the emergency one; no lights flashed.

But she knew that whoever it was, he or she was coming to tell her about Luke. About what had happened to him this time.

Had he survived?

Tears stung her eyes just as another pain struck her. She dropped to her knees and clutched her stomach, as if she could somehow hold the baby inside her. She hadn't been able to do that the first time she'd miscarried.

And the last…

The baby had simply stopped breathing, stopped growing, and Willow hadn't even noticed. Until it was too late…

"Come on," she murmured in encouragement. "You're a fighter." This baby had already moved more than the other two ever had. "You can hang in there for me." More tears rushed to her eyes. "For your daddy…"

But had his or her daddy hung in there for them? Was he still alive?

"Luke…" she moaned.

A knock rattled the door. She knew it wasn't him. She knew that emergency vehicle had taken him away from her. From them…

She clasped her belly, which had gone taut with the cramp. Finally the pain subsided.

"Willow!" a deep voice called as the door rattled with another knock. "It's Braden Zimmer. Are you okay?"

She tried to stand, but her legs were shaking so badly she thought she might fall. She was so scared—scared for Luke, scared for their baby.

"Willow!" Braden called out again with alarm in his deep voice. "Are you alone? Are you hurt?"

She was hurting because another cramp gripped her belly, making it tighten so much that she cried out.

And the door, which Luke had locked behind himself when he left, burst open, the jamb splintering.

Braden rushed inside, another man right behind him. He dropped to his knees beside her. "Are you all right?"

She shook her head.

The other man, the Hotshot who'd taken Dirk's place on the team, stepped around them and moved around the house. "Is someone in here? Someone hurting you?"

She shook her head again. "I'm alone..." Now that Luke had left. And she wondered if she might be alone forever. If something had happened to Luke and something happened to their baby...

She gritted her teeth at the pain, but another cry slipped out.

"What is it?" Braden asked.

Her voice cracked as she replied, "The baby..."

Braden gasped. "Call 911," he told the other man.

But she grabbed his arm. "Just get me to the hospital." Using his arm, she tried to pull herself to her feet. The pain had subsided, so she was able to stand. But the fear was still there.

For all of them...

"Why are you here?" she asked. "What happened to Luke?"

Braden led her outside to where his truck was idling in the driveway. It was a crew cab, so he opened the rear door on the driver's side for her.

But before she climbed onto the running board and into the back seat, she studied his face in the light spilling out of the cab. "Braden, tell me..."

"He crashed—just down the road," he said.

"Is he…?" Her voice cracked with fear and emotion. She couldn't say it. Couldn't even let herself think it…

"He was swearing he was fine," Braden told her. "He was just worried about you."

A pang struck her heart. Even after all the times she'd hurt him, he still cared about her. He still thought first of her.

"Owen took him to the hospital," Braden said. "He's probably already there."

Another pang struck her, but this was in her abdomen as a cramp clutched at her. She cried out.

"Now let's get you there," Braden said as he lifted her onto the seat. He closed the door on her and called out to the man who was still inside the house.

That man shook his head. He was staying behind. Why?

She couldn't ask the question—not until the pain receded. And Braden was already halfway to the hospital before it eased.

She asked, "Why was Luke worried about me?" Had whoever set the fire and shot at them at Dirk's been the reason he'd crashed? Had Luke figured that person was coming after her next?

"He was worried that whoever sabotaged his truck might have done something here, to the house," he said.

Maybe that was why the other man had stayed, to check for that sabotage. He was the new Hotshot, the one nobody else seemed to trust. Was that with good reason?

"I didn't notice anything out of place," she said. This time. But then she'd been more focused on Luke and his injuries. Anybody could have been out there.

She shivered as she considered that the killer could

be *anyone*. And she'd left her bag, with her gun inside it, in the house.

She was unarmed. But surely she could trust Braden Zimmer. He was the Hotshot superintendent. But she couldn't say if he was truly Luke's friend. Luke probably wasn't able to tell friend from foe anymore, not after everything he'd been through.

He had to be okay. And their child had to be okay, too.

But she knew what that pain was. Contractions…

And even if she'd gotten pregnant earlier than she had originally thought, it was still too soon for her to go into labor. No matter how much a fighter the baby was, he or she might be far too premature to survive.

And if Willow lost another baby—or Luke—she wasn't sure that she would be able to survive again. While she'd always considered herself strong, it was too much.

Too much pain.

Too much loss.

Chapter 19

Luke's life was in danger. More so than ever before.

If something happened to Willow and the baby...

His life wouldn't be worth living anymore. No matter if he finally proved his innocence.

He'd been worried and asking Owen about her even before they'd brought him off to Radiology for X-rays. He'd been coming back to the ER just as a nurse and a resident had wheeled her in, bent over in the wheelchair clutching her stomach. He hadn't been there for her during the other miscarriages, but he had a feeling that must have been how she'd looked. So afraid and in so much pain...

Fear and pain washed over him as well, overwhelming him. She could not lose *this* baby. While he'd been hurt to lose a child, to lose that little piece of his heart the child had already claimed, it had devastated Willow. Each loss had taken away much more than the baby she'd carried—they seemed to have taken away a part of the essence of who she was, her very soul.

He scrambled off the edge of the stretcher and hurried to her side. "Are you okay?" he asked anxiously. "What's wrong?"

She jumped up from the chair and threw her arms around him. "You really are okay!"

"Yes," he assured her. "And according to the X-rays I'm fine." Except for another concussion and the fractured ribs that he'd already had from the first crash.

"When I heard the sirens, I knew it was you," she said, her voice cracking.

"Is that why you're here?" he asked. And his palms slid from her waist over her belly, which was taut as if she was cramping. "Did I cause this?" Or had it been all the stress from earlier, from someone shooting at them? He shouldn't have left her; he should have made certain that she and their baby were in no danger. But he'd thought leaving them alone would keep them safer.

"Let's find out what *this* is," Cheryl said as she just about tugged Willow free of his arms. Willow's supervising nurse had obviously heard and believed the rumors about him. When he started to follow, she held up a hand to hold him back. "She didn't invite you to join her."

He nearly shivered at the coldness on her face and in her voice. Cheryl had once been his friend, too, but clearly her loyalty was with Willow. But he willingly stepped aside and let her lead Willow away from him. He didn't want to argue and delay treatment she might desperately need.

But he also wanted to make sure she and the baby were okay. Had she gone into early labor like she had with their first baby, when her pregnancy wasn't far enough along for the baby to survive. Would Willow survive if she lost this one, too?

He wasn't sure that he would.

The curtain that Cheryl had pulled around the ER bay where she'd led Willow opened again. And Willow held out her hand to him, almost imploringly. "Come here. They're going to do an ultrasound to find out what's going on."

His heart swelled with hope that she was reaching out for him instead of pushing him away. But maybe for her own safety she should have pushed him away.

But he couldn't stay away, not when there was a chance to see the baby inside her, to see how the baby was doing.

He wouldn't let her go through that alone again like she had before. Maybe that was why she'd grown to resent him so much, because he'd never been there for her when she'd needed him.

Cheryl helped her onto the gurney and pulled an ultrasound machine closer to the bed. "I don't know why we haven't done this sooner," she said with a quizzical glance at Willow.

But maybe Willow hadn't wanted to see the baby and get attached only to lose it, too.

"I had one scheduled with my OB for next week," Willow said.

Would she have invited him to that one? She'd never mentioned it. But then they hadn't done a whole lot of talking about the future any time they'd been together the past few days.

"I called your OB to come here," Cheryl said.

"It's so late," Willow protested.

Luke hoped it wasn't too late—for the baby, for them. They'd nearly been killed earlier tonight at Dirk's, and then he'd hopped in that truck without realizing it had been sabotaged. What if Willow's SUV had been as well?

"You know that obstetricians are always on call," Cheryl said. "Babies don't keep bankers' hours." She was so gentle as she lifted Willow's sweater and squirted the lotion on her skin. Then she moved the wand from the ultrasound softly across her belly.

A ragged sigh escaped Willow's lips. "The baby's heart is beating…"

It echoed loudly in the curtained area and it moved on the screen. The baby moved, too, kicking and punching as he or she somersaulted around her womb.

"Your baby is active," Cheryl said with a little chuckle.

"And the cramps?" Willow asked.

"Braxton-Hicks," a female voice said as Willow's obstetrician stepped inside the curtain. "I don't think you're in early labor."

"How early would it be?" Willow asked. "How far along am I?"

The doctor stepped closer to the ultrasound and appeared to be making measurements. "I would say twenty-four weeks."

Luke gasped. So they had made the baby before that final night, long before she'd thrown him out. Even though they hadn't been talking to each other much during that time, they'd still connected physically.

"This baby is already farther along than the others," Willow murmured. "But still too early to come. Are you sure these are just Braxton-Hicks contractions?"

"We'll monitor you for a while yet, but it doesn't look like the baby's in any distress. Now you…" The doctor looked at her flushed face. "Are you all right?"

She wasn't. And that was his fault, just like her losing those other babies had been his fault, too.

"Her blood pressure is high," Cheryl answered for her and reported the reading she'd taken.

The doctor nodded. "Yes, that is high. We definitely need to monitor you."

Luke cleared his throat and spoke the question that had been haunting him. "Could stress have caused her prior miscarriages?"

The doctor glanced at him. "Studies have shown that stress can cause complications."

He knew how much he had already complicated her life, so that pressure was back on his chest, weighing heavily on his heart. He'd been right earlier when he'd left her—that just his presence put her in danger.

He didn't want to risk the baby's life or hers. He knew he needed to turn around—to leave her and not come back until he had stopped the person who was trying to kill him. But even then he wasn't sure that she would be willing to take a chance on him again, not when he had already cost her too much. She would probably never forgive him for those other losses, just as he would never forgive himself.

He forced himself to turn and reach for the curtain.

But the doctor asked, "Do you want to know the baby's sex?"

Luke froze. He'd only wanted to make sure that the baby was okay. Finding out its sex made it too real and too hard if the baby didn't survive. That was probably why Willow hadn't had an ultrasound before tonight. She'd been worried about getting too attached again. But they hadn't known that the first one was a girl until she was gone and the second one a boy...

He'd already lost one son and one daughter. He couldn't lose another child. This baby had to survive, and one way he could make sure that was possible was to make sure Willow was no longer in danger.

So he had to walk away like he had before. He had to leave her, for her sake and their baby's, even though it would probably kill him.

A hush came over the crowd at the Filling Station and everybody turned toward the door that must have just opened. It was late, but on a Friday night, the place stayed busy until closing time. Owen James swiveled on his bar stool to see who had drawn such attention. A quiet curse slipped through his lips.

Of course, Luke hadn't stayed in the hospital earlier. Once he'd learned Willow was okay, he'd wanted to leave immediately. So Owen had brought him back to the firehouse less than an hour ago with orders that the guy get some rest. And he'd left Stanley and Annie guarding him.

So much for them...

Luke's presence here might put him in danger. Everybody continued staring at him as he walked slowly through the crowded bar and headed toward Owen.

"What do you want?" Owen asked as Luke slid onto the stool next to his. "A beer?"

Luke snorted derisively. "I'm not here for a beer and you know it."

Owen had hoped his friend had quit drinking, but he had a feeling that wasn't what Luke was talking about right now.

"I'm here to find out who the hell's been trying to frame me and now has been trying to kill me," Luke said, loud enough that if that person was in the suddenly quiet bar, he or she had probably overheard him.

"And you think that person is here?" Owen asked.

Luke swiveled his stool around to stare back at the patrons staring at him. "He or she almost has to be one of us…" But then he glanced behind the bar, at Charlie, for some reason.

Owen had wondered if it was a fellow firefighter, because who else could have walked right into the firehouse without anybody noticing. Who else would have even known about Luke's prescription?

Owen glanced around the bar again.

Because the team was on standby for a wildfire that had started in New Mexico, all of the Hotshots had remained in Northern Lakes after the meeting Braden had called. And most of them were here in the bar tonight except for Braden and his brother-in-law.

And Dirk…

A pang of loss struck Owen. He would miss his friend forever. Just like so many other friends he'd lost during his deployments. He didn't want to lose Luke, too.

The man already looked like hell with dark circles rimming his eyes. His hair was mussed, and his face bore a grimace—probably from the pain of his fractured ribs and his concussions.

"So why are you here?" Owen asked. "Are you daring that person to make another attempt to take you out?"

Luke uttered a ragged sigh and gruffly admitted, "I'm not sure I could survive another one."

"Neither am I," Owen said.

"But I have to figure out who it is," Luke persisted. And once again he stared back at all those people staring at him. "It could be anyone," he said. "They wouldn't even have to be stationed here in Northern Lakes..." His gaze seemed to home in on Trent Miles then.

But he wasn't the only one stationed elsewhere. He focused on the Hotshot with the bushy hair and beard. "How well does anyone really know Ethan Sommerly?"

Ethan was an enigma who preferred living alone in the woods of the Upper Peninsula as a forest ranger.

"Or Trent Miles?" Luke asked. "I've heard rumors that he used to be in a gang in Detroit."

"And you know how accurate rumors are," Owen reminded him.

He grimaced again, but then he added something Owen hadn't known. "He tried to date Willow before I did."

"What?"

"Before she moved here," Luke explained. "When they both worked in Detroit."

He was relying on rumors again, but Owen repeated, "I heard he's dated a lot of women. So I don't think he would have been too upset that she'd turned him down. And if he was, why would he have waited three years to go after you?"

Luke nodded. "True. He would have gone after me right away if he was jealous."

And Owen's impression of Trent was that he was too self-assured and confident to be jealous of anyone.

"What about Rory?" Luke asked. "He lives closer to Northern Lakes than Ethan or Trent."

And Rory VanDam lived even more like a hermit than Ethan, in a lighthouse on a remote island. Maybe that little contact with other humans would have made him an easy target for Louanne. But Owen doubted it. He doubted that any one of their team could have killed Dirk.

Even Luke. Especially Luke. He and Dirk really had been the closest of friends, the closest of the team. That was why it was even more cruel that someone was trying to frame him for the man's death.

"And let's not rule out the female team members," Luke said. "They're both damn strong."

Hank was nearly as tall as the guys and leanly muscled, while Michaela was more petite but freakishly strong for her deceptively delicate-looking frame.

"If you're looking specifically for whoever had the affair with Louanne, Hank and Michaela have only ever dated men," Owen said. "Not married women."

Luke sighed. "Yeah, the only person I know who's actually dated married women is Braden's good buddy, Trooper Gingrich." As soon as the words slipped out of his mouth, Luke tensed, and his blue eyes widened with shock. "You don't think…"

Owen snorted just like ol' Marty always did. "I don't think he's smart enough to pull off what's being done to you. And if he was, Braden would be his target. Not you…"

Luke's shoulders slumped. "True. Braden is the one he hates." And whose wife—first wife—Marty had slept with. So he had no reason to go after Dirk's wife or after Luke. "Except I was the one who made myself an easy target for a few months there."

Owen reached out and squeezed his shoulder. "You were going through a lot. I can't imagine losing Courtney, and we've not been together as long as you and Willow have been."

Owen could not imagine the pain Luke was going through right now. He and his team weren't the only ones who knew about it, though. Thanks to the small-town gossip mill, everyone in Northern Lakes knew Luke's business.

Or thought they did…

So hopefully the person taking advantage of his current vulnerable state of pain and distraction was not a member of their team. But who else could it be?

Who could possibly want to destroy Luke so badly that they would first try to frame him for murder and then try to murder him?

But if someone really wanted to destroy Luke, that person would go after Willow. Because from seeing how worried he had been about her and the baby, Luke obviously cared more about Willow and their unborn baby than he cared about himself.

Willow touched her face, but it was chilled now, like the rest of her body. Yesterday, at the hospital, she had been flushed with embarrassment over her overreaction.

Braxton-Hicks…

She should have known that was all the cramps had been. But after what had happened before, she'd been scared—so scared that she might lose this baby, too.

She'd thought a baby was all she needed to make her happy. But when Luke had walked away…

Her heart had ached for the loss. He hadn't been interested enough in their baby to stay and find out that he was having a son.

Another son…

The doctor had assured her that his heartbeat was strong—that he looked strong and healthy. She had also added that Luke didn't need to be too concerned about stress affecting this pregnancy since Willow was already so far along.

Further along than she'd realized. But then after that last miscarriage, her cycles had been so sporadic that she'd had no way of keeping track of them.

But Luke had left before the doctor had been able to offer him any assurances. Because he was worried that he was stressing her out?

Or putting her in danger?

She shivered and glanced over to the hearth where only dust stirred from the old ashes inside it. She hadn't had the energy to make a fire when Cheryl had driven her home. She'd laid down on the couch and fallen asleep for hours. Nearly for a day because when she'd awakened a while ago, it had been almost night again. Yet she was still so tired, her eyes barely able to focus, that she wasn't certain what had awakened her.

A noise?

Or the cold?

A blast of it struck her now, blowing through the curtains at the window near the fireplace. She gasped with shock. She hadn't opened that window.

Had Braden or the Hotshot who'd been here with him opened it? He'd stayed behind, apparently to fix the doorjamb, because it was repaired so that her door locked again. Would he have opened a window while he was working?

With as chilly as it had been outside, Willow doubted it. But why was it open? Had someone broken into the house while she was gone? Or while she'd been asleep?

Shaking and disoriented, she looked for her purse with her gun. She hadn't brought it to the hospital with her. She'd left it here.

She hurried over to the table near the front door. Her purse was there, but when she grabbed it up, she felt the unfamiliar lightness of it. Usually it was heavier than this, heavier because of the gun.

She dumped out the contents on the table and confirmed her fears. The gun was gone.

Someone had taken her weapon away. Was that someone still inside the house? About to use that weapon on her and her baby?

Chapter 20

She had been so afraid that he wouldn't come. Almost as afraid as she'd been that he would, and that she was putting him in danger. So when the door rattled with a knock, she wasn't certain if she should open it or not.

"Willow!" he called out, his voice gruff with fear and urgency.

She ran to the door, unlocked and pulled it open. Then she flung her arms around him and clung to him.

And he gasped.

Remembering he had fractured ribs, she jerked away from him. "I'm sorry!"

Luke turned away from her. But only to close and lock the door. "Are you okay?" he asked. "Did you check the house?"

She shook her head. She had been too afraid to move away from the door. Without her gun, she wouldn't have been able to protect herself from an intruder.

Luke had no gun either, but that didn't stop him from searching the house.

"Luke," she murmured, fear for his safety overwhelming her. "Don't…" She started after him, but he was already back before her shaky legs could follow him.

"I didn't find anyone inside," he said.

She pointed toward the window just as the wind ruffled the curtains.

Luke stalked over to it, pulled down the pane and twisted the lock. "It doesn't look like anyone's tampered with it."

"I didn't open it," she insisted.

Before he stepped away from the window, his gaze fell on the pewter frame of their wedding portrait. The cracks of the broken glass zigzagged through their smiling faces. "Did you…?" His voice trailed off with a rasp.

She shook her head. "No, I found it like that a few days ago…"

"So somebody keeps letting themselves in and out of the house?" he asked.

She nodded. "I wasn't sure…until tonight."

Luke tensed. "Did you see someone inside?" he asked.

She drew in a shaky breath before replying. "No. But somebody took my gun."

He cursed.

"Just the same way Louanne must have taken yours…" Then she'd tried to kill Owen with it but had wound up dead instead. Willow shivered. Even though he'd closed the window, she was still cold. And guilt hung heavy on her shoulders. Because she'd thrown him out, he'd had no place to go but the couches of his friends and the bunkroom at the firehouse.

Would any of this have happened if they hadn't been separated?

"I'm sorry," he said. "I'm sorry that I've put you in danger." He glanced down at her belly then. "That I put you both in danger."

She shook her head. "*You* didn't. Whoever framed you, whoever tried to kill you—"

"Kill us," he corrected her. "Those shots weren't fired just at me last night. And that fire…" He shuddered now. "You could have died, too, just because you were with me. That's why I should leave." But he didn't move toward the door. He stayed standing near the fireplace, staring at her. "Just by being here, I'm putting you and the baby in danger," he said.

"But when we were together, even in danger, we kept each other safe," she pointed out. Well, not exactly safe, since he'd nearly been strangled and shot. "Alive, anyway," she added in a murmur.

And a slight smile tugged up his lips.

"Stay," she implored him. And she held out her hand toward him.

He stared at it for a long moment before finally reaching for it. She entwined their fingers and tugged him toward the bedroom. But he planted his feet, resisting her efforts to lead him to bed. And he pulled his hand free of her grasp.

"This isn't a good idea," he said.

She expelled a shaky breath. "Probably not," she agreed. But she didn't care.

"I don't want to hurt you or the baby."

"You won't," she assured him. "You know, from the previous pregnancies, that having sex doesn't harm the baby."

"That's not the only way I can hurt you," he said.

"I told you that we're safer together," she said.

"Is that why you called me instead of the police?" he asked.

"If I had called the police, Trooper Gingrich would have accused you of breaking in and stealing the gun," she said. "And I know you didn't."

He set the picture back on the mantel, where it had always been. Then he stepped closer to her and touched her face. He skimmed his fingertips along her jaw and tipped up her chin. His mouth brushed across hers so gently that her breath caught. She parted her lips and he deepened the kiss. And as always, passion ignited.

She didn't have to pull him to bed now. He lifted and carried her. She tensed and tugged her mouth from his. "You're hurt."

"I'm hurting," he agreed. "But not because of my ribs or my head."

When he laid her on the bed, she saw that his erection was straining against the fly of his worn jeans. He wanted her as badly as she wanted him.

Needed…

She needed him. Maybe that was why she kept pushing him away. Raised to be independent, she hated that she needed someone as much as she needed him. But at the moment, she didn't care about being vulnerable or proud. She cared only about him.

She reached up to pull him down onto the bed with her. He resisted, and panic flashed through her that maybe he didn't need her as badly.

But he only hesitated for a moment before he dragged his shirt over his head. Then he unbuttoned and unzipped his jeans and pushed them off, along with his boxers. When he was fabulously naked but for the bandages wrapped around his ribs, he joined her on the bed.

She stared at the bandages. He was lucky he hadn't been hurt worse or killed. She was lucky that she hadn't lost him forever. "Luke..."

He cut off her words with a kiss. His lips moved softly but passionately over hers before his tongue slipped inside her mouth and stroked hers.

She gasped as desire overwhelmed her. She wanted him so badly. How had she gone months without him—without his touch, without his kiss?

Tears stung her eyes, but she squeezed them shut, refusing to cry. And it wasn't just because of her pride. She didn't want to distract him, didn't want to worry him...

She only wanted to love him. So she gently pushed him onto his back. And she moved her mouth from his, down his swollen neck to his shoulders. She kissed every inch of his injured body, wishing her touch could heal him.

He'd been through so much. But instead of soothing him, her caresses had his body tense and hard. When she tried to use her mouth to release that tension for him, he gently pulled her away.

"No..." he murmured in a raspy whisper.

And as always, he made love to her first. He pulled off her clothes and lavished his attention on her sensitive breasts. He kissed and caressed and stroked the nipples with his thumbs and then his tongue.

She shuddered as she came. Then his fingers pushed aside her panties and stroked her until she came again.

"Luke..." She felt like sobbing with the pleasure he'd given her. But she wanted to focus on him, on his release. She pushed him back onto the bed, then she straddled him. Careful of his ribs, she moved her hands to his arms, sliding them down his bulging biceps, over his hard forearms to his hands. They entwined their fingers, and she used them to brace herself as she moved her hips, rocking back and forth against him.

He let her set the rhythm. But sweat beaded on his brow and upper lip as he obviously struggled to hang on to his control.

So she moved faster, harder, and as she did, the tension wound inside her—the same tension that had his muscular body so taut beneath hers, as if he might break at any moment.

And she was worried that he would. That he'd been so wounded that he might break. But he pulled his hands from hers to stroke them over her body, down from her breasts to the most sensitive part of her.

And she came again.

He tensed and clutched her hips in his big hands as he finally gave in to his need for release. He shouted her name. But then he tensed again, as if cutting off something else he'd wanted to say.

He used to tell her that he loved her when they made love. Did he still? Or had she pushed him away too many times for him to trust her with his heart again?

She moved off him, but not away from him. Instead she clutched him close, her arms around his lean waist. She didn't want him to slip away from her again…as he had the last time they'd made love.

She didn't want him to leave.

Ever.

Luke needed to leave. His presence was only putting Willow in more danger—no matter what she said. Somebody had taken her gun for a reason, and he hated to think what that reason might be.

To kill him?

Or to kill her?

She should have called 911 instead of him. But he was glad that she'd called, glad that she trusted him again even though she shouldn't. He wasn't protecting her. He wasn't keeping her safe. Instead he'd lost control again and made love with her.

He wanted her so badly, even now, after that powerful orgasm. His body was tense, lying next to hers. She'd fallen asleep. But Luke could not. He had to be alert to any sign of danger.

The person who'd taken her gun might return…to take her life. So he couldn't leave—not unless he found someone to take his place protecting her.

Owen?

He felt like he could trust Owen. But Owen wasn't a bodyguard. He was just a firefighter, like Luke.

She should have called the police. There were other troopers aside from Gingrich. They needed to speak to someone else, to someone who would have an open mind—who hadn't prejudged him based on all those damn rumors.

But there were more than rumors. The car, the gun…

And now Willow's gun was missing.

He hadn't been thrilled she carried one, but now that she didn't have it, he was worried. At least she'd had that for protection when he'd been gone. Now she had nothing…if he left.

He was probably just looking for an excuse to stay here—in their home, in their bed—with her. The smart thing would have been taking her away from here, to someplace safe in town. Cheryl would let her stay with her.

They could trust her. Couldn't they?

Hell, could they trust anyone? Even each other?

She'd called him, so maybe she was over her doubts. But she hadn't asked him back home to stay. She'd only called because she'd been scared.

He was scared, too. Not just that she was in danger, but he was worried that they might never get back to where they'd once been, so happy, so in love...

He held in a wistful sigh, not wanting to risk waking her. She needed her rest.

But Luke wouldn't be able to rest until he figured out who the hell was trying to frame him. He or she must have taken Willow's gun to carry out the next step in his or her sadistic plan to destroy him. He couldn't let Willow get hurt in the crossfire.

He needed to get her to leave—not just their house, but maybe the town as well. She had friends in Detroit. Maybe she would be safer there, with them. She would be safer anywhere he wasn't.

When she woke up, he was the one who would tell her to get out. She might not agree to do it for herself, but she would for the baby. She had to.

Luke was so tense that he nearly jerked when he heard the noise. It wasn't very loud, was as if someone was moving stealthily around outside. But he heard the crunch of gravel under heavy footsteps. Someone was coming toward the front door.

He slid out of bed and pulled on his jeans. He had no weapon—nothing to protect himself from an armed intruder. But he didn't care. He would readily give up his life for Willow's.

Before he hurried into the hall, he pulled the bedroom door closed. He didn't want to wake up Willow. Didn't want to frighten her if what he'd heard was just the movement of a four-legged trespasser.

Hopefully it was a real animal moving around in the

night, not a human one. But now there was a noise at the door, as if a key was being turned in the lock.

His key, or at least a copy of it.

Damn it...

Wanting to surprise whoever was at the door before they got inside the house, Luke moved to the window that had been opened earlier and opened it again. Then he slipped out onto the porch near the front door.

Not even a sliver of moonlight shone in the night sky, so it was dark—so dark that all Luke could see was a shadow. A tall, broad-shouldered, two-legged shadow.

It had moved away from the door, as if the person was walking away from the house. Maybe he'd heard Luke moving around, had heard the window open.

Barefoot, Luke could move silently, so he followed the shadow as he moved away from the house. He wanted to see who it was—who'd tried to break into his home.

But when his bare foot hit the gravel drive, he sent a stone skittering forward. And the person began to turn around. Luke had to act before the person could aim the stolen gun at him, before he could fire. So he launched himself at the shadow, knocking the person to the ground.

They rolled around in the dark, grappling for the upper hand. When Luke had a chance, he swung. But his weren't the only fists flying.

Despite the power of the punch to his jaw, Luke held on to consciousness. He wasn't fighting just for his life. He was also fighting for the lives of Willow and their baby.

Trick's phone went straight to voice mail, unsettling Braden. He cursed with frustration. His brother-in-law was supposed to be guarding Luke. Why wasn't he picking up?

He should have just been sitting in his truck, parked on the road near Luke's house. Owen had called, had given Braden a heads-up that Luke had left the Filling Station—not to return to the firehouse, but to go out to his house. And that he'd left in a hurry.

Owen had been worried about him, but Braden had assured the paramedic that he had it all under control, that he had someone protecting Luke. But maybe he should have let Owen go as backup…for Trick.

Maybe Braden had needed someone protecting his brother-in-law, too. The last time Trick had acted as a bodyguard, someone—probably Louanne—had drugged him. The only thing that had gotten hurt was his pride over that incident and he'd vowed to be more alert from now on.

But that didn't mean that he couldn't have been hurt again. And this time more seriously than just some wounded pride.

Chapter 21

Willow awoke again—cold and alone and scared. This time she knew what had awakened her—the sound of grunts and cursing from outside the house. She pulled on her robe and rushed out of the bedroom.

But the only weapon she'd had was gone.

And so was Luke.

He had to be outside, tussling with whoever had trespassed on their property. But he was armed with only his fists. And because of his concussion and damaged ribs, he was especially vulnerable.

She needed to do something. Needed to help him…

But if she ran outside, she could risk distracting Luke—risk his getting hurt more. So instead of reaching for the door, she reached for her cell. And this time, she punched in 911. If Trooper Gingrich responded to the call, he would know that he'd been wrong about Luke.

That there really was someone out there trying to

hurt him. She only hoped Luke wasn't hurt too badly before help arrived. She prayed that it wouldn't be too late to save him.

Tears of fear and frustration streamed down her face.

If Luke was killed because of her...

She would never forgive herself.

Blood oozed from Luke's swollen knuckles. He'd fought hard—for himself and for his family. But his knuckles weren't the only thing that was bruised. His eye throbbed, the vision in it blurred. He could barely see the person sitting across from him, on the other bunk in the jail cell.

"Why the hell were you sneaking around my house?" Luke asked Trick McRooney.

Trick hadn't been in town long, so Luke hadn't considered him a truly viable suspect in framing him. But maybe he'd been around and Luke hadn't noticed.

Trick stared back at him through two swollen eyes. "I wasn't the one sneaking around."

"I heard someone walking around outside and when I got up, that person was trying to open the door," Luke said.

"I wasn't near the door," Trick said through gritted teeth. He had a swollen lip, too.

"What the hell were you doing at my house?" Luke demanded.

"My job."

"There was no damn fire at my house," Luke said. But there could have been, just like there'd been at Dirk's garage, and weeks ago at Courtney Beaumont's store. The killer could have set a fire at Luke's house, too, and he'd been so preoccupied with Willow that he wouldn't have even noticed. He narrowed his eyes and studied his cellmate. How much did anyone really know about Trick McRooney?

Trick had been around the night of the fire at the store, too. Had he been in Northern Lakes before Dirk had died? Could he have had anything to do with Louanne?

"I was doing my other damn job," Trick muttered.

"What other job?"

"For Braden," he said. "When you work for your brother-in-law, it's hard to refuse to do anything for him."

"What exactly did he have you doing?" Luke asked, but he suspected he already knew.

Trick confirmed those suspicions. "Babysitting you…"

Luke cursed.

"You can't deny that you need a keeper right now," Trick argued. "Somebody to keep you alive…"

Luke touched his swollen eye and flinched. "He should have asked someone else." And then it occurred to him why Braden hadn't; he didn't trust anyone else on the team besides his brother-in-law.

What the hell was going on within the ranks of the Huron Hotshots? Luke dropped back onto the bunk and grunted as pain shot through his ribs. "Braden needs to fire you," he murmured. "You're not very damn good at the job he gave you."

"Somebody was messing around at your front door," Trick said. "But it wasn't me. I moved closer to the house to investigate when you jumped me."

Luke tensed and sat back up. So there had been somebody trying to get inside. "Who was it? Did you see them?"

Trick shook his head. "It was too damn dark to see

even my own damn hand in front of my face," he said. "That's why you got the jump on me."

Luke snorted. "Yeah, you keep telling yourself that, but people are as likely to believe you as they are me when I tell them that I'm innocent."

"I believe you're innocent," Trick said. "And so does Braden and even Owen believes you now."

Luke released a breath he hadn't realized he'd been holding, and the pressure on his chest eased slightly. But only slightly…

"Now if only I could get Gingrich to believe me," he said.

"Hey, he didn't believe me either," Trick pointed out.

Willow must have called the police because Gingrich had shown up even before he and Trick had identified each other. He'd pulled them apart only to toss them back together in the back seat of his car, then arrested them.

"Don't take it personally," Luke told him. "Ol' Marty hates every Hotshot because he hates your brother-in-law so much."

"He has been going after you extra hard," Trick remarked.

Luke shrugged and grunted as a pang shot through his ribs. "I haven't taken it personally…"

Gingrich always looked to the Hotshots for suspects to whatever crime occurred in Northern Lakes. He'd actually thought one of them might have been the arsonist terrorizing the town all those months ago.

And he'd seemed disappointed when he'd been proven wrong. Luke needed to prove him wrong this time, too.

He focused—with his one good eye—on Trick again. "So you've been following me?" he asked.

The auburn-haired Hotshot nodded. "Yeah, but it's not been easy to keep track of you. I lost you most of yesterday and didn't know where you were until Owen found you in the ditch again."

But then he must have followed him from the hospital to the Filling Station and then home again without Luke noticing. Trick was better at his job than he was giving himself credit for being. "Did you see anyone else following me?" he asked.

Trick shook his head now. "No, but Braden hadn't wanted me to get too close. He didn't want you to see me."

So maybe Braden wasn't entirely convinced of his innocence. Had he had Trick following Luke for his protection, or to catch him in a crime?

But the only role Luke had played in the crimes recently happening in Northern Lakes was victim. He hadn't been the only one. Dirk had died. Owen nearly had. And Willow...

What would happen to Willow now that Luke wasn't there to protect her and she didn't have her gun?

If only her father was in town.

He jumped up from the bunk and clutched at the bars of the cell door. "I need to get the hell out of here."

"I'm sure Braden's working on getting us out," Trick said. Fortunately the superintendent had arrived just as Gingrich had been driving away with them in the back seat.

But Luke wished he'd stayed with Willow instead of coming to post their bail. "What about our phone calls?" Luke asked.

Neither of them had been offered one.

"I'm sure Braden's working on bail," Trick said again. "You don't need to call a lawyer."

"I wasn't going to call a lawyer." He needed to call Willow and tell her to get the hell out of their house, the hell out of town.

Or Owen…

He could call Owen to protect her. He trusted Owen a hell of a lot more than he did the police trooper. His last conversation, at the Filling Station, replayed in Luke's mind. He and Owen had considered Gingrich a possible suspect in his framing. Maybe they shouldn't have discounted him as quickly as they had.

"How was he so close…?" Luke murmured to himself.

"What?" Trick asked. "I told you I was following you."

"Gingrich," Luke said. "Even if Willow woke up and called 911 the minute I left the bed…"

Trick sat up, too. "He could have been following you, too," he said. "You are his number-one suspect."

"But you didn't see anyone else following me," Luke reminded him.

And Trick shivered slightly. "It doesn't make sense."

No. It didn't.

"He got there too fast." So he must have been close. But how close?

And where the hell was the trooper right now?

Had he gone back to the house, to Willow?

Fear rushed over Luke, fear for his wife. And he began to pound on the bars. "Hey! Let me out! Let me out!"

Trick joined him at the bars. "Man, what the hell's the matter with you? You can't seriously think that a police officer has been framing you."

"I don't know what to think," Luke admitted. "I just want to make sure my wife is safe." But he had a horrible feeling that even if he was let out now, he would be too late to save her. She was in danger.

Grave danger.

Ever since Luke had rushed out of the Filling Station, Owen had been uneasy. When he'd called Braden to express his concern, the Hotshot superintendent had assured him he had it covered. Someone was watching Luke.

Protecting him…

So Owen had left the Filling Station to join Courtney at her store, and they were now upstairs, in their bed. But his mind kept returning to Luke.

Owen guessed his protector was Trick, just as Braden had had Trick McRooney following him when he'd been in danger. But there had been someone else following Owen then. Louanne Brown and maybe her accomplice.

And just like he had, Luke obviously had someone else following him, too. Someone who knew when he'd be alone and vulnerable to an attempt on his life.

Louanne was gone now. So it had to be her accomplice. But that wasn't the only person who always seemed to be around Luke.

Trooper Gingrich seemed to have switched the target of his animosity from Braden to Luke. He was going after Garrison even harder than he ever had his old high-school nemesis.

But then, Braden had always been too strong for Gingrich to take down. Now, Luke…

He was a tough guy. But he had one weakness. His wife.

Since their separation, he had been distracted and vulnerable. But he hadn't been so distracted that he hadn't realized that Gingrich had it in for him.

He'd also remarked that the only person he'd known who'd gone after another man's wife was Marty Gingrich. Could he have been the one having the affair with Louanne?

Could he have been her accomplice?

They'd dismissed Luke's suspicion earlier. But it kept coming back to Owen now.

"What is it?" a female voice murmured as Courtney lifted her head from his shoulder and stared up at him. "You're not sleeping."

He couldn't. Not with his friend in danger.

And not when he might know from whom that danger was coming...

He had his arm around Courtney, but he slid it from beneath her now. "I need to go."

"Go where?" she asked. "What's going on?"

"I don't know," he said. But he had a bad feeling— had had one since that conversation with Luke at the bar. "I don't have any proof, but..."

She tensed. "You figured out who Louanne's real accomplice is."

"Luke figured it out," Owen said. And he never should have dismissed his suspicions.

"Who?" Courtney asked.

"Trooper Gingrich."

Courtney didn't doubt it. But she hadn't when he'd told her that he didn't think Luke had anything to do with the attempts on his life and hers. She'd trusted him.

And he wished he'd trusted Luke's instincts. He hoped it wasn't too late to help him. He hoped that Trooper Gingrich hadn't already gotten to Luke or, worse yet, Willow.

Chapter 22

Willow had wanted to go with Braden to bail out Luke. But the Hotshot superintendent had assured her that he would get Luke and his brother-in-law released. She hadn't pressed charges. She wasn't sure why Trooper Gingrich had insisted on arresting them for disturbing the peace.

The only peace they'd disturbed had been their own. And hers.

She'd been so frightened that the person after Luke had been trying to take his life again. Now she realized Luke had been right when he'd refused to call the cops after what had happened at Dirk's house. And she wished she'd never called them either. How had the trooper arrived so quickly? Had he been watching their house?

Watching Luke?

Or her?

She shivered with a sudden chill. She'd closed the window Luke must have gone out since the slide lock had still been extended across the doorjamb. She'd even dressed in jeans and a heavy sweater, but she was still so cold. So scared...

For Luke.

For their baby...

Someone had taken her gun. She hadn't told Gingrich that, figuring he would just blame Luke if she had. And then her husband might never get released from jail.

But a knock at the door had hope lightening the weight on her shoulders. He was here. He was back. She rushed to the door and pulled it open, then stopped short in the doorway, staring into Trooper Gingrich's intense face.

"Where's Luke?" she asked.

"Locked up," he said. "Where he should be."

She shook her head. "No. No, he shouldn't."

"You called the police on him," the trooper reminded her.

"I called the police *for* him," she clarified. "I heard him fighting with someone outside, and I was scared for him."

"You should be scared *of* him," the trooper said. "If only you'd taken out that restraining order against him."

"I'm not afraid of him," she said. But she was beginning to fear Gingrich. Usually he came across as bumbling and incompetent, but there was something about him, something so determined that chilled her even more deeply than she'd already been chilled.

"It'll still work," he said.

Her head was beginning to pound with confusion. "What are you talking about?"

"The murder-suicide," he said so matter-of-factly that she couldn't believe he was serious.

But then he pulled out her missing gun, and she knew that he was deadly serious. He intended to kill her and frame Luke for it.

She stepped back into the house. But Gingrich followed her, kicking the door shut behind himself. "This isn't going to work," she told him. "You have Luke in jail."

He snorted. "He'll get out soon. Braden Zimmer will get to that idiot prosecutor. They'll make sure no charges are filed." He grinned. "He's going to feel like an even bigger idiot than he is when Luke Garrison kills you and then himself."

She shook her head. "Luke won't hurt me. He won't hurt our baby."

"He won't have to," Gingrich said as he slid off the safety and cocked the gun. "As soon as he pulls into the drive, I'll kill you. Then, if he isn't distraught enough to kill himself, I'll kill him."

Her heart pounded furiously with fear over his diabolical plan. She had to figure out a way to save herself, their baby and Luke. But she was frozen to the spot, the barrel of her gun pointing directly at her.

"This—this won't work," she insisted. "He isn't coming back here." She hoped that he wouldn't. But he was worried about her—because she'd called him about that damn missing gun. It wouldn't have mattered had she called the police; it wasn't as if Gingrich would have admitted to stealing her weapon.

Taking it had been part of his plan to set up Luke. And because Luke was worried about her, he probably would come back. But Gingrich didn't have to know that.

She shook her head and sighed. "Luke and I are separated. He doesn't live here."

"He's been spending a hell of a lot of time here lately," Gingrich said.

And she shivered as she realized that the trooper had been watching him—watching them. "Not anymore," she replied, bluffing. "We had a terrible fight. He thinks this baby is someone else's."

Instead of being discouraged, the trooper grinned. "That makes it even easier to explain his killing you."

"He's done with me," she said. "He won't be coming back here."

"Then we'll just have to make sure that he does," Gingrich said. And he thrust the gun closer to her. "Where's your cell phone?"

She shook her head. "No. I won't call him." She wouldn't lure the man she loved to his death. And hers...

"I want to file a complaint," Luke told the prosecutor who Braden had gotten out of bed at the crack of dawn to come to the state police post. "Trooper Gingrich has been harassing me for weeks. He had no right to arrest me when I was on my own property."

"He claims your wife swore out a complaint against you," the prosecutor said. "That she's the one who called the police on you and Mr. McRooney."

Luke paused for a second, wondering if he was telling the truth. But she had called him earlier that night— when she'd awakened to find the window open and her gun missing. She'd called him, not the police. And Luke told the prosecutor as much.

The older man cocked his head, as if unable to believe what Luke was saying. But Braden chimed in.

"There's no way Willow Garrison wanted her husband arrested. She wanted to come down with me to make sure there were no charges pressed against him or my other Hotshot."

"But why would the trooper lie?" the prosecutor asked.

And that suspicion he'd had earlier, when talking to Owen at the Filling Station, returned to Luke...bigger than before. Too big for him to easily dismiss.

The prosecutor was a short guy, barely over five feet tall, so Luke easily looked over his gray-haired head and met Braden's gaze. His boss's eyes had widened, too.

"It's him," Luke said.

"It can't be." Braden shook his head. "Marty's a dick, but to try to kill someone..."

"What are you accusing the trooper of?" the prosecutor asked. "Lying...or more?"

More. So much more. "Let's start with the lying," Luke said. "Call my wife. See if she backs up his story." He'd had nothing on him but his jeans when he'd been arrested, but Braden had brought him a shirt, socks and boots from the firehouse.

Fortunately Luke had had his cell phone in the pocket of his jeans. He fished it out now and punched in the contact for Willow's cell. He also hit the speaker button, but when Willow's voice emanated from the phone it was the message she'd recorded for her voice mail.

"Is she working?" Braden asked.

Luke shook his head as fear gripped his guts. "No. She's taken some time off."

"Sleeping?" Braden asked.

But Luke doubted it.

"Maybe she just doesn't want to talk to you," the prosecutor suggested.

"You try," Luke told Braden.

His boss had his wife's contact information. As superintendent, Braden had emergency contacts for every member of his team. He punched in the number, then cursed. "Straight to voice mail again."

Luke held out his hand. "I need your keys. I need your truck." He had to get to Willow, before Gingrich did.

But Braden hesitated. "I'm still working on getting Trick out of jail."

Luke hadn't been trespassing, since he owned the property. So the charges against him had been easy to get dismissed, especially when it was pointed out that Willow had no restraining order against him. But Trick had been trespassing. "I'm not pressing charges against McRooney," Luke said. But he wasn't waiting for him either. "Keys," he implored Braden. "I have to check on her."

Braden was a man in love, too, so he understood and passed over the keys. "You need to be careful, though."

Luke touched his head, which still had a dull ache from his concussion. "I know."

Nobody knew better than he did just how damn dangerous Gingrich was. The man had nearly killed him a few times. It had to be Gingrich. It made so much sense.

"Am I free to go?" he asked the prosecutor.

The older man hesitated a moment—a moment too long. Tension wound through Luke, along with his fear. He needed to get to Willow, needed to make sure she was okay. Finally the guy nodded. "Yes. And I will be speaking to your wife and to Trooper Gingrich."

"Me, too," Luke said as he headed out the door. He only hoped he didn't find them together. He wanted Gingrich nowhere near his wife.

He was heading toward Braden's truck when his cell vibrated. Relief flashed through him when he saw that Willow was calling him back. "Thank God you're okay," he said.

But the voice that greeted him wasn't Willow's soft one. "She will be…if you do what I tell you to do."

Dread curled inside him as he recognized the trooper's voice. "What do you want, Marty?" he asked. And he really wanted to know. The guy had a grudge against Luke's boss, not Luke.

"For you to confess."

"To what?" he asked. "To your crimes? You're the one who had the affair with Louanne. You're the one who plotted with her to kill Dirk. You're the one who's been trying to frame me. And when you failed at that, you tried to kill me."

"No," the trooper said. "That's not true. And you'll make that clear…if you want to see your wife and baby again."

Luke cursed. "You son of a bitch! Leave her alone. She's already been through too much."

"Yes, she has," Gingrich agreed. "So don't put her through anymore. Get your ass back out to your house and come alone."

"No!" Willow shouted. "It's a trap!"

She hadn't had to tell him that, but she'd risked her safety to warn him. And he cursed as he heard a sharp slap. Anger and fear surged through him.

"Don't!" Luke yelled into the phone. "Don't hurt her. I'll do whatever you want. Just don't hurt her!"

"Get over to your house," Gingrich said.

Luke had already clicked the fob for Braden's truck and unlocked the doors. He jumped into the driver's side. "I'm on my way."

"And come alone," Gingrich repeated. "She'll be dead the minute I see anyone but you."

"You better not hurt her," Luke warned him. "Or I will kill you—slowly, painfully…"

Gingrich snorted. "You're in no position to make demands or threats, Garrison. I have the upper hand."

He had—because nobody had suspected him. But now Luke and Willow knew the truth. So Marty had no intention of letting either of them live.

Luke could only hope that the trooper didn't kill Willow before Luke had a chance to get home—to her and their baby. But even if she was still alive when he got there, Luke wasn't sure how he'd be able to keep her that way. And survive himself…

Gingrich had had months to come up with his plan and put it in motion to destroy Luke. Luke only had minutes to figure out how to outsmart the murderous lawman.

This is going to work…

His plan wasn't falling apart. Nobody was on to him.

But Willow had not seemed surprised, nor had Garrison. But Marty wasn't worried anymore that they'd figured it out, like he'd been worried about earlier. Luke had been around so often, so many times that Marty had called Louanne and stopped by to see her, that he must have overheard something or seen them together. Fortunately he must not have said anything to anyone else because nobody had investigated Marty. And nobody would. Luke and Willow Garrison would soon be dead.

And everybody would just think that their deaths had been the result of domestic violence. It happened all the time. And he'd already set up Garrison to look unstable and out of control. Nobody would figure out what had really happened. Who had really been behind their deaths.

Luke must have been alone when he'd taken Gingrich's call because Marty hadn't heard anyone else in the background. Luke would come alone. He loved his wife.

Gingrich glanced across the living room to where she sat on the couch, hunched over, her arms wrapped around her middle. He'd been holding her at the door, where he was. But she'd started doubling over with pain.

Was she going into labor now?

She wasn't that big yet. So it would be too soon. He felt a flash of panic. But then he reminded himself that she was going to die, anyway, and the baby would die with her. She had to die...

Just like Luke Garrison had to die.

"Why are you doing this?" Willow asked, between gasps for breath. She sounded as if she was getting hysterical.

Marty hated when women cried. His wife cried all the time now because she either knew or suspected he'd cheated on her again. But she hadn't left him yet, and she probably wouldn't. "It's not my fault," he said. "Louanne Brown was the one who came after me."

"She wanted you to help her kill her husband?" Willow asked.

He shook his head. "No. She had that all planned out on her own. She even went after Owen on her own. She was so worried that Dirk said something in those last moments, that he'd given her up."

"So you have nothing to do with that," she said. "You're not a killer."

He wasn't.

Yet.

But he had to be now.

"That's Luke's fault," Marty said as anger and frustration rushed through him. "He just wouldn't die…"

"But you don't have to kill him," Willow said. "You don't have to kill anyone."

"It didn't work," Marty said. "I tried framing him. But it didn't work. That damn lazy prosecutor would not file charges against him."

"Because Luke's not guilty," she said. "Why would you make it look like he is?"

"Because when he was staying there, he must have seen us or overheard our calls. He'd been so out of it then that he probably wouldn't have realized we were having an affair, and this whole thing would have died with Louanne," Marty said. "But she had to open her damn big mouth. She had to say something about the affair…" And that had gotten his wife thinking and worrying and crying…but if she believed it was Luke Garrison and not him…

"But why Luke?" Willow asked. She wasn't panting anymore. She wasn't doubled over. Had she been faking this whole time?

Marty narrowed his eyes and studied her. Was she playing him? Trying to distract him?

He had her gun, though. And when he'd used the keys Louanne had lifted from Luke to let himself in last night, he'd made sure there were no other weapons in the house.

She grimaced and leaned forward, and he realized she must have just had time in between her contractions. She was definitely in labor.

Too soon.

He felt a pang of pity for her. And, hell, even for Luke. "I didn't have a choice," Marty insisted. "Louanne had taken advantage of the fact that Luke had been crashing on her couch. She'd taken and copied his keys in case she needed access to his gun and car. And when she thought Owen might be on to her, she used them. *She* used Luke."

And now he had to…

He had to wrap this all up, so that people would stop asking questions. So that Andrea would believe Luke Garrison had been having the affair with Louanne and not him. Maybe then she would stop crying…

A noise drew his attention and he whirled back toward the door with the gun in his hand. Willow's gun.

A truck had pulled into the driveway. One of the big, black pickups with the US Forest Service emblem on the door. It looked like Braden's truck, and a big man sat on the driver's side. The passenger side and rear seat looked empty.

The truck stopped and the driver's door opened. The big man who stepped out was Luke Garrison. He had come alone—just like Marty had told him.

He tightened his grasp on the gun. Luke was big and strong. He'd survived crashes, an overdose and a near-hanging. But even he couldn't beat a bullet, and unlike the last time Marty had fired at him, nobody would be firing back. Willow didn't have her gun now. He did.

"It'll be over soon," Marty assured her. "It'll all be over soon."

And everyone would believe that it was a tragic case of murder-suicide. That Luke Garrison had lost it all.

Chapter 23

Luke stood behind the open driver's door, in case Gingrich just started shooting like the rest of the team had worried he might. But Luke had figured out Marty's plan to make his and Willow's deaths look like a murder-suicide. His stomach lurched at the thought and with fear that Willow might already be dead.

He couldn't have lost her. Not again.

"He's at the door." A deep voice emanated from the cell phone Luke had left lying on the seat of the truck on speaker. "She's on the couch."

He lifted his hand to his face, so Gingrich wouldn't see him talking, and asked, "Is she…?"

"Looks fine, just scared," Owen replied. "She noticed us back here and kept distracting him. We'll get her out."

But they needed a distraction now—something to draw Gingrich's attention to the front and keep it there.

And Luke was it. He leaned into the truck and pressed his hand against the horn.

The front door opened, and Marty's free hand, the one not holding a gun, waved at him. Not a friendly wave but a wave to stop.

Luke pressed a little harder on the horn before easing off it. Now Marty gestured with the gun. "Get the hell in here!" he said. "Now!"

Luke drew in a deep breath and stepped around the door. Gingrich wouldn't shoot him here—in the driveway. He needed to get him inside, but Luke walked slowly toward the door, giving the others time to get Willow out.

She had to be alive…

Owen wouldn't have lied to him. If she was already gone, they wouldn't have let him start toward the door. They would have taken down Marty then. Wouldn't they?

The closer he got to Marty, the more agitated the man looked. He was unraveling, but he didn't seem to know it. Sweat beaded on his bald head and ran down his face, turning the collar of his tan uniform shirt brown. He wore his vest beneath the shirt, the outline of it visible the closer Luke got. Marty had protection. Taking him down wouldn't be easy.

"Get in here!" the trooper shouted, his voice shaky. He glanced around Luke, as if looking for other vehicles to come barreling down the driveway.

Maybe he'd realized that Luke wasn't stupid enough to have followed his orders. That he wouldn't have come alone.

He'd been tempted, but then he'd remembered what Willow had said about them being safer when they were together. Well, the same went for his team. They were his family. None of them would have betrayed him, just as he wouldn't have betrayed them. So he'd reached out and trusted them to help him. And they had his back.

They had Willow's, too.

Through the front window, he saw Owen and Trent quietly carrying her out the back. And the breath he'd been holding slipped raggedly out through his lips.

Gingrich stepped back inside the house, then turned and cursed. "What the hell! What the hell did you do, Garrison?" And the gun he held was pointed directly at Luke's chest—at his heart.

But even if he pulled that trigger, Luke's heart would be safe…with Willow. All that mattered to him was her life and the life of their unborn baby.

He closed his eyes and braced himself for the bullet.

"Don't!" Braden shouted as he saw Gingrich's finger twitch against the trigger. He'd slipped around the side of the house. He hadn't been about to let Luke face this madman alone, no matter how much he'd insisted he could handle it. "Don't shoot him!"

The gun barrel swung toward Braden. He lifted his hands, trying to show he posed no threat. But Marty had always considered him a threat—to his popularity, to his athleticism, to his academics.

They'd been rivals since they were little kids.

"Let Luke go," Braden said. "This is about me, not him."

Gingrich snorted. "You are so damn full of yourself, Zimmer. Believe it or not, not everything is about you!"

Braden hoped that it was true—that it wasn't his fault that Marty had targeted a member of his team. "It's not about Luke either," Braden insisted. "He's done nothing to hurt you."

"He was supposed to help me!" Marty said and the barrel swung back toward Luke. "He was supposed to take the fall, so nobody would ever have to know…"

"About you and Louanne?" Luke asked. "You were her lover?"

Marty lifted his free hand to his face and wiped away some sweat. He was perspiring so profusely that it had to be running into his eyes. Maybe he wouldn't be able to see well enough to shoot Luke.

But Luke was too close. He was bound to get hit if a bullet came out of the barrel of the gun pointed at him.

Braden had to get between them.

But Marty was focused on Luke now. "I didn't know what she was planning," he insisted. "I didn't know she intended to kill her husband. She'd already messed with the cable when she told me. She wanted me to help her cover it up." He shook his head. "I told her that nobody suspected anything. But she was worried about Owen, worried that Dirk had said something to him… or to you."

Luke shook his head. "Dirk never said anything about their marriage. I had no idea—"

"But you were close and you were always around, so she was worried that you overheard something," Marty said. "She wanted to take out Owen and make it look like you were involved—that way nobody would hear what he had to say and nobody would listen to you."

Luke shuddered. "She was vicious."

Marty's mouth curved into a faint grin. "She was exciting and smart and sexy."

Braden nearly shuddered now. He hadn't seen Louanne as any of those things. "She's gone now," he pointed out. "It's over, Marty. Put down the gun."

The barrel swung back toward him. "Don't tell me

what to do!" Gingrich shouted. "You're not the captain of my team anymore. You're not the boss of me!"

"Your boss knows," Luke said. "Other troopers are on their way."

Luke wasn't lying. They'd called the police but only after they'd arrived at his house. He hadn't trusted anyone but his team to help him rescue his pregnant wife.

And given how duplicitous Marty had been this entire time, Braden didn't blame Luke for not trusting the police to help.

The gun shook in Marty's hand. "You screwed this up!" he yelled at Braden. "You screwed this all up like you have everything my whole life!"

Luke stepped closer to the trooper. "It wasn't him," he said. "I figured out on my own that it was you. Braden had no idea."

Gingrich snorted again. "Yeah, right."

"It doesn't matter," Braden said. "It's all over. Put down the gun, Marty."

But the madman tightened his grasp on his weapon. "Stop telling me what to do!" he shouted. "You're not the boss of me. I'm not one of your loyal team like gullible Garrison here."

"Is that why you went after Louanne?" Braden asked. "You wanted to hurt a member of my team? Is that why you've been sabotaging equipment? You just want to mess with me?"

Gingrich groaned. "I told you that not everything has to do with you. But you're just too damn full of yourself to believe it."

Luke chuckled. "He just doesn't get it."

Gingrich nodded. "Yeah, yeah…"

"He doesn't know that this is between you and me,"

Luke said, and he stepped even closer to the troubled trooper. "You've spent months trying to ruin my life."

Gingrich looked nervously at Luke now. So did Braden. He understood that Luke had every reason to be furious with the trooper. The man had tried to destroy him, had threatened his wife and unborn baby.

"Oh, no…" Braden murmured just as everything got out of control.

Her heart pounding with fear and dread, Willow struggled against Owen James. "Let me go!" she protested as he tried loading her into the back of the paramedic rig he'd parked around the block from her house. "I'm fine!"

But Luke wasn't. Luke had walked headlong into danger—into Trooper Gingrich's trap. But Luke had sprung a trap of his own on their would-be killer. He'd brought in his team and made sure she was rescued.

So there was no way in hell she was going anywhere until she knew he was safe.

"You need to get checked out," Owen said. "You don't want to risk your pregnancy."

"I was faking the contractions," she assured him. The only pain she'd felt had been in her aching heart, as fear had caused it to pound wildly.

Fear for herself, for their baby, for Luke…

Her heart was still racing frantically—because Luke wasn't safe. He was still in there—with that deranged gunman.

Owen narrowed his eyes and studied her face. "You were faking?"

She nodded. "I didn't want him touching me and pointing that gun at me." Her gun. She shuddered as she remembered how close the barrel of it had come to her, to their baby. "And I was hoping I could put enough distance between us to get away from him."

Even though she'd gained the distance, she'd been too scared to risk running—worried that he would shoot her in the back if she tried to escape.

But she should have known that Luke would have come up with a way to save her. He had always tried so hard to make her happy. That was why she'd pushed him away—because she hadn't wanted to be happy, hadn't felt she deserved to be after she'd lost those babies.

But Luke deserved to be happy. He deserved to live. And he was willing to give up both those things for her. He would do anything for her—even die.

Tears burned her eyes and rolled down her face. "Please, Owen, make sure he's okay."

Owen squeezed her hand. "He will be. Braden is with him. They'll figure out a way to disarm Gingrich. Or they'll stall him until the state police get here."

Sirens whined in the distance; they were on their way. But she still worried they wouldn't get here in time to save her husband.

"He's crazy," she murmured.

"He's in love," Owen said.

"What?" she asked. "I was talking about Gingrich." She doubted he'd ever loved anyone but himself.

"Luke," Owen said. "He's in love with you. That's why he came up with this plan."

She didn't deserve his love, not after how she'd treated him. And while he cared about her and their baby, she wasn't sure if he loved her like he once had or if she'd destroyed that love.

"Luke is a hero," she said. "He would do this for anyone."

Even Braden.

If it came down to his life or his superintendent's, Luke would take the bullet meant for Braden.

Owen squeezed her hand again. "He did this for you."

She tugged free of Owen's grasp and put her hands on her belly. The baby moved beneath her palms, kicking and shifting inside her womb. He was so active, so strong...

Like his father.

Luke had to survive.

For their baby's sake and for hers...

She couldn't lose Luke again.

"Gingrich is crazy," she said. And the sound of those sirens would probably set him off even more. He would know that it was all over—that his stupid plan hadn't worked. "I'm afraid—"

Before she could even fully confess to her fear, shots rang out. And she echoed them with her scream—because she knew that if anyone had been hit, it was Luke.

So she screamed his name over and over...

Chapter 24

"Shhh…" Luke said as he pulled Willow into his arms. Her body trembled against him, but then he was shaking, too. He had come so close to nearly losing her. To nearly losing the baby, too.

But they didn't know yet if he or she was safe.

Over her head, he stared into the back of the paramedic rig. "Why is she still here?" he asked Owen. "Why haven't you brought her to the hospital?"

She should have been there, hooked to monitors, having ultrasounds, making sure she and the baby were all right.

"She refused to go," Owen said. "Until she knew you were all right."

She clung to him. "I—I thought he shot you…"

Luke shook his head. "No…"

Not that he hadn't tried. But Luke had been faster. He'd grabbed Gingrich's wrist and jerked his arm up just as the crazy lawman had squeezed the trigger. So the bullets had fired up into the trees.

Then Braden had helped Luke wrest the gun from Gingrich and take him down to the ground. He'd left his superintendent to handle the madman as he'd rushed down the driveway and around the block, drawn to Willow's screams.

He moved his hand down her back, trying to soothe her. "I'm fine. I'm not hurt at all."

Not any more than he'd already been.

"He was going to kill us," Willow said, her entire body trembling.

"I know…" And he felt sick over putting her in such danger. He looked up at Owen again. "You need to bring her to the hospital. Now."

He needed to know that she and the baby were really all right. They'd both been through too much—because of him. And she would be put through more if Owen didn't get her out of here before the troopers interrogated her.

Owen must have realized the same thing because he jumped down from the rig and caught her shoulders, pulling her away from Luke. "You really need to get checked out," he insisted. "For the baby's sake…"

Her breath caught and she nodded. "Okay." But she reached out and grasped Luke's shirt, trying to tug him along. "Come with us…"

He shook his head. "I have to talk to the police."

"You need to be checked out, too," she said.

He shook his head again. "I'm fine."

But he wasn't. He was sick over what he'd put her through—not just now, but all the years they'd been married. He'd stressed her out so much over his job.

He knew he had a decision to make. But would it

matter if he gave up his job? Would she take him back? Or had too much damage already been done to their relationship?

Would she ever forgive him for all he'd already cost her, for all he'd cost them?

Where was Luke?

Willow had been at the hospital for what felt like hours, but he hadn't shown up. He hadn't come to check on her or on their baby.

Had the police arrested him? Had they believed Gingrich over the truth?

She'd given a brief statement a while ago. She'd assured the female trooper to whom she'd spoken that Gingrich had admitted to his affair with Louanne Brown and that he'd been responsible for the attempts on Luke's life.

She'd come so close to losing him. Or had she already lost him when she'd been so cruel to him, blaming him for her miscarriages, for not being there when she'd needed him? She'd needed him the most today, and he'd certainly been there for her, risking his own life for hers and for their child.

Tears stung her eyes, and she squeezed her eyelids shut to hold them back. She'd already cried too much, so much that she was dehydrated. Not that her tears had caused that. She was physically drained and had been admitted for observation.

Of course, she thought her doctor was being overly cautious. She could have gone home after she'd received an IV to rehydrate her. But she shuddered as she remembered to what she would be going home—the scene of a crime.

Not that anyone had died at her house.

Luke hadn't been shot. And he'd made certain that nobody else had. Braden had stopped by to tell her that, to tell her what a hero her husband was.

But she already knew that. What she didn't know was where her hero was. And why was his boss here and not him.

She stared at Braden, who clearly looked uncomfortable paying her a visit. His face was flushed, and he couldn't quite meet her gaze.

"I'm sorry," he said. "I've never liked Marty, but I had no idea how unhinged he is. That he would have pulled something so horrible…"

"Like trying to frame Luke," she finished for him. And she shuddered to think of how close he'd come to succeeding. For a little while even she had had her doubts about her husband.

And a pang of regret for that struck her already aching heart. Her heart ached for Luke.

"Like trying to kill him," Braden said. "And you. Are you really all right?"

She nodded. "I'm fine. My doctor is just being extra cautious given my previous miscarriages."

"Luke blames himself for those," Braden told her.

And that pang of regret and guilt intensified to a stabbing pain. That was her fault. She had blamed Luke.

"That's probably why he's given me his resignation," Braden continued.

"What?" Willow was more shocked by this news than she'd been over Gingrich showing up with her gun. "Why would he do that?"

"For you," Braden said. "For the baby."

She shook her head. "I didn't ask him to do that. I didn't want him to quit."

"You need to tell him that," Braden said.

She needed to tell him more than that. But first she had to find him. "Where is he?" she asked, and she moved to slide off the bed. But the IV tugged at her skin. She could remove it. She was probably rehydrated now. But that wasn't the only thing connected to her.

A blood-pressure cuff encircled her arm. She imagined it would be up right now if it performed the automatic check of it.

Braden reached out, as if to push her back into the bed. "I didn't mean to upset you. Luke is doing this because he thinks this is what you want."

That was her fault. Everything was her fault. She hadn't talked to him like she should have. She'd bottled up her pain and grief and then lashed out at him.

Unfairly.

She'd been so unfair to him.

"If he's done this for me, why isn't he here?" she asked. Where the hell was Luke?

She needed to talk to him. Not just about his quitting his job, but everything else.

The baby.

Their marriage.

Her love for him.

His love for her.

Maybe he'd quit out of love, but that love would turn to resentment soon enough if he gave up his career for her. But being a Hotshot was more than his career. It was part of what made him the man he was—the man she loved.

Fury coursed through Owen and he slammed the locker shut. "What the hell are you doing?" he demanded.

"What the hell are *you* doing?" Luke asked him. "You nearly took off my hand."

He'd wanted to stop him from packing up his stuff, wanted to stop him from leaving. "You can't do this!"

Luke clenched his jaw so tightly that a muscle twitched in his cheek. Through gritted teeth, he murmured, "I have to."

"You don't want to." That was obvious.

"I have to," Luke said. "I can't risk upsetting Willow any more than she's already been. I can't risk her losing another child."

Owen cursed. But he couldn't argue with his friend, like he wanted to. He couldn't be selfish—again—because he realized how selfish he'd been.

The last few months—hell, the last couple of years—they'd all known that Luke had been hurting. But they hadn't wanted to pry. Owen wished now that he had pried—both with Luke and with Dirk. Maybe Dirk wouldn't be dead and Luke leaving...

"Are you sure this is what she wants you to do?" Owen asked. And he knew he was grasping at straws. He was being selfish again. But he'd already lost Dirk; he didn't want to lose Luke, too.

Luke shrugged, then continued shoving his stuff into the duffel bag sitting on the bench in front of the lockers. "It doesn't matter. It's what I have to do—for her, for the baby..."

"But what if she doesn't take you back?" Owen asked. And he hated that he sounded almost hopeful. "Would you stay?"

Luke shook his head. "No. I wouldn't be able to keep doing a job that had cost me everything that really mattered to me."

And Owen suddenly understood. If Courtney wanted him to quit, he would. But Courtney loved him just as he was, scars and all, and would never ask him to change.

But he knew what he and Courtney had was rare. Well, not so rare anymore. A few other members of his team had found a love like his.

If only Luke's had been…

Then he wouldn't have to give up the team. But Garrison clearly loved his wife more than he loved his job.

"I hope she appreciates the sacrifice you're making for her," Owen said.

Luke shrugged. "It doesn't matter…"

But Owen knew he was lying. It mattered a hell of a lot. Luke had obviously made his extreme sacrifice in the hope that Willow would give him a second chance, that she would let him come home.

He couldn't imagine how devastated his friend would be if Willow refused. She could hurt him more than Marty Gingrich had. She could completely destroy him.

Chapter 25

Nobody really understood why he'd done what he had. But nobody understood the loss he and Willow had suffered with those miscarriages. They'd lost two babies, but they'd lost more than that. They'd lost the unbreakable bond they'd once shared. And Luke had finally realized why.

That he hadn't done enough to prove his love to Willow and to their babies. Giving up the job he loved was hard, but it was nothing in comparison to the pain of the last few months, to not being with her.

But as Owen had pointed out, giving up his job didn't guarantee him a second chance with Willow. She might not be willing to take a risk on him no matter what he did for a living.

And he hadn't quite figured that out yet. He'd never had a backup plan. All he'd ever wanted to be was a Hotshot firefighter.

But now there was something he wanted to be even more: Willow's husband.

And a father...

He very badly wanted to be a father to the baby she carried. At least he thought she still carried the baby. Hopefully she hadn't miscarried again because of the stress that Gingrich had caused her.

The stress that Luke had caused. If only he'd figured it out sooner.

If only he'd made sure that Willow was never alone and vulnerable. But he'd left her alone the last couple of days. He'd wanted to give her time to recover from her ordeal before he put her through another one.

Before he pressured her to give him—and their marriage—another chance.

Had he given her enough time?

If she'd lost the baby, there would probably never be enough time. He doubted she could handle another miscarriage. He doubted he could.

So when he lifted his fist to knock at the door to his house, his hand was shaking. He was almost as scared as he'd been when he'd known Gingrich had her, that he was holding her hostage.

Gingrich was the one being held now. Without bail.

The prosecutor had not hesitated to file charges against the former lawman. And a grand jury had not hesitated to hand down the indictment.

Gingrich would never threaten or hurt Willow again. But Luke could. If he wasn't careful...

He had to be so careful. Maybe coming here had been a mistake. Maybe it would be smarter to give her more time to recover.

Although waiting the last two days had nearly killed him.

He forced himself to turn away from the door, back

toward the truck. It was Dirk's. He and Stanley had worked together to repair it. Maybe that was what he would do—start restoring vehicles for a living.

That couldn't be too dangerous.

Apparently turning away from the door had been dangerous, though, because something struck Luke's back. Fortunately it hadn't been hard. He swiveled around to see a pillow lying on the brick walk behind him.

"You're lucky I wasn't holding something harder," Willow said, her green eyes bright with anger.

"Are you okay?" he asked.

"No," she replied.

And he hurried toward her. "What's wrong? Did you lose…?" He couldn't say it; the words stuck in his throat.

"My husband?" she asked. "Yes, I lost him."

And Luke knew he'd made a terrible mistake. No matter what he did, it didn't look as though Willow intended to give him another chance. But he had to know. "What about the baby?"

She pressed her hands to her belly, which looked even bigger now. "He's fine," she said.

And a pang struck Luke's heart so hard that it took his breath away. He would have a son.

But how much a part of the boy's life would Willow allow him to be?

"I—I want to be here for him," Luke said.

"And what about me?" she asked. "Do you want to be here for me?" It wasn't anger making her eyes bright now, but tears.

"Do you want me to be?" he asked. Hopefully…

She shook her head.

And his heart cracked wide open with pain. He had blown it.

"Not like this," she said. "I want you to want to be with me for me—not for the baby."

His head pounded with confusion. "I don't understand. Of course, I want to be with you for you." He stepped closer to her now, but she still blocked the doorway, as if unwilling to let him back inside their home.

"And I want to be with you," she said, her voice cracking. "But you're not you anymore."

"I stopped drinking weeks ago," he said.

"You never had a problem," she assured him.

"And I quit my job," he said.

She reached out and shoved him back. "That's the problem," she said. "I want you to be the man I fell in love with, the man I married. My hero..."

"I don't understand."

"Being a Hotshot isn't just what you do," she said. "It's who you are, who I love."

"But you worrying about me, the stress—it isn't good for the baby," he reminded her.

She shook her head. "I have been more stressed this pregnancy than any of the others, and you haven't been off fighting a wildfire. You've just been gone."

"Because you said that was what you wanted," he reminded her.

"I lied," she said.

Her admission struck him harder than the pillow had. Hell, harder than the truck had that struck the ditch and then the trees. He was stunned. So stunned that he couldn't talk. He couldn't move.

She stepped back from the door and gestured for him to come inside. But he wasn't sure that he should. He wasn't sure that he wanted to...

* * *

Willow held her breath. The look on Luke's handsome face nearly made her double over with pain. She'd hurt him. She'd hurt them.

Months ago and every day since that she hadn't apologized to him. She'd been worried that he wouldn't forgive her. And apparently she'd had cause for that worry.

"We promised each other that we would never lie," he reminded her.

"I didn't know that I was," she said, trying to figure out how to explain what she was only just beginning to understand herself. "I was hurting so badly that I thought I wanted to be alone."

And she was afraid that he was going to leave her alone now, for good. But he finally stepped inside the house and closed the door.

"I never really blamed you for losing those babies," she continued. "I blamed *me*."

He shook his head. "You did everything right. The rest. The vitamins. It was me…"

She reached out then and cupped his face in her hands. "No. It wasn't. You are the sweetest, most loving and supportive man." Tears stung her eyes, blurring his handsome face. "And I don't think I deserve you." She snorted derisively at herself. "I *know* I don't deserve you."

"Willow—"

She pressed her fingers against his lips. "I'm so sorry for the way I treated you. I didn't know how to grieve. I didn't know how to express myself but in anger…"

He reached out for her hand and entwined their fingers. "You are a lot like your dad…"

She smiled. "He is who he is," she said. "But I don't have to be like him. I can change."

"I love you just the way you are," he assured her.

And broke her heart. She really didn't deserve him. "I'll work on how to be a better person, a better mother, a better wife…if you'll give me another chance."

"I came here to ask you for one," he said.

"Why?" she asked. "I have been horrible to you."

"You've been hurting," he said, as if that excused her treatment of him.

It didn't.

"So have you," she said. "And I was selfish. I couldn't give you what you needed."

"All I need is you," he said. And he leaned down and brushed his mouth across hers.

She tasted tears. She wasn't sure if they were hers or his. She threw her arms around his neck and clung to him. She didn't deserve him, but she was still too selfish to give him up.

He picked her up and carried her. And she felt the heavy, frantic beat of his heart against her side. He wanted her as badly as she wanted him.

They pulled their clothes off—themselves and each other—until they were naked. Physically. Emotionally, they'd already bared themselves.

And it hadn't been nearly as hard as Willow had thought it would be. She loved Luke. And, more importantly, she trusted him. With her life and with her heart.

He pressed a kiss to it, moving his mouth across her breast. Then he took the nipple between his lips and gently tugged at it.

She arched up from the bed and moaned as desire rushed through her. They had always had so much passion. But now there was even more intimacy between them, in every kiss, every caress…

There was even more tenderness.

She loved him so much. And she kept telling him that between kisses, between caresses...

He groaned. "Willow... I can't... I'm losing control..."

She pushed him onto his back and straddled him, taking him deep inside her. Finally the emptiness was filled—with him and his love. She moved, and he clutched at her hips. But he didn't stop her; he just guided her to a rhythm that drove them both out of their minds and beyond their control.

She screamed his name as she came. And hers escaped his throat in a deep groan as his big body shuddered with release beneath hers. She collapsed onto his chest, panting for breath.

His hands stroked down her bare back. "You're amazing..."

She shook her head, and tears slipped from beneath her closed eyes. "No, I'm not. I'm terrible. And I've been so terribly unfair to you."

"Shhh," he said. "I understand that you were in pain. And I know I helped cause that."

"You did nothing wrong," she insisted.

"Neither did you."

And finally she accepted that. What had happened had just happened. "It was nobody's fault," she realized. And her breath shuddered raggedly out as the burden she'd been carrying so long finally slipped off her shoulders. There was no reason for it. No explanation. And no blame...

And finally, while she would always grieve those babies, it was just grief. It wasn't mixed up with the anger and the guilt anymore.

Luke held her closely, as if he'd felt her new lightness and thought she might drift away from him. But that was not going to happen again. "I will never push you away," she promised him. "I will never take our love for granted."

He pressed a kiss to her forehead. "And I will never walk away again. I will never leave you."

She sighed again with such relief. "I will hold you to that promise," she said. "The only time you can leave is to fight a wildfire with your crew."

He tensed beneath her. "What? I told you I quit."

"Braden told me," she said. "And I couldn't believe it. You love your job."

"I love you more."

"But it's not just a job," she said. "Those Hotshots are your family."

He snorted. "Some family…"

"They all feel badly for ever doubting you," she assured him. "They don't want you to leave and neither do I. Being a Hotshot is who you are, the hero I love. I don't want you to give that up—ever—for any reason."

"Even age?" he asked, and she heard the levity in his voice. He was teasing. "You want me fighting fires at a hundred?"

"As long as you're not on oxygen," she said with a smile. "That could be dangerous."

"The job is dangerous," he reminded her.

"And you're a professional with a good team backing you up," she said. "You're not in any more danger doing your job than I probably am doing mine."

He shook his head. "That was only dangerous when you were working the ERs in Detroit. That's why your dad gave you the gun."

She shuddered. "I don't need that anymore. All I need is you."

"And all I need is you," he replied.

"Remember we promised never to lie to each other,"

she admonished him. "You know you need your job. You love it."

"I love you."

"I know. I have always known," she said. She was the one who hadn't shown her love. "I haven't always deserved your love, but that's going to change—starting now."

"Willow—"

She cut off his words with her lips, kissing him deeply. Then she skimmed her lips along his jaw and lower as she showed him just how much she deserved his love.

He showed her his love—over and over—until they were both exhausted. Before she closed her eyes though she studied his handsome face. "You will ask Braden for your job back."

"If you're sure…"

She had never been more certain of anything. She loved her husband so much, and she knew that no matter what dangers they faced, as long as they faced them together, they would survive. "I am," she said. "You promised you would never leave me, so you'll be fine."

"Better than fine," he said. "I am so damn happy."

"Me, too," she said, and she didn't feel even a flicker of guilt over it. She felt nothing but her husband's love.

"Can I take back my resignation?" Luke Garrison asked.

Braden glanced up from his desk and uttered a ragged sigh of relief. "I'd been hoping you would."

He'd needed some good news.

Even though Marty Gingrich would be behind bars for a long time, that only solved one of Braden's problems. He wasn't the one who'd been sabotaging the equipment.

He wouldn't have taken Marty at his word about that or anything else, but another piece of equipment had broken down and almost broke Trick when the truck lift he'd been riding on earlier today had malfunctioned and sharply plummeted.

Since he'd been using a chain saw at the time, he was damn lucky he hadn't cut off one of his own limbs instead of a tree limb.

"I heard you almost lost a man," Luke said as he stepped closer to Braden's desk and studied his face. "Another *accident*?"

"Yeah," Braden said.

"Bullshit," Luke said. "I was there when you questioned Marty about sabotaging our equipment."

Braden shrugged. "You know stuff's been happening. Look what happened to Dirk."

"That was Louanne trying to collect the huge life insurance she took out on him," Luke said. "What's this sabotage stuff?"

Braden sighed another ragged sigh. "I can't have too many people finding out about this."

But word was getting out. Luke's resignation wasn't the only letter he'd received lately. The US Forest Service had sent him a warning about all the damaged equipment and accidents. Any more incidents and he risked losing his team to another superintendent.

"I won't tell anyone," Luke said. "But Willow. We have no secrets."

"She may not want you coming back if you tell her," Braden warned him.

Luke shook his head. "She trusts me to stay safe. And being aware of the sabotage will help. You really should let everybody know." Then he tensed and stared at Braden, his blue eyes wide with shock. "You think it could be one of us."

"I don't want it to be," he said. "If only it was Marty."

"He would have gloated his ass off if it had been him," Luke said.

"And it would have ended when he got locked up," Braden added.

"But Trick's accident happened after that…"

Braden nodded. "So you know there's a risk," he said. "You sure you want your job back?"

"I'm sure," he said. "I'm going to be damn careful, but I'm sure."

Braden's shoulders slumped with relief. "Thank you, for coming back."

"Thank Willow," he said. And he turned for the door.

"Hey, Luke," Braden called out to stop him. "What do you think?"

Luke hesitated a moment before turning back to him. "About the accidents?"

He nodded.

"I don't think they're accidents either."

"Do you have any idea who might be behind them? Any idea who might not be who we think they are?"

Luke cocked his head. "What?"

Braden shook his head. "Just something somebody said once…"

Luke shrugged. "I thought I knew everybody so well, but if I had, they would have known me, too. They would have known that I wouldn't betray my wife or Dirk or any other member of the team."

"They should have known," Braden agreed. "You're a good man." He thought everybody on the team was a good person, though.

But somebody wasn't what they seemed...

"You're a good man, too, Braden," Luke assured him.

He sighed again but not with relief. "I'm not sure I'm doing the right thing."

"You've been investigating," Luke said, as if he knew. "You're trying to figure out who's behind the sabotage."

"How do you know?"

"Trick," Luke replied. "That's why you brought him in."

"You figured that out?"

Luke nodded and started for the door. But then he stopped himself and turned back. "And if I figured it out, the person behind the sabotage might have, too. That could be why the last person who got hurt was Trick."

That was Braden's concern, too, that he had put a target on his brother-in-law. And they were still no closer to finding the saboteur.

"You'll find him," Luke assured him.

Braden hoped his returning team member was right. And that they found him before Trick got hurt any worse.

* * * * *

#2199 COLTON'S ROGUE INVESTIGATION
The Coltons of Colorado • by Jennifer D. Bokal

Wildlife biologist Jacqui Reyes is determined to find out who's trying to steal the wild mustangs of western Colorado. She enlists the help of true-crime podcaster, Gavin Colton. He's working on a series about his notorious father but he can't help but be drawn into Jacqui's case—or toward Jacqui herself!

#2200 CAVANAUGH JUSTICE: DEADLIEST MISSION
Cavanaugh Justice • by Marie Ferrarella

When his sister goes missing, small-town sheriff Cody Cassidy races to her home in Aurora. All he finds is heartbreak...and the steady grace of Detective Skylar Cavanaugh. Once firmly on the track of a killer, Cody and Skylar discover they have more in common than crime. But a murderer is on a killing spree that threatens their budding relationship.

#2201 PROTECTED BY THE TEXAS RANCHER
by Karen Whiddon

Rancher Trace Adkins is wary when Emma McBride shows up on his doorstep. How could he let a woman convicted of murdering her husband into his home? But he's never believed in her guilt, and the simmering attraction he's always felt toward her remains. Despite his misgivings, he agrees to let her stay until she gets on her feet, unaware that someone is after her.

#2202 REUNION AT GREYSTONE MANOR
by Bonnie Vanak

Going back to his hometown is painful, but FBI agent Roarke Calhoun has inherited a mansion, which will help save a life in crisis. But returning means facing Megan Robinson, the woman he's always loved. She also has a claim on the mansion, which puts them together in a place full of secret dangers...and a love meant to burn hot.

SPECIAL EXCERPT FROM

(H) HARLEQUIN

ROMANTIC SUSPENSE

*Rancher Trace Adkins is wary when Emma McBride
shows up on his doorstep. How could he let a woman
convicted of murdering her husband into his home?
But he's never believed in her guilt, and the simmering
attraction he's always felt toward her remains. Despite
his misgivings, he agrees to let her stay until she gets on
her feet, unaware that someone is after her.*

Read on for a sneak preview of
Protected by the Texas Rancher,
the latest thrilling romance from Karen Whiddon!

Was she really considering allowing herself to be
captured by the man who'd killed Amber? Even though
he'd insisted he hadn't murdered Jeremy, how did she
know for sure? She could be putting herself into the
hands of a ruthless monster.

The sound of the back door opening cut into her
thoughts.

"Hey there," Trace said, dropping into the chair next
to her, one lock of his dark hair falling over his forehead.
He looked so damn handsome her chest ached. "Are you
okay? You look upset."

If he only knew.

"Maybe a little," she admitted, well aware he'd see straight through her if she tried to claim she wasn't. In the short time they'd been together, she couldn't help but notice how attuned he'd become to her emotions. And she to his. Suddenly, she understood that if she really was going to go through with this risky plan, she wanted to make love to Trace one last time.

Moving quickly, before she allowed herself to doubt or rationalize, she turned to him. "I need you," she murmured, getting up and moving over to sit on his lap. His gaze darkened as she wrapped her arms around him. When she leaned in close and grazed her mouth across his, he met her kiss with the kind of blazing heat that made her lose all sense of rhyme or reason.

Don't miss
Protected by the Texas Rancher *by Karen Whiddon,*
available October 2022 wherever
Harlequin Romantic Suspense books and
ebooks are sold.

Harlequin.com